How to Age Disgracefully

ALSO BY CLARE POOLEY:

The Authenticity Project

Iona Iverson's Rules for Commuting

How to
— Age —
Disgracefully

CLARE POOLEY

PAMELA DORMAN BOOKS / VIKING

VIKING
An imprint of Penguin Random House LLC
penguinrandomhouse.com

Simultaneously published in hardcover in Great Britain by Bantam,
an imprint of Penguin Random House Ltd., London, in 2024

First United States edition published by Pamela Dorman Books/Viking

Copyright © 2024 by Quilson Ltd
Penguin Random House supports copyright. Copyright fuels creativity, encourages
diverse voices, promotes free speech, and creates a vibrant culture. Thank you for
buying an authorized edition of this book and for complying with copyright laws
by not reproducing, scanning, or distributing any part of it in any form without
permission. You are supporting writers and allowing Penguin Random House to
continue to publish books for every reader.

A Pamela Dorman Book/Viking

LIBRARY OF CONGRESS CONTROL NUMBER: 2024933309
ISBN 9780593831496 (hardcover)
ISBN 9780593512036 (ebook)

Printed in the United States of America
1st Printing

Set in Simoncini Garamond Std
Designed by Cassandra Garruzzo Mueller

This is a work of fiction. Names, characters, places, and incidents
either are the product of the author's imagination or are used fictitiously,
and any resemblance to actual persons, living or dead, businesses, companies,
events, or locales is entirely coincidental.

For my mother, Janet (80),
and my daughter, Matilda (15).
Proof that incredible,
inspirational women come in all ages.

———

Do not go gentle into that good night,
Old age should burn and rave at close of day.

DYLAN THOMAS

How to Age Disgracefully

Prologue

Police Constable Penny Rogers had been right on the bumper of the minibus, siren wailing and lights flashing, for several miles before it finally pulled on to the hard shoulder of the motorway. Were they completely deaf and blind? As she approached the vehicle and saw the mismatched group of people staring down at her through the grimy windows, she realized that perhaps they actually were. At least half the passengers looked to be well over the age of seventy, and a few—bizarrely—under the age of five.

The minibus's hydraulic door opened with a reluctant clunk and a shudder, revealing a red-faced and slightly sweaty middle-aged woman in the driver's seat.

"Why did it take you so long to pull over?" asked Penny as she climbed on board, not bothering to disguise her irritation.

"So sorry, officer. I was looking for a service station for another urgent toilet break. You have *no idea* how many of those we need with this lot." The woman jerked her head toward her passengers, who were all staring at Penny with an unnerving, silent intensity.

To add to the surreal nature of the scene, the three children were dressed as policemen. Were they taking the piss?

"It's a miracle we get anywhere, to be honest," continued the driver. "So initially when you started flashing all those lights and the traffic began moving out of our way, I thought maybe you were giving us a helpful escort. But then I realized that you couldn't have known about the state of Kylie's nappy, or Ruby's weak bladder, and you were being rather insistent, so I thought it best to stop."

"I don't think you're allowed to disclose sensitive and personal medical information like that without permission, Lydia. Or a warrant. Does she have a warrant?" said a small but fierce-looking lady who Penny presumed must be Ruby.

"I wasn't speeding, was I?" continued the driver.

"No. In fact, if anything, you were driving dangerously slowly. But we've been asked to apprehend this vehicle. I believe someone in this minibus is wanted by the Met for questioning," said Penny.

The color drained from the driver's face, and she rubbed her hands along her thighs, creating faint sweat marks on her pale-blue jeans, before gripping her knees tightly and gulping.

"Oh gosh," she said. "Is he pressing charges? I'd thought he might. I just snapped, you see. After twenty years of dismissive comments, criticisms or—even worse—being completely overlooked and ignored, I'd just had enough. Although I admit it was partly my own fault."

"It was not your fault, Lydia," chanted several of the passengers in unison, employing the weary tones of an oft-repeated mantra.

The driver ignored them, pulling a tissue from her sleeve and using it to mop away the beads of moisture which were breaking out on her forehead.

"That photo montage was the final straw—the one that broke

the camel's back, I guess you could say," she said in a croak. "Are you going to arrest me? What on earth are the girls going to think? Their own mother, a common criminal . . ."

Penny looked down at the photocopied picture she was holding, then back at the driver, who was now weeping all over the faux-leather steering wheel, playing havoc with her eye makeup. She wondered what this most improbable felon could possibly have done, but she didn't have the time, or the energy, to find out. She walked a few paces down the aisle, scanning the faces of the bus occupants on either side.

"Lydia, my dear," said an extremely old man halfway down the row of passenger seats to the blubbing bus driver. "I don't think they're looking for you. It's me they're after. You know, it's almost a relief after all these years. It had become an addiction, I think. But the stakes had to get higher and higher to create the same rush. I should have stuck to bingo, like an ordinary pensioner. I think the only way I was ever going to be able to stop was to get taken down. And now, it seems, that time has come. Bang to rights."

The man started to get to his feet, holding his hands out in front of him, waiting for Penny to cuff him. In the seat next to him, an angelic-looking blond boy was fast asleep, his badly fitting policeman's helmet falling down over his face. His arms were wrapped around an ancient, unrecognizable breed of dog. As if he could sense the drama unfolding around him, the boy opened his eyes and stared at Penny in horror.

"HIDE EVERYTHING! IT'S A FUCKING RAID!" he shouted, waking the dog whose bark, it transpired, was much bigger than one would expect. Penny took a few paces back in shock. The whole bus erupted into applause.

3

"Shut UP, Maggie Thatcher!" said an old lady at the back, who obviously had dementia and no idea who the current prime minister was, or that she wasn't on this minibus.

"Bravo, Lucky! We knew you could do it!" said the man whose anticipated arrest had been interrupted. Then, spotting the expression on Penny's face, he added, "Sorry. It's just those are the first words we've ever heard him say, and he's nearly five. Not an ideal choice of vocabulary, obviously. Better if he'd started with a 'hello,' or a 'thank you,' but hey-ho. You work with what you're given."

"What did he mean—*hide everything*?" said Penny, rubbing her forehead where she could feel a tension headache brewing, exacerbated by the tequila slammers she'd drunk at last night's pub quiz. Next time she'd leave the Met to do their own legwork.

"Who knows, dear girl. Lucky's past is a bit of a black box. He's the most inappropriately named child you can imagine," said the old man. "Anyhow, he wasn't referring to me. None of my ill-gotten gains are aboard the vehicle. Well, not many, at least."

"Look," said Penny, with a sigh. "I have no idea what you've been up to, and I'm quite honestly not sure that I want to know, but it's not you I'm after. Or her," she said, nodding at the still-weeping bus driver.

"Did Social Services send you?" said a voice from the back of the bus, a teenaged boy with a gorgeous baby—who, given the resemblance, must have been his little sister—on his lap. "I honestly had no choice, and I swear I'll never, ever do it again."

"If you're here on behalf of the council, then tell them it's not criminal damage, it's art. They're just a bunch of philistines who can't tell the difference," said the woman Penny thought was Ruby.

4

She was almost entirely covered by a voluminous mound of multi-colored knitting.

Penny's temples throbbed harder. She could feel the headache building, pressing against her skull.

"Well, I'm not going in for questioning again," said another old lady with electric blue hair that made her head look uncannily like a police siren. "How many times do I have to tell you lot, they all died of natural causes? I'm just extraordinarily unlucky with husbands."

"Not as unlucky as them," muttered the old man.

"WILL YOU ALL PLEASE STOP CONFESSING!" Penny shouted. She held up the photocopied picture in her hand and waved it at them all. "THIS is who I'm looking for."

Everyone went silent. Almost as one, they turned and stared at the seat immediately behind the driver. The empty seat. Then, they all swiveled to look toward the open bus door, and the motorway beside them.

Penny turned, too. The traffic had slowed to a near crawl, as it always did when drivers spotted a patrol car. Did they think she wasn't aware that they never usually drove so cautiously?

A car horn blared, long and angry, and it was obvious why.

Who would have imagined that anyone so old could leap over the central reservation quite so athletically?

THREE
MONTHS
EARLIER

Daphne

So, how are we going to spend my seventieth birthday?" said Daphne to Jack. Which was, obviously, ridiculous, since Jack hadn't been in a position to respond for the past fifteen years.

Daphne not only spoke to Jack regularly, she also talked to her house plants and to the people in the photographs dotted around her apartment, and she often shouted at actors and presenters on the TV. She didn't, however, talk to the neighbors. Ever. Unless an urgent administrative issue cropped up, like the recent redecoration of the building's "common parts."

"Common parts?" she'd said to Jack in outrage, waving the letter from the building's management company at the ceiling. "What kind of a descriptor is that? Sounds like something you'd find in a second-rate brothel."

But, while Daphne avoided engaging with any of the other residents—or anyone at all, actually—she did know all about them. She could argue that she enjoyed the feeling of connection with the community that this gave her, but the reality was that she liked the sensation of power that an imbalance of information imbued. When you know more about someone than they know about you, it puts you in control. And it makes you safe.

Daphne's source of information was a website she'd come across, about a year ago, called OurNeighbours.com. An extraordinary number of local residents appeared to have signed up to the sub-group that covered their end of Hammersmith, and she'd discovered that, if she joined them, she was able to lurk furtively, eavesdropping on everyone's strongly held opinions, without ever having to declare herself.

Every morning, while she ate her toast and marmalade, Daphne would scroll through the latest posts, watching video surveillance footage of Amazon parcels being stolen from people's doorsteps, reading heated debates about traffic-calming systems and residents' parking, or looking at the *awful*, tasteless, often broken items people put up for sale, expecting some fool to pay good money for them.

Yesterday morning there'd been an argument about urban foxes. Were they friends, who should be left food in our gardens, or mange-ridden vermin who spread disease and caused damage? As always, the debate had rapidly descended from reasonable and measured into a slanging match resulting in one resident threatening a call to the police and the RSPCA, and another offering to cover his neighbor's garden with fox poo to see how she liked it. Finally, after several posters being misnamed "Karen" for some reason, an admin had removed the whole thread from the site, and everyone had gone back to talking about rubbish collection.

Daphne loaded up the website, trying not to get toast crumbs on her keyboard. What was waiting for her on her birthday morning?

The talk today was surprisingly, and annoyingly, genial. A cleaner looking for work, a woman seeking advice on retrieving a wedding ring from a kitchen sink U-bend, and someone selling a dining-room table and chairs to a community of people who were highly unlikely to own a dining room. Since Daphne's second-favorite website was Rightmove.co.uk, she knew that every local dining room had long since been converted into a home office, a gym or a "media center." What, she wondered, did one *do* in a media center? Mediate? Meditate? Who knew?

Daphne kept scrolling through the recent posts, but was finding it impossible to concentrate. *Seventy*, she kept thinking. *Seventy*. Could she really be that old? She certainly didn't feel it, and couldn't yet believe it. How on earth had she got here? Where had all that time gone?

This wasn't where Daphne had expected to be at this stage of her life. She'd rather imagined that she'd spend her older age surrounded by loving friends and family. Well, perhaps not *loving* friends and family, but at least a group of familiar people connected by history, genetics, or shared finances and real estate. Yet, here she was, utterly alone, stalking her neighbors and talking to her plants. Except for the yucca, which she'd never entirely trusted.

Her apartment, admittedly, was gorgeous, with views of the majestic, winding Thames, with Hammersmith Bridge to her right, Putney Bridge to her left, and the imposing, salmon-pink, terra-cotta-clad Harrods Furniture Depository on the opposite bank. But while it had initially felt like a place of safety—a cocoon—it had gradually become a prison, however luxurious. Since she'd moved in, fifteen years ago, she'd only ventured out once or twice a week to buy groceries, and recently she'd had the feeling that the walls were closing in on her, that eventually she'd be mashed, together with all her furniture, into a tiny cube.

Maybe it was time, whatever the consequences might be, to

reengage with the world, to make some friends? Or at least some acquaintances. And what better day to start than her birthday?

The problem was, Daphne didn't actually *like* other people very much, and she had no idea how one went about making friends as an adult, in any case. You couldn't exactly ask someone to play hopscotch with you, or give them one of your Sherbet Lemons. They'd probably report you to the authorities, or bad-mouth you on OurNeighbours.com.

Daphne needed *a plan*, which shouldn't be a problem since she was, after all, one of the best strategists she knew. She and Jack had spent hours standing in front of elaborately mapped-out flowcharts, uncapped pens in hand, interrogating them from all angles, adding in options, contingencies, backstops, firewalls. Stress testing, then redrawing until the names, places, times, code words, arrows, and symbols would infiltrate her dreams, whirling around and coalescing in alternative patterns, which sometimes provided a breakthrough.

It was probably when she'd loved Jack the most, those long evenings when she would toss him an idea and he'd catch it, reshape it slightly, and throw it back, the to-and-fro volley continuing until they'd created something spectacular together.

Could she do it without him?

Of course she could! She'd always been the real brains behind the operation. Not that Jack, or anyone else, would have acknowledged that. And, in any case, this was hardly a complex project, was it? Make some friends. A five-year-old could do it!

Daphne pulled a coat and handbag from the pegs by her front door. She would buy herself a whiteboard and some colored pens. Then she would construct a plan.

Art

A rt Andrews always put a call in to his agent on the first Monday of the month, but for the last few months his agent had been strangely unavailable. According to his ferociously protective assistant, he'd been in an important meeting, or visiting a set, or playing golf, and, despite her assurances, he'd not called Art back. Even his NHS GP was not this difficult to get hold of.

Art was beginning to suspect that he was being deliberately avoided. He believed the modern expression was "ghosted." He'd been one of Jaspar's first clients, about forty years ago, but he'd spent more of his career "resting" than acting, so he'd never been anywhere near the top of his agent's priority list. Now it seemed he wasn't on the list at all.

For a while Art had found himself a niche, playing grumpy old men in wheelchairs and heart attack or stroke victims in hospital-based TV dramas. He had also become fairly renowned for his extremely convincing late-stage Alzheimer's. How many actors could drool realistically on demand?

If Art were offered a part, it was very rare that he was alive by the end of his episode. On more than one occasion he'd been smothered with a pillow by a close family member. Sometimes, he wasn't even alive at the beginning of an episode. He had spent numerous hours playing a dead body, over which siblings argued about their inheritance while he tried desperately not to sneeze. In his last job, he'd been one of the White Walkers in a *Game of Thrones* spin-off, and just had to shuffle forward as part of an undead pack, until he was incinerated by a dragon in postproduction.

But recently, even these less-than-glamorous opportunities appeared to have dried up.

Art picked up the phone. He was not going to let his career die without a fight. He dialed his agent.

"Shelbourne Talent Agency," trilled Jaspar's assistant.

"Hello," said Art. "This is Mr. Shelbourne's consultant speaking. I'm calling with the results of his recent medical tests. Is he available?"

"He didn't mention any medical tests," the assistant said, sounding hesitant, verging on vaguely suspicious. "Can I take your number and get him to call you back?"

"I'm afraid it's rather urgent and very . . . sensitive," said Art. "And I have a patient ready prepped in theater for an extremely tricky phalloplasty." Thankfully, Art had appeared in several episodes of *Casualty* and *Holby City* over the years, during which he'd been examined by many arrogant, overbearing medical consultants, so the part was coming naturally. He should add it to his CV.

"Uh, OK, I'll put you through, Dr. . . . ."

"Clooney," said Art, which was the first name that came to mind.

There was a pause on the line, then Jaspar said, "Dr. Clooney?"

"Hi, Jaspar. It's Art," he replied.

"Oh, for goodness' sake," said his agent. "Why the subterfuge? And couldn't you have done better than *Clooney*?"

"Sorry, dear boy," said Art. "It's just you've been rather tricky to get hold of recently."

Jaspar sighed, which wasn't a promising sign. "I'm afraid the work hasn't been exactly *pouring in* for you recently, old chap. But you are"—there was a pause, and Art could picture Jaspar checking Art's somewhat dusty CV—"seventy-five years old. You should put your feet up! Learn to play golf! Spend more time with your grandchildren!"

Art had never actually met his grandchildren, but this was hardly the time to revisit that old wound.

"But I don't want to retire, Jaspar," he said. "I've got so much life left in me." *And almost nothing left in the bank account*, he could have added. "And seventy-five isn't exactly *old*, is it? The president of the United States is older than me. The Queen, God rest her soul, carried on working right up until she died at ninety-six. The Rolling Stones are my age, and they're still performing to packed-out stadiums."

"I bet their insurance premium is massive," said Jaspar, which was hardly the point.

"Do you not have anything I could do?" said Art, trying not to sound as if he were begging. Which he was.

"Hold on," said Jaspar, with another long sigh, but at least it was punctuated by the sound of rustling paper.

"Nope. The only thing I can see that could work is a request for entrants for a TV talent show. It's called *Me and My Dog*. They wondered if any of our talent have equally talented dogs and might be able to put an act together. I don't suppose you . . . ?"

"No," said Art. "I'm afraid not."

"Shame. There's a hundred thousand pounds' prize money to play for. And there's the visibility, obviously. Well, that's all for the moment, I'm afraid," said Jaspar, in what Art recognized as his *I'm wrapping this up now* voice. "But I'll be sure to call you the minute I find anything appropriate."

This, Art knew, was highly unlikely.

"Sure," he said. "Thanks, Jaspar. Speak soon."

Art hung up and went to the cupboard for his emergency bottle of whiskey, before remembering that he'd drunk it in a fit of despair during another long dark night of the soul spent stalking Kerry on Facebook. He put on his coat and headed for the off-license.

As Art turned the corner onto King Street, he spotted a rather sweet-looking old lady, with white hair in a messy bun and the petite physique of a retired ballet dancer, carrying a ridiculously large whiteboard. She kept shifting it from one arm to the other, only narrowly avoiding assaulting passing pedestrians.

Art believed in helping people more disadvantaged than himself. It was the right thing to do, and it made him feel like a *good person*. The problem was, recently he'd been unable to find anyone more disadvantaged than he was. But here, right in front of him, was a lady who was almost as old as him, and significantly smaller.

"Can I offer you a hand with that?" he said, in his most chivalrous tone.

"Do I look like I'm unable to manage by myself?" she replied, not at all sweetly.

"Actually, yes," he said.

"Do you think I'm incapable because I'm old? Or because I'm a woman?" she said, fixing him with a steely glare.

Art considered giving up and leaving this grumpy old bag to her own devices, but now he'd resolved to earn himself some karmic merit points, he wanted to see the whole thing through.

"I don't think you're incapable at all," he said. "I just think you're much smaller than that whiteboard. I'll help you carry it home, if you like?"

"And let you know where I live?" she said, scowling at him as if he were some kind of criminal. Which he wasn't. At least, not entirely. "What kind of fool do you think I am? Anyhow, if I did want help, I wouldn't ask someone so . . ." She paused, looking him up and down, before choosing the word "unfashionable."

Unfashionable?!?

"Look, I'm just trying to help," said Art. "It's obviously far too large for you to transport by yourself." Art picked up the end of the board that was now resting on the pavement.

"GET YOUR HANDS OFF MY PROPERTY!" yelled the woman, causing every pedestrian within a ten-meter radius to stop and glare at him.

"Fight! Fight! Fight!" shouted two youths on bicycles, before collapsing over their handlebars in fits of giggles, then cycling off.

"Now, move out of the way, before I call the police," said the woman.

"Certainly, my lady," said Art, affecting the deep bow he'd perfected when cast as a random, nonspeaking courtier in an episode of *Blackadder*, and shuffling backward off the pavement, where he was sworn at, and nearly mowed down, by a man on a moped with a Deliveroo bag strapped to his back like an improbably fast-moving tortoise.

He watched the woman walk off down the road, sending pedestrians ricocheting out of her path, stopping every three or four meters to put down the whiteboard, then pick it up again in a slightly different position.

If Art had been just a smidgen less charitable, he'd have been willing her to drop it on her foot.

Daphne

aphne positioned her new whiteboard a few meters in front of her bed. That way it would be the first thing she saw when she woke up in the morning, which would keep her focused. She pulled the cap off the fat black marker she'd bought and lifted the nib to her nose, inhaling the smell of purpose, of potential, of the future.

Make some friends, she wrote, the squeak of the pen on the board giving her a little frisson of anticipation. She'd missed having a challenge, and was under no illusion about what a challenge this was, as her little interaction with that irritating, interfering, and patronizing old man on King Street had reminded her. She'd spent most of her life distrusting people, assuming that everyone must have some kind of ulterior motive for every decision they made. After all, she usually did. However, she imagined that in order to make friends, you probably had to show them some level of trust. Give them the benefit of the doubt, and not threaten to have them arrested.

Be more trusting, she wrote in blue. Then, remembering how she'd yelled at her recent Good Samaritan, she added no shouting or glaring in parentheses. She surveyed her words, head cocked to one side, before uncapping a green pen, adding an aster-isk after the word glaring, then writing *unless severely pro-voked at the bottom of the board.

Now, where was she going to find these strangers who she had to trust and not shout or glare at?

Volunteering? she wrote in red pen. But surely the whole point was to meet people with whom she had at least a little in common? She was far too selfish to spend her time helping the needy, and disliked, in principle, anyone who did. She picked up her white-board eraser and scrubbed the word out.

Take up a hobby? she wrote in its place. But what? The only hobbies she'd had in the past were not the type that made you friends. Quite the reverse, in fact.

Join a club? she added to the list, then snorted, remembering the Groucho Marx quote, "I refuse to join any club that would have me as a member." Wasn't that the truth?

Use the internet? she wrote with a flourish, before putting the caps back on her new pens and lining them up at the base of her board. She took a few paces back and stared at her beautifully color-coded work.

"Use the internet," she read out loud. That was something she could start on right now, wasn't it?

Daphne was a huge fan of the internet. Young people today had no idea how lucky they were, having all that information at their fingertips. In the early days of Daphne's career, her job had been gathering information. She'd spent *days* searching through micro-fiches in the local library, tailing possible leads, grilling informants, and flirting with policemen. Now, much of the information she'd required would have been right there, on the internet. You just needed to know where to look. And she always knew where to look. Surely, the World Wide Web could snare her a friend or two?

She walked over to her huge, square, leather-topped partners' desk. Ironic, since she didn't have a partner to sit on the other side. She flipped up the lid of her laptop, which revealed the last website she'd been on: OurNeighbours.com. She moved the cursor up to the search bar and typed two words: **make friends**.

Almost immediately, a slew of posts containing the words "make" and "friends" highlighted in bold appeared on her screen. She scrolled down the page until her gaze snagged on the words **ARE YOU OVER SEVENTY?** As a matter of fact, despite her feeling nothing of the sort, she now was. **WOULD YOU LIKE TO MAKE SOME NEW FRIENDS?** Seeing the question posed so baldly, Daphne still wasn't entirely sure that she did, but she had resolved at least to give it a go, so she read on.

WHY NOT JOIN THE SENIOR CITIZENS SOCIAL CLUB AT THE MANDEL COMMUNITY CENTER? CALL OR TEXT LYDIA ON 07980 344562, she read. She looked back at her whiteboard, and the words Join a club? She stared at the post for several minutes, drumming her fingers on her desk. Perhaps she should try this social club. Mandel Community Center was just around the corner: a squat, dilapidated-looking carbuncle of a building, nestled among the prettier Victorian houses between King Street and the A4. She could go just the once, and if it was terrible, as she suspected it would be, she need never go again.

Daphne looked over at her phone, which was sitting on an art deco console table near her front door, tethered to the wall. She hadn't called *anyone* apart from tradespeople for well over a decade, and just the thought of phoning a complete stranger and trying to sound like the kind of social, outgoing person she'd want in her club made Daphne feel queasy. It would be humiliating.

No, a more detached communication would be preferable. Then she could keep it simple and to the point. But her phone didn't have the capability of texting anyone. She didn't want to fall at the first hurdle. Not at her age—she could break a hip.

Daphne had owned a mobile, of course, back in the day. A state-of-the-art BlackBerry, which had allowed her not only to text, but to send emails! But she'd had to dispose of it when she'd moved here, on April 26, 2008. She'd stopped the van containing the salvaged remnants of her previous life, and had tossed her beloved BlackBerry into the dark, cold depths of the River Thames.

She hadn't replaced it. After all, the clue was in the name: *mobile*. If you never went anywhere, or talked to anyone, what was the point?

Still, it was her birthday. And not just any old birthday—a BIG one. So tomorrow she would buy herself a belated present: a brand-new mobile phone. And then she would join a social club.

The man in the mobile-phone shop wasn't a man at all. He was very much a boy. He even had acne, including one spot with a generous head of yellow pus that was just begging to be squeezed. Daphne considered offering to help, but thought that might be overstepping the boundaries. It would be reckless to go from little social contact at all to manhandling other people's unsightly dermatological features in one fell swoop. *Baby steps, Daphne.*

The man-child looked up at her as she stood at his desk. Was he *smirking*? She suspected he was.

"I'd like to buy a mobile phone," said Daphne. "And I believe I am in the correct establishment."

"Totally," said the boy. Definitely smirking. "What sort of phone would you like?"

This question stumped Daphne somewhat, and she refused to display total ignorance in front of this child, so she quickly scanned the display of phones around her. She couldn't see anything that remotely resembled her old BlackBerry. Everything seemed to be Apple these days. Why was all technology named after crumble ingredients?

"I'd like the red one," she said, pointing at a slim, modern-looking phone on a display stand. She'd always liked red. It was very *her*.

"That's an iPhone Fourteen Plus, with a dual-camera system, face ID, and five hundred and twelve gigabytes of storage," he said. "I'm not sure you need that much capacity. What do you want to use it for?"

This was an extremely impertinent question. It was entirely Daphne's business how she used her new phone. Fortunately, she remembered the words she'd written on her whiteboard the day before—no glaring—and rearranged her face into a benign smile, of sorts. Given the slightly alarmed look on the salesboy's face, she hadn't entirely succeeded.

"It's perfect," she said. "Box it up, and I'll pay cash."

"Whoa! Slow down," he said, holding his palms out toward her, as if she were a skittery horse which might bite. She had a strong urge to do exactly that. But she needed the phone.

"You'll have to have a contract," continued the boy, pulling up a screen on his laptop, and swiveling it around so she could see it.

"I'll need name, address, bank details, date of birth, credit check, etcetera, etcetera."

"I'm sorry, extremely young man, but we've only just met, and there's no way I'm giving you all that intrusive and sensitive information. This is a standard commercial transaction. You tell me how much that phone costs, I give you the cash, you put it in a bag, and I go home. *Capisce?*" she said, adding a little touch from *The Sopranos* as a flourish.

The boy sighed. "OK, we'll do a pay-as-you-go. That'll be nine hundred and forty-nine pounds, plus the cost of a SIM card."

Daphne tried very hard not to look shocked as she mentally calculated how much cash she'd shoved from the safe into her handbag that morning.

"Do you know how to use it?" said the boy.

"Look, why is it that whenever people see someone my age, they assume that they're totally useless with technology?" she said. "It's terrible stereotyping, not to mention rude and patronizing."

"So, you know how it works?" said the boy.

"No," said Daphne.

Two hours later, the mobile-phone salesboy had a migraine and had to take the rest of the day off work.

Daphne, meanwhile, was the proud owner of a smartphone that she knew how to operate, had sent her first text message since 2008—to someone called Lydia—and was on her way to creating a social life.

Art

rt's pace slowed as he reached the greengrocer. Right there, on the pavement, were huge baskets of fresh fruit and vegetables. Glossy green apples, bunches of bananas, carrots, and a pyramid of plump pumpkins, ready for Halloween. Art felt his fingers itch. It would be so easy just to reach out, pick up one of those delicately arranged peaches, and pop it up his sleeve. He could already feel the soft, fuzzy skin against his palm.

This was the problem with having too much time on his hands. He couldn't be trusted with it. He clenched and unclenched his fists, then thrust them deep into the pockets of his overcoat, where they couldn't do any damage.

Yet again, Art cursed his agent. Along with the whole film and TV industry. How come, when one quarter of the UK population was over sixty, they made up such a teeny-tiny percentage of available roles? The producers, directors, and writers seemed determined to airbrush wrinkles from their glossy, make-believe worlds. Unless they were vital to forward a plot point, illustrate a backstory, or provide a minor, two-dimensional villain.

Art walked on, staring at the pavement, and didn't look up again until he was past the row of shops, next to the local community center. He paused at the noticeboard outside. Right in the middle of all the various announcements and advertisements was a poster posing the question ARE YOU OVER SEVENTY? in bold black type.

Indeed, he was. At least someone seemed to want to attract a person of his age. He presumed they were selling funeral plans or retirement homes. He read on.

WOULD YOU LIKE TO MAKE SOME NEW FRIENDS?
WHY NOT JOIN THE SENIOR CITIZENS SOCIAL CLUB
AT THE MANDEL COMMUNITY CENTER?
CALL OR TEXT LYDIA ON 07980 344562.

Maybe he should join this club. Perhaps they'd supply free food and drink! Cake, even. And if he could spend several hours in a warm community center, he would save on his heating bills. Now it was nearly November, his house was freezing.

Art pulled out his phone and took a photo of the notice so he could call this Lydia. It would be good for him to keep himself busy. Get some of that dangerous time off his treacherous hands. He'd persuade William to come along for moral support, and so he wouldn't look entirely friendless.

William had taken more persuading than Art had anticipated. In the end, he'd had to play the sympathy card by relaying the whole humiliating conversation with Jaspar, and then suffer his oldest friend's gales of laughter as he said "Dr. Clooney" and "phalloplasty" on repeat.

Now, two days later, they were standing opposite the community center, ready to join the inaugural meeting of the social club. A whole afternoon to be spent with like-minded people doing . . . what, exactly? Something interesting, he was quite sure.

Art was poised to skip over the road, as exuberant as a small child clutching a helium balloon, when he saw something—someone— who deflated his mood entirely.

William tried to move forward, but Art thrust a rigid arm in front of him.

"Wait!" he said. "This isn't a good idea after all."

"What are you talking about?" said William. "You're the one who wanted to come! And now we're here. So let's go."

"It's her," said Art, pointing at the woman opening the door to the hall. "I'm not joining a club where she's a member. She's dangerous."

"Dangerous?" said William, craning his neck to look at the woman opposite them. "Don't be ridiculous. She's not much younger than us. And she's tiny. She looks rather sweet, actually. If a little overdressed."

William stepped from the pavement into the road, before being yanked backward again by Art.

"You may think that," said Art, urgently. "But she's ferocious. Possibly evil. She abused me terribly during an argument about a whiteboard."

"Where were you? In a classroom?" said William.

"No! I was just walking along King Street when I saw someone who needed a hand. You know how I like to help?" said Art. William just rolled his eyes, which was a little unsupportive, frankly.

"Anyhow, when I offered to carry her whiteboard for her, she was horribly rude. And ungrateful. She even threatened to have me arrested," said Art, the memory making his shoulders tense with indignation. "And she called me unfashionable."

William snorted, and stared in a meaningful way at the jacket Art was wearing, which had a large hole under one armpit and a stubborn gravy stain on the lapel.

"Don't be such a wimp, Art," he said, in a conciliatory tone. "It sounds like a mistake and a misunderstanding. I'm sure the first thing she'll do when she sees you is apologize. Let's go. You promised me cake."

"OK," said Art, reluctantly. "But if there's no cake, we're leaving."

Lydia

When Lydia had applied to the local council for the job of running a new senior citizens' social club three afternoons a week, she'd imagined herself surrounded by a group of genial, grateful, and enthusiastic geriatrics. They'd tap their feet to old Beatles tracks and teach her how to do the Twist. They'd play gently competitive games of bingo and spend happy hours collaborating over giant jigsaw puzzles.

However, as Lydia looked around her group of assorted seniors, she just couldn't fit them into the jolly scenes she'd imagined.

"I'm really sorry, but I'm pretty sure dogs aren't allowed in the hall," she said to a woman who'd introduced herself as Pauline-Retired-Headmistress.

"You're *pretty sure*," said Pauline, glaring at her as if she were a schoolgirl found smoking behind the bike sheds. "That's not quite good enough, is it? Show me where, specifically, in the building regulations it says *No Dogs Allowed*, and until then, she stays."

Pauline turned her back on a stuttering Lydia, walked over to the tea table, and sat down on a chair, tying her dog's lead to the chair leg.

Lydia had spent the weekend reading *The 7 Habits of Highly Effective People*, in preparation for her new job, but she still felt completely out of her depth, and not in the slightest effective. Thank goodness she was British and could resort to the tradition of tea-making when the going got a little tough. That was an effective habit she *had* properly mastered. Lydia poured tea for each of her six inaugural club members, adding milk and sugar as requested, and referring to her list of names as she did so.

In addition to Pauline, there was Art—an actor, apparently, although she didn't recognize him—and his friend William, a retired paparazzo. Then Ruby, who'd arrived with a giant bag of wool and knitting needles which she waved around in a somewhat threatening manner. Next to Ruby was Anna, who had hair colored in the most extraordinary shade, and used a walking frame on wheels to plow her way forward, regardless of who or what was in her way. And, finally, Daphne, who said little and gave the impression of finding everyone beneath her. She was wearing giant fake emeralds around her neck, which seemed completely over the top for afternoon tea. Unless you were at the Ritz, which this most definitely was not.

Lydia finished handing round the tea, along with generous slices of the chocolate fudge cake she'd baked for the occasion, and sat down. Everyone stared at her, in silence, and it became obvious that she was expected to say something.

"Err, so what kind of activities would you like me to arrange for you?" she said. "I do have a small budget, but some of the best activities are completely free, aren't they?" She looked around the table at six blank faces. "I was thinking maybe bingo? Bridge? A knitting circle, perhaps? Painting? Or we could do some singing?"

They all stared at her, silently.

Please, someone say something, she thought.

"To be frank, you're guilty of some heinous clichés here," said William. "Why does everyone assume that once you get past the age of seventy, all you want to do is play bingo and knit?"

There was a murmur of agreement from the assembled circle, except for a mumbled "What's wrong with knitting?" from Ruby.

Lydia sighed. "Well, what activities would you like to include, then?" she asked.

"Skydiving," said Art, through a large mouthful of cake.

"Target practice," said Daphne.

"That figures," muttered Art, and Daphne shot him a glance that was surprisingly malevolent from one so petite.

"Speed dating," said Ruby. "And knitting."

"Karate," said William.

"Synchronized swimming. Or go-karting," said Anna, banging her walking frame against the floor for emphasis.

"Oh, for heaven's sake," said Pauline.

Where did she even start? With the limitations of their budget, or the Health and Safety implications of taking six pensioners skydiving?

"More tea?" she said.

"Thanks, Lydia," said Art, proffering his empty cup. "But do you think next time we might have something a little stronger? Cocktails, maybe?"

"Good idea!" said William, slapping Art on the back, causing some of his refilled tea to slop into the saucer. "I could wheel my cocktail trolley along, if your budget won't stretch that far. I live just around the corner."

"Cocktails!" shrieked Pauline, before Lydia could even try to work out how to suggest that a bunch of geriatrics getting plastered on spirits might not have been what the council had in mind when they'd proposed a social club.

"Alcohol? In the afternoon? On a weekday? That really is completely inappropriate," continued Pauline.

Lydia spotted Daphne rolling her eyes, then watched as she reached into her handbag and pulled out a packet of cigarettes. With mounting alarm, Lydia saw Daphne flip open the packet, tap out a cigarette, and insert it into a cigarette holder—did people still use those? She put it in the corner of her mouth. She wasn't going to light it, was she? Oh God. She actually was.

"PUT THAT OUT!" shrieked Pauline. "Disgusting habit, not to mention illegal in a public space. I honestly wish I'd never come."

Art said something to William in a whisper, making William giggle.

"If you have something to say, please share it with the whole class!" said Pauline, her eyes narrowed into tiny slits.

"Thank you, Pauline," said Lydia, trying to sound more forceful and in control than she felt. "But this isn't one of your classes."

"Well, that's obvious," said Pauline. "I'd hardly have been rated Outstanding by Ofsted if my classes had been run like this. Do you have any formal qualifications or training? You have absolutely no natural authority. What on earth were the council thinking, putting you in charge?"

Pauline prodded her finger accusingly in Lydia's direction, and

Lydia, who always tried to think only the best of people, was side-swiped by a sudden and nasty emotion.

Go to hell, you ungrateful old bat, she thought and, at that very second, there was a huge crash as a section of the Mandel Community Center ceiling, right above Pauline's head, collapsed.

As soon as the dust had cleared, settling in great mounds on the tea table, which now resembled a scene from *Scarface*, it was clear that Pauline had indeed gone to hell, or thereabouts.

Lydia was *almost* certain that it was impossible to kill someone with the power of thought, but it did seem like an uncanny coincidence of timing.

They sat, frozen in time and covered in dust, still holding their teacups, like the petrified remains of the inhabitants of Pompeii. No one was able to break the oppressive, stunned silence. Pauline, face a mottled purple and mouth agape, lay rigid in her upended chair, sensibly shod feet in the air. There was a flurry of movement next to her as the small dog, which Lydia had entirely forgotten about, shook itself free of the debris and began to whine.

Before Lydia was able to adjust to the situation and decide what to do, Daphne took control—calling an ambulance, moving everyone away from the jagged, gaping hole in the ceiling and checking Pauline, in vain, for any signs of life.

It was fair to say that Lydia's first day back in paid employment in twenty years had not been an unmitigated success. Was it too much to hope that things could only get better?

Ziggy

Ziggy thought back to the days when he'd grumbled about having to get out of bed and dressed in time to leave for school at eight thirty a.m. He'd had no idea how lucky he was.

On Mondays, Wednesdays, and Thursdays, his mother left home at five a.m. One of the three jobs in what she laughingly called her "portfolio career" involved cleaning offices before they opened for the day. So, on those mornings, Kylie was entirely his responsibility.

Kylie didn't believe in staying in bed for as long as possible, like any normal person. Oh no. She'd wake up by five thirty a.m. at the latest and issue an alarm far more penetrating and insistent than any electronic device. Ziggy would then have to get her up and change her nappy. A poo-filled nappy had to be the rudest possible awakening to a new day.

Breakfast, before Kylie, had been a hurried bowl of Coco Pops, eaten with one hand while the other scrolled through Snapchat or TikTok. Now it was an endurance test involving trying to get more mashed banana and baby porridge into Kylie's mouth than over her face and hair, or on the floor.

But then, just as he'd start wondering, for the millionth time, how he'd let himself get into this mess, Kylie would give him one of her wide, gummy smiles, reach her plump little hands toward him like curious starfish, and say "Dada," and—for at least the next ten minutes—it would all feel worthwhile.

Ziggy steered Kylie's pushchair through the estate as though it were a force field. He kept his eyes trained down on his schoolbag, slung over the handlebars, and walked as fast as he could, trying to get out before he was spotted.

It was impossible to survive on Ziggy's estate without pledging allegiance to one of the rival gangs, who found the local teenagers useful as lookouts, messengers, and couriers. They were less likely to be stopped and searched than an adult and, even if they were, would most probably be released on caution. Before Kylie, Ziggy had found the extra money this occasional errand-running brought him tantalizing. For the first time in his life, he'd been able to afford some of the labels he'd always lusted after, so long as he hid them from his mum. But now the stakes were so very much higher. Being found carrying one of Floyd's packages might not land him in an adult prison, but it would most definitely lose him custody of his daughter. So now Ziggy did everything he could to avoid being seen, and given a job to do.

Ziggy let out a long exhalation as he made it through to the main road unchallenged, and charged toward Mandel Community Center. Kylie attended the council-funded nursery there five days a week, so that he could finish his final year at school, and his mum could keep working to support them all. He couldn't be late for registration again.

Ziggy rounded the corner and stared at the community center in alarm. It was covered in what looked like police tape, and a group of men wearing hard hats and high-visibility vests were wandering around with clipboards. It looked like a cross between Kylie's favorite TV show—*Bob the Builder*—and his mother's—*Silent Witness*. He turned Kylie's pushchair one hundred and eighty degrees and pushed through the doors with his back, pulling Kylie behind him.

"What the fff-lip is going on out there?" he said, biting the swear word back just in time. Janine, the head nursery nurse, had told him that if he swore *once more* in front of the children, he'd be banned from entering the hall without a gag. He suspected she might not be serious, but didn't want to find out, just in case.

"It's because of that incident yesterday," said Janine, gesturing toward the room next door. "At the Senior Citizens' Social Club, on the other side." The way Janine said "other side" reminded Ziggy of his Liverpudlian grandmother, who'd had a strong belief in the afterlife, where she now resided.

"Part of the ceiling came down, and someone *died*. They reckon it was a massive stroke that killed her, rather than the ceiling collapse itself. Although I bet the two things were related," said Janine.

Ziggy kissed Kylie on the top of her head and watched her crawl at high speed toward the toy box.

"Crikey," he said, using one of Janine's approved expletives. "Well, at least it didn't affect the nursery. I mean, those relics must be on their way out, in any case."

"That's really not appropriate, Ziggy. Every life is precious," said Janine, giving him the same hard stare that she used on the toddlers before sending them to the naughty step.

Ziggy cursed himself. That thought had just popped out before he'd had a chance to consider it. His mum was always telling him that if he just paused for a few seconds to think about the consequences before he opened his big mouth, or unzipped his trousers, he'd still be spending his days playing *Call of Duty* and hanging out at the skateboard park, rather than pushing swings and playing endless games of peekaboo. *Just count to ten, Ziggy, honey. Then put it back in your pants.*

This was not how Ziggy had envisioned his life turning out. He'd dreamed of being the first in his family to go to university, and then a job in tech—maybe in Silicon Valley, even, where he'd have a house with a swimming pool and a girlfriend with a Hollywood smile and perfect boobs.

Ziggy loved Kylie, obviously. He just wished she hadn't appeared in his life until a bit later on. Then he might have been able to give her all the things he'd wanted as a child, but had never had. Her own bedroom, and a garden with a swing set and a Wendy house. Nerf guns, a PlayStation, and the latest designer trainers.

"Who are they?" asked Ziggy, nodding toward the men with clipboards.

"They've been sent by the council," said Janine. "They said it's safe to keep using the hall for the time being; they've just taped off one end of the room next door. But I heard them say they might need to close us down for *months* for refurbishments. What am I going to do? I need this job, Ziggy."

Ziggy felt sick. It had taken him and his mum *ages* to find this council-funded nursery place. The few hours of freedom it gave him each day was the only time he got to feel like a normal teenager. Without Mandel Community Center, Ziggy's former life was pretty much over, and his future was utterly screwed.

Daphne

The first hour of the Senior Citizens' Social Club had been every bit as dire as Daphne had been expecting. More so, even. Why was it that people assumed you could throw a total group of strangers together and, just because they were approximately the same age, they'd get along? It might work with five-year-olds, but not with septuagenarians who'd accumulated vastly different life experience, bad habits, and entrenched opinions. It had been clear to Daphne, within minutes, that she had nothing whatsoever in common with any of her fellow "club members." And thank the Lord for that, frankly.

One of them, to Daphne's horror, was the badly dressed, irritatingly helpful man she'd yelled at the other day on King Street. What were the chances of that? She'd considered trying to make amends, but she didn't want to reveal any form of weakness in front of this group of strangers. And besides, he kept glaring at her as if she'd kidnapped one of his children and sent him their ear in the post, rather than just been a tad tetchy. The man obviously had no backbone.

But then, just as Daphne had resolved never to walk through the door of Mandel Community Center again, things had looked up.

For a start, their mundane tea party had descended into a general slanging match, aided by Daphne herself who, given that she'd barely been out of her apartment for fifteen years, had forgotten the city had instituted a public smoking ban in 2007. Not that it would have made much difference if she had remembered. She'd never been one for following rules.

And then, just as she'd started to contemplate stabbing her own hand with a cake fork to ease the burden, a riveting and entirely unexpected death! For a while, it had felt just like the old days! She'd put on a good show of pretending to care whether Pauline had a pulse, and had called the emergency services while Lydia—who was a complete wimp, to be honest—had wailed and Pauline's mangy old dog had howled.

Two paramedics had arrived, who were so handsome that Daphne had considered feigning a life-threatening illness herself. They'd reassured the hysterical Lydia that it looked very much like Pauline had died from a massive stroke, which could have happened at any time. The ceiling collapse appeared more dramatic than it actually was, and certainly couldn't have killed Pauline on its own.

Now Daphne was rather looking forward to the next club meeting, although it was unlikely they could keep up this level of excitement and action, sadly.

Daphne spread some marmalade on her toast, picked up her plate along with her laptop, and took them back to bed, so she could scroll through OurNeighbours.com in comfort.

Today's chat, it transpired, was all about Pauline! For the first time in decades, Daphne felt the thrill of being on the inside looking out, rather than on the outside looking in. She had been there, in the room where it had happened.

According to the chat, Pauline had been killed when the entire local community center had collapsed on top of her. Metaphorical fingers were being pointed everywhere. There was much blaming of the local council, for underfunding and egregious breaches of Health and Safety regulations. They didn't use vocabulary like "egregious," of course. Most people on the site could barely spell. She'd never seen so many misuses of "their," "there" and "they're." Pauline, God rest her pedantic soul, would have been horrified.

The usual suspects proffered conspiracy theories involving terrorists; the racists muttered about the hall having been constructed by "foreign" contractors; and one young man, who Daphne suspected had received one too many detentions from Pauline back in the day, believed it was a revenge attack.

The only thing taking the edge off Daphne's enjoyment, apart from the toast crumbs which kept scattering over her sheets, despite every effort to keep them on the plate, was an unsettling sense that *time was running out.*

Pauline, after all, was almost exactly the same age as Daphne. She was a salutary reminder that life was so often shorter than one might have anticipated. Daphne could go *at any time.* And what would she leave behind? Nobody at all to miss her, not even a mangy dog. Just a collection of rather nice furniture, clothes, and jewelry that would end up being sold for a pittance by philistines on OurNeighbours.com. The thought made her unbearably and unexpectedly sad.

Daphne remembered the newspaper article she'd spotted a couple of months ago. Just an innocuous couple of paragraphs on one of the back pages. Words which had stopped her breath and made her feel both devastated and hopeful simultaneously. Words which had shed an entirely new light on her situation.

Perhaps, given her new circumstances, it wasn't too late to change the ending to her story. Was it possible that she could share what was left of her life with someone else? Maybe find a man with perfect manners, the ability to follow instructions, and most of his own teeth? She had always made her gums a priority and had no intention of settling for someone who'd been lackadaisical with theirs.

Daphne walked over to her whiteboard, uncapped the red pen, and on the right-hand side, next to the words Make some friends, she wrote, in firm, decisive letters, AND FIND A PARTNER.

She stared at it quizzically. The question, of course, was: How?

The social club might be a source of some amusement, unexpected drama, and surprisingly good cake, but it was looking unlikely to provide her with friends, let alone a lover. She was going to have to spread her net much, much wider and, once more, employ the power of the World Wide Web.

Daphne typed how to find love on the internet into her search engine. This was a mistake. Before she could blink, she was bombarded with ads for dating websites. There were just *too many* of them. She typed in which is the best online dating site? and started to read, making neat notes on the reporter's notepad she kept on her bedside table.

First, it seemed she had to define her objectives. Was she looking for romance, or a hook-up? She Googled "hook-up," which, it transpired, was all about sex. Daphne hadn't had sex for over fifteen years, and wasn't sure it all still worked. Perhaps everything had gone rusty and seized up, like an old bicycle left in the rain.

She wasn't much convinced by the idea of romance, either. She didn't want anyone composing terrible poetry for her, singing up at her window, or turning up with sad-looking flowers from the local garage. No, she just wanted someone to talk to other than herself. Or her plants. Or, God forbid, Art and William. Someone to share dinner with, and discuss what was on the telly, like they did on *Gogglebox*.

What was the website for that?

Daphne narrowed her search to the sites that focused on *meaningful relationships*. However, these seemed to be obsessed by *getting to know each other*. Exchanging information about skills, careers, hobbies, families, and so on. That was hardly going to work, was it?

Daphne had plenty of skills—leadership, planning and organization, code-breaking, nose-breaking, troubleshooting, actual shooting, to name just a few. But she couldn't exactly talk about any of them. Not without opening a whole squirming can of worms. She had no hobbies that would portray her in a good light, and no family, not since Jack had gone.

Just the thought of Jack floored her. She was usually so good at keeping all of that locked in her mental filing cabinet. This was what happened when you started letting people in, and letting parts of yourself out. It hurt. Like the nerves of a limb coming back to life after a near brush with frostbite. Daphne banged her laptop shut in frustration, sending more toast crumbs flying.

This was all a waste of time. How could you create a future when you had no present you enjoyed and no past you would admit to?

Lydia

ydia felt totally responsible for Pauline's dog since, even if she hadn't actually killed its owner with the power of thought, she had been the person *in charge* when her death had occurred. Had she been somehow culpable?

The council had sent her an online Health and Safety training module to complete before she could start the job. She'd tried to concentrate on the litany of mundane questions, regarding fire exits, food allergies, slippery floors, and wheelchair ramps, but *Antiques Roadshow* had been playing in the background, and she'd become distracted by trying to work out if the presenter, that lovely Fiona Bruce, had had Botox and fillers, or if she was just naturally blessed.

Lydia had taken her eye off the training module for a few minutes to check Wikipedia. Fiona was, apparently, fifty-nine. Six years older than Lydia, despite looking significantly younger. During her wave of resulting despondency, had she accidentally skipped over a section on ensuring that the ceiling of your venue was structurally sound?

The paramedics, who'd loaded Pauline into the ambulance with a blanket pulled over her head, had assured Lydia that the ceiling collapse hadn't been the cause of Pauline's death. But Lydia couldn't shake the overwhelming guilt. So she'd taken Pauline's poor orphaned dog home with her, just for the time being.

"What on earth is that ugly looking dog doing here?" said Jeremy as he shrugged off his navy cashmere overcoat and loosened his tie. He sank into his favorite leather armchair, in the corner of the open-plan kitchen that had once thrummed with activity, but now felt far too large for just the two of them, their voices echoing off the marble worktops.

"Her owner's just died," replied Lydia, feeling a twinge of guilt again. "One of the old ladies at the social club I'm running. I thought we could look after her for a while."

"Doesn't she have any friends or family who could take her on?" said Jeremy, frowning at the dog, as if she had engineered the situation herself just to irritate him.

"Not according to her neighbors," said Lydia. Pauline's neighbors hadn't seemed much affected by the news of her death. In fact, Lydia was pretty sure one of them had even *smirked* a little. Maybe Lydia hadn't been the only one to find herself at the sharp end of Pauline's tongue.

"Well, she can't stay long," said Jeremy, brushing his wavy brown hair, streaked with silver, back off his face. Jeremy was inordinately proud of his still-full head of hair, and looked down on the balding pates of lesser middle-aged men, both metaphorically and—on account of being a couple of inches taller than six foot—often literally.

"The last thing we need, now that the girls have left home, is the responsibility of a dog. Just when we're able to travel anywhere at the drop of a hat," he said.

"But we don't travel anywhere, Jeremy. Do we?" said Lydia. "At the drop of a hat or not."

"But we *could*," said Jeremy. "If we wanted to. But not if we have a dog. Besides, even if I wanted a dog, I wouldn't want that one."

"What's wrong with her?" said Lydia, hoping the dog wouldn't answer her question by farting, which she seemed to do alarmingly frequently.

"What's *right* with her?" snorted Jeremy. "She's too old, totally unkempt, and nervy."

"Of course she's nervy," said Lydia, trying to shake the thought that Jeremy had just described her. No wonder she felt such an affinity with the dog. "You keep frowning at her."

"She's not going to live very long, which I suppose is a bonus. But she'll cost an arm and a leg in vet's bills," said Jeremy, now frowning at them both. Lydia decided not to tell Jeremy about the small fortune she'd already spent at the incredibly chic pet boutique in Brook Green on a dog bed, lead, bowls, and various chews and toys.

"If I were to choose a dog, which I wouldn't, it would be something well bred. Sleek and intelligent. A black Labrador, maybe. Although they tend to be a bit greedy and run too fat." Was it her imagination, or had he just flicked his eyes toward her tummy when he'd said that? Lydia put the packet of crisps she'd been about to open in the bin. "What breed is she, in any case?"

"A bichon frise," said Lydia. This wasn't true, but Lydia suspected a posh-sounding breed would go down much better with Jeremy than the more accurate "mongrel of indeterminate parentage." Labels, in Jeremy's world, were important.

"Well, whatever she is, she's not staying here," said Jeremy. His phone pinged, and he stared at the screen, then said, "I've got to make a call. I'll be in my study."

"He's been doing that a lot recently. Taking phone calls in the evenings and at weekends, in private," said Lydia to the dog, once she'd heard the familiar click of Jeremy's study door closing. She opened the kitchen bin and retrieved the packet of crisps she'd thrown away, brushing the potato peelings and coffee grounds off it. Needs must.

"And did you notice that the only time he's smiled since he came back from the office was when he looked at that text message? Should I be worried? Or am I just jealous, because nobody ever calls to speak to me?" she said, through a mouthful of salt-and-vinegar crisp.

The dog didn't reply, obviously, but she did stare at Lydia intently, her head on one side, as if she were considering her question carefully.

"He didn't even ask your name, did he?" said Lydia. "Which is a shame, as it's possibly the only thing about you that he'd approve of."

Lydia really didn't want to send her new confidante away. For a start, finding a good home for her was going to be difficult, for all the reasons Jeremy had cruelly, but accurately, outlined. And, even for such a short time, Lydia had rather enjoyed having her around. She'd found coping with an empty nest, now the girls were both at the university, even harder than she'd expected. She'd been rattling around her large, lonely house since term started, totally surplus to requirements. At least now when she talked out loud, she didn't feel quite so unhinged.

Lydia wasn't sure exactly when she'd lost herself. Before she'd married Jeremy, she'd been Lydia Armstrong, an in-demand food stylist. She'd spent her days arranging the perfect selection of corn-flakes for the final money shot of a TV commercial, as the milk was poured into the bowl from a white ceramic jug. Or creating the most delicious-looking slice of pizza, stringy cheese dripping from its sides as it was lifted into shot, surrounded by a photogenic family of four with improbably white smiles. She'd been independent, con-fident, attractive.

Then she'd given up her surname. Followed, when the girls ar-rived, by her job. And she'd even stopped being referred to as Lydia much of the time. She was "Mummy" or "Darling" or "Mrs. Rob-erts." Sometimes she lost any form of name at all, and became just an adjunct: "Sophia's Mum," or "Jeremy's Plus-One." When she pic-tured scenes from the past, she felt like the Lydia she was looking at was a completely different person. She couldn't remember what it felt like to be her.

At least a dog would make her feel needed again. Perhaps, once he'd got to know her better, Jeremy would change his mind? Maybe, for the time being, Lydia could find someone to share responsibility for her care. That way, she could look after her just a couple of days a week to start off with. After all, Jeremy hadn't explicitly ruled out that scenario, had he?

The social club was due to meet again tomorrow. If anyone had the courage to turn up again, she could ask if they might be willing to help out.

Art

rt paused outside the community center to look at the noticeboard. A large poster had been placed aggressively in the middle, surrounded by a patchwork of more reticent faded and peeling notices, and covering up Lydia's advertisement for the social club.

IN THE LIGHT OF RECENT EVENTS,
THE COUNCIL IS HOLDING A GENERAL MEETING TO DISCUSS
THE FUTURE OF MANDEL COMMUNITY CENTER.
ALL WELCOME.

"Have you seen the sign outside from the council?" said Art to the assembled club members, crowded into the half of the room that hadn't been cordoned off.

"Yes," said Lydia as she placed a homemade cake on a plate in the center of the table. A Victoria sponge. A classic of its genre. The Dame Maggie Smith of baked goods. It was worth showing up just for that. Even if it meant having to be polite to the whiteboard-wielding witch, who hadn't yet even looked him in the eye, let alone apologized. Art snuck a hopeful glance at the ceiling above Daphne's head, but it looked irritatingly sound.

"I can't believe it," continued Lydia. "This is the first paid job I've had in decades, and it might be over before it's even properly begun."

"Well, if we keep on losing members at the rate we've been doing so far, there won't be any of us left to socialize, anyway," said Anna.

"Yes, what have you got in store for us today, Lydia? Electrocution by dodgy wiring in the kettle? Listeria in the butter icing? Carbon monoxide poisoning from the ancient boiler?" said Daphne, who looked as if she were relishing the prospect of more death.

"It's not funny," said Lydia, setting out seven cups and saucers, before going slightly pale, and taking one away again. "We should actually take a moment to remember Pauline, may she rest in peace."

Art, who was always good at spotting an opportunity, grabbed it.

"Quite right, Lydia," he said, trying to sound vaguely mournful. "Luckily, I've brought a bottle of whiskey, so we can all have a toast to our dear friend." He suspected he might have laid it on a little thick with the "dear friend"—dialogue improvisation had never been his forte—but he plowed on, pouring a decent shot of whiskey into each of the teacups.

Lydia frowned. "I don't think Pauline would have approved, at all, of alcohol on a weekday, in the afternoon," she said. "She made that quite clear, just before she . . ." Lydia gulped and went silent.

"It's Friday," said Ruby. "Which counts as the weekend, doesn't it?" She put down her knitting and picked up her cup of whiskey. The knitting, sprawled over Ruby's lap, looked very much like a half-finished bright-red hat, but far too big to fit on any normal-shaped head. Art wondered if he should suggest she use some kind of knitting pattern. She obviously didn't have a clue what she was doing.

"Thanks, Art," said William, reaching for a cup. "Anyhow, Pauline liked nothing better than a bit of disapproval. She'll be loving this." He raised the cup to the ceiling, and they all looked up, as if expecting to see a spectral Pauline hovering up there, glaring down at them, threatening them with lines and detentions from the hereafter.

"Now, talking of Pauline, I have a favor to ask you," said Lydia. "It's about her dog."

Until that moment, Art hadn't noticed the dog sitting next to Lydia's chair. She looked a little depressed. Bereft. Or perhaps she always looked like that. Living with Pauline would have been enough to give anyone a miserable resting face.

"I was wondering whether, given the unfortunate circumstances . . ." said Lydia, lifting up the dog and putting her on her lap.

"You mean, given Pauline's sudden death," said Daphne. "Let's not speak in euphemisms."

". . . whether anyone might volunteer to help look after Pauline's dog," continued Lydia, stroking the dog's head. The dog didn't seem to be enjoying the public display of affection much. Art didn't blame her. She was probably feeling patronized. Perhaps he should warn Lydia that geriatrics generally didn't like being patted on the head.

"I thought if three of us shared her care, we could each do a couple of days a week, until we can find a more permanent solution," said Lydia.

"Ha! I can barely look after myself, let alone a dog as well," said Art. Then he stopped, remembering the conversation he'd had the week before with his agent. *A TV talent show.* Me and My Dog. *A hundred thousand pounds' prize money. And the visibility.*

This, he realized, with a growing sense of excitement, could be the answer to his financial issues and his flatlining career. He squinted at the dog. She didn't look ideal, obviously. She wasn't exactly telegenic, but then neither was he any longer. And she did have a real advantage: she was only part-time, and temporary. If he wasn't able to turn her into a prize-winning performer within a few weeks, he could just give her back!

Art had watched animal wranglers on set many times. It was all just a case of arming yourself with endless dog treats and using the right tone of voice. Honestly, how hard could it be?

"Only joking!" he said, effecting a screeching U-turn with a forced laugh. "I'd be delighted to help."

"Me too," said Daphne, the last person he'd have expected to be charitable, but perhaps she and this grumpy, old, antisocial dog would have much in common.

"Oh, that's so good of you both," said Lydia, clapping her hands. Art took advantage of her good mood to top up everyone's cups with another generous slug of whiskey.

"What's she called?" said Art, reaching over and grabbing the brass tag hanging from the collar of his new sidekick.

"Aarrrghh!" he said, dropping it as if it had scalded him.

"What is it?" said Anna.

"Her name!" said Art. "Look! It says *Maggie Thatcher.* Who would do that to a dog?"

Daphne laughed so hard that she spilled some of the whiskey she was holding into her saucer. She picked the saucer up and emptied it straight into her mouth. She saw Lydia staring at her. "Might as well cut out the middleman," she said, with a wink.

"I presume Pauline was a fan of the Iron Lady," said Lydia.

"That figures!" said Art. "But we can change her name, right? How about Marilyn Monroe?"

"I vote for Helen Mirren," said Anna. "She's a fabulous example of how to age gracefully. Very aspirational."

"Where's the fun in aging gracefully?" said Daphne. "Personally, I intend to age as disgracefully as possible."

"Well, you're making a fabulous start," said Art, before he could stop himself.

"We can't change her name just to suit us," said Lydia. "It's not fair on the poor thing. She's already lost her owner; we can't take her name away from her, too."

"Women have been made to change their names to suit their husbands for centuries," said Daphne, glaring at Lydia as if she'd personally invented the patriarchy.

"If you don't want to use her whole name, just call her Maggie," said Lydia. "But we need to be consistent, so no calling her by other names or nicknames, OK?"

Art and Daphne both nodded.

"I've written down some basic guidelines for Maggie's care, so it'll be easy for her to move between homes," said Lydia, reaching into her handbag and pulling out some sheets of paper. "There's some details about her daily routine, then some general rules, like not allowing her on the furniture or in your bedrooms. And she must sleep in a proper dog bed, definitely not on your bed. And strictly no human food. It's not good for her."

Lydia handed around the papers, while Maggie Thatcher took

advantage of the diversion and snaffled a whole slice of Victoria sponge off her plate.

Lydia's phone, face down on the table, buzzed and skittered a little across the Formica surface. Lydia picked it up and stared at the screen. She frowned and rubbed her eyes, as if trying to erase what she was seeing.

"Are you OK, my dear?" said William.

Art would dearly have loved to know what the message Lydia had just received had said, but Lydia put it straight into her handbag and knocked back her whiskey in one gulp. Her cup rattled against the saucer as she placed it down with a shaking hand.

"I'm fine," she said, with a tight smile.

Art had seen many unconvincing performances in his day. In fact, he'd given a fair few of them himself. So he knew an act when he saw one.

Lydia was most definitely not fine.

Ziggy

Ziggy often viewed his life like the lines of a computer program.

Until year eleven, just after his sixteenth birthday, he'd been following a neat, predictable, stable line of code. A line which led, he'd hoped, to university, then a well-paid job somewhere far, far away from the run-down council estate he'd lived on his whole life.

But a series of decisions—what his computer science teacher would refer to as "if-then-else statements"—had led him down an entirely different branch, plunging his avatar into a parallel universe. One from which, it seemed, there was no return, no loop back to the beginning.

Only the first decision had been his—led entirely, according to his mum, by his hormones. When he and Jenna had found themselves in the stationery cupboard during the junior prom, and he'd realized that his lucky condom was still in the pocket of his jacket which was hanging over the back of his chair in the main hall, Jenna had told him not to worry, that she could take the morning-after pill. His decision had been, *just this once*, to take the risk.

The other decisions had not been his at all.

Jenna had decided not to go to the chemist the next morning, on account of her chronic hangover. The day after that was a Sunday, and her parents had planned a family visit to her grandparents. She could hardly tell them why she needed to stop at a pharmacy, could she? By day three, the stationery cupboard liaison had felt like a drunken dream, her fear had ebbed away, and, besides, it was all a bit late by then, wasn't it?

After that, there had been a series of nondecisions. Jenna hadn't decided to keep track of her menstrual cycle. She hadn't decided to see a doctor when she'd finally realized there'd been no sign of her period for months. She hadn't decided to let Ziggy know that anything was up. In fact, she hadn't made any decision at all until she was twenty-six weeks pregnant and could no longer zip up her school skirt. The decision had, by then, been made for her. And for Ziggy.

The final decision had been very much his mother's.

When Jenna and her mum had come round for the most awkward cup of tea in the history of the universe, and Jenna's mum had talked, through a mouthful of fruit cake, about adoption, Ziggy's mum wasn't having any of it. Before Ziggy could refill the teapot with boiling water, his mother had announced that Ziggy was just as responsible for Jenna's situation as she was, and would not be an absent, feckless father like his own had been. Before he could reply that "absent and feckless" seemed a wholly sensible strategy in the circumstances, she appeared to have agreed that she, and Ziggy, would bring up the baby and Jenna need have no responsibility at all, unless she wanted it. Which she didn't. And who could blame her?

So, like the heroes of his favorite children's book who had walked through a wardrobe into Narnia, Ziggy had been propelled from a stationery cupboard into a parallel universe which he hadn't chosen and didn't understand and from which he couldn't escape.

And, to make it all so much more painful, Ziggy got to watch his former life play out in front of him, in the form of Jenna, who'd moved schools for a fresh start, but who he often saw about town and on social media. She still traveled everywhere with a gang of "besties," still dated boys who weren't single fathers, went to parties, took all the risks, and made all the mistakes that teenagers were supposed to make. Jenna, who still had a future.

The bell sounded for the end of the lesson. Pens were zipped back into pencil cases, books and files swept into schoolbags, and chair legs scraped across the floor as the class fled for the door.

"Don't forget, I want to see your coursework by Monday!" shouted Mr. Wingate to a sea of departing backs which coalesced into small groups, none of which contained Ziggy.

In his past world, Ziggy had been a magnet. Wherever he went, he would attract small groups of friends, like iron filings drawn to a charge. But now his polarity had been reversed, and they skittered away from him as he drew near.

"Ziggy! Hold up! May I have a word?" said Mr. Wingate.

Several faces turned back, etched with a momentary curiosity, before resuming their exit. Ziggy ran through a mental list of what he might have done wrong. A missed piece of homework? A messed-up test paper? Computer science was his best subject, and he was pretty sure he was on top of it, despite everything. Top of the class, even.

"Pull up a chair," said Mr. Wingate, gesturing at the space opposite his desk at the front of the room.

Ziggy dragged a chair into position, resting his schoolbag next to his feet, and waited.

"I was wondering," said Mr. Wingate, steepling his fingers in front of his aquiline nose and peering over the top of his glasses, "whether you were considering reading computer science at the university?"

For a few moments, Ziggy was catapulted back into his old universe—the one where he'd had ambitions, and choices, where his future had been a blank screen just waiting for a new line of code to be inputted.

But, just as quickly, his reality returned, along with a wave of guilt. That universe might have been full of possibility and excitement, but it didn't have Kylie in it. And how could he possibly wish for that?

"I'm not applying for uni," he said, looking down at his hands. "It's not really an option, because . . ."

"I know about your situation, Ziggy," said Mr. Wingate, in a completely different voice from the one he used to issue instructions from the front of the class. "But it needn't stop you. You could find a course in London. Or if you wanted to go farther afield, which might be good for you, the universities all have arrangements for single parents. Accommodation and affordable childcare."

"But what about the money?" said Ziggy, trying to extinguish the small flame of hope that Mr. Wingate had ignited before it could take hold. Hope, he had learned, was more painful than acceptance. "I can't afford it."

"You could get a student loan," said Mr. Wingate, "and maybe even a scholarship or bursary."

"I need to think about Kylie," said Ziggy, firmly, more to himself than to his teacher. This had, after all, been his mantra for the past six months.

"If you get yourself a brilliant degree, which I think you can, it would be way better for Kylie in the long run," said Mr. Wingate. "Your earning potential would be much higher, and think what a wonderful role model you'd be for your daughter."

Ziggy opened his mouth to protest, but Mr. Wingate, who was used to railroading dissenting students, soldiered on.

"Look, I would really like to give you a couple of extra sessions each week after school. I could help you with your UCAS application and, with a bit of additional focus, I think a scholarship is a real possibility. Just think about it, Ziggy. Will you do that for me?"

"Sure," said Ziggy. "And thanks."

The Ziggy who picked up his bag and left the room was a slightly different one from the Ziggy who'd entered it less than an hour before. At least one person in his world hadn't completely written him off. Mr. Wingate believed in him, and had even offered to give up his own free time to help him. Ziggy allowed himself, just for a while, to feel like the future mapped out by his teacher might even be possible.

As he approached Mandel Community Center, Ziggy deliberately looked away from the noticeboard, and the council's doom-laden poster boldly occupying its center. He couldn't even think about the possibility of the nursery closing down, on top of everything else.

The nursery and the Senior Citizens' Social Club both ended at the same time, so the hallway was filled with people representing the whole spectrum of ages. A physical manifestation of "from cradle to grave."

"I nearly got mown down on the pavement just now, by an old woman in a leather biker jacket with lilac hair, riding a pimped-up mobility scooter," he told Janine as he strapped Kylie into her buggy.

"That would be Anna," said another old lady, dressed incongruously in flared jeans. Her white hair was in a bun in which she appeared to have stored a Biro, and she wore a brightly patterned silk scarf tied at her neck. She was pulling an emerald-green tweed coat with a fur collar off one of the pegs on the wall. Ziggy presumed the fur was fake. Surely nobody wore the remains of actual dead animals anymore?

"Anna used to be a long-distance lorry driver," she continued. "It screwed her back and left her with an extremely macho wardrobe and an almost pathological need to own the road. She's just as bad with the walking frame on wheels she uses indoors. She nearly pinned one of the toddlers to the wall on her way out just now."

Ziggy had no idea how to reply to that, so he didn't. Before he lost his nerve, he blurted out the words he'd prepared in his head and rehearsed for Janine, all the way back from school.

"Uh, Janine, I was wondering if there's any way Kylie could stay an extra hour, just a couple of days a week. My teacher wants me to apply to do computer science at uni. He's offered to help me after school," he said in a rush, then held his breath.

"Oh, Ziggy, honey," replied Janine, in a tone he already knew meant no. "I would, honestly, but we only get the hall from eight a.m. until four p.m. After that there's a whole rota of activities— karate, NCT classes, Alcoholics Anonymous. You name it. And I can't work any later, in any case. I have commitments, too. I'm sorry."

Ziggy knew she was. And he'd known that this would be the answer, but he'd owed it to Mr. Wingate, and to his past self with all those dreams, at least to give it a go.

"Sure. No worries," he said. "I just thought I'd ask."

"Wait," said a voice behind him. He turned to see the old woman with the tweed-and-fur coat. "Computer science. I presume that means you're good with technology? The internet? Stuff like that?"

"Uh-huh," said Ziggy. "I guess. I'm definitely the best in the class."

"I'm Daphne," she said. "Perhaps I could look after your little sister?"

"Daughter," said Ziggy and Janine simultaneously.

"Good God, you're not old enough to be a father. You're barely old enough to shave," said the lady, voicing the thought that Ziggy knew everyone had, but most were too polite to say out loud.

"Well, you're not young enough to wear those jeans," replied Ziggy. "You're barely young enough to be alive."

Ziggy cursed his big mouth, yet again. If he hadn't misheard, this old lady was, for some unknown reason, offering to help him solve his problem, and he'd just insulted her.

"Sorry," he said. "That was really rude of me. What were you saying?"

The woman's glare softened a little. "I said I could take your daughter back to your place after nursery twice a week and wait with her until you get back from school."

"Do you have experience with babies, Daphne?" asked Janine.

"Dear girl, how could one possibly get to my age without having experience with babies? And besides, I'd only be in charge for an hour, right? And she's just a tiny little thing. How hard can it be?" said Daphne.

"Uh, I'm not sure it's a good idea," said Ziggy. Surely he couldn't entrust his daughter to a complete stranger? "Besides, I really can't afford to pay for babysitting."

"I wouldn't dream of charging you anything . . ." said Daphne.

Ziggy weighed up his vague concern versus the offer of free childcare. An almost imperceptible nod from Janine tipped the scales in favor of Daphne.

"OK, you're on," he said, hoping he wouldn't live to regret this.

"Great. But you'll need to do something for me in return," said Daphne.

"Uh, like what?" asked Ziggy. Maybe he could help with weeding her garden or picking up prescriptions from the chemist. A few trips to the library, perhaps?

"Do you know anything about internet dating?" she said.

Daphne

irror, mirror, on the wall, who's the cleverest of them all?" said Daphne to her ornate mirror, which had once hung over the fireplace of some grand stately home, and always looked faintly surprised to find itself in Hammersmith. As, indeed, was Daphne.

For the first time in over a decade, Daphne was feeling proud of herself. She'd achieved so much over the past couple of weeks. She had always thought of herself as someone who, once she'd made a resolution, would *get things done*. Swiftly and efficiently. And here, once more, was the proof.

On Daphne's seventieth birthday, she'd had no friends, no one who loved her or needed her, and no children or grandchildren. But within two weeks, she'd managed to secure herself a social life three afternoons a week, an occasional baby, and an expert to help her find a lover. How was that for progress?

Daphne had even volunteered to help look after Pauline's ugly dog. She hadn't done this out of the kindness of her heart, obviously. It was a cunning strategic move. She'd realized that when people took a dog out for a walk, they got *noticed*. Passersby stopped to give the thing a stroke, ask its name, and exchange stories about their own overindulged pets. So, given Daphne's resolution to reengage with the world, a dog seemed like a sensible addition to the plan.

Also, dogs were notoriously indiscriminate when it came to doling out affection, so this could be a practice run, a starter relationship of sorts. The dog could give Daphne unconditional love, while also acting as bait. So long as it was only a part-time arrangement, and she could return it if it didn't have the desired effect or started to irritate her.

There was only one fly in the ointment: the council, who were threatening the future of the community center. The Senior Citizens' Social Club was not her scene at all—all those old people drinking tea and being irritatingly polite to each other—but it was proving a helpful stepping stone, as evidenced by her impressive progress to date. And, if she were to stop attending, she wanted that to be *her choice*. Not dictated by some small-minded bureaucrat.

She was going to have to attend this ghastly council meeting. No one was closing down the Senior Citizens' Social Club on her watch.

The nursery side of Mandel Community Center was packed, and the debate about the future of the building and its occupants had been raging for over an hour, with no real sense of direction or purpose, let alone any reasonable resolution. There was brightly colored children's artwork on the walls, hanging mobiles, and garish toys and furniture pushed into the corners to make way for several rows of foldable plastic chairs. Which all made a rather surreal contrast with the monochrome, suited, pompous council members who sat at a table on a raised stage, facing their audience.

To date, Daphne had managed to ascertain the following:

1. Mandel Community Center had been underfunded
   since its inception. In fact, it had originally been
   named after Nelson Mandela, but the A had
   dropped off the sign in the late 1990s, and it had
   been cheaper to rename the hall than to replace
   the signage.
2. The building appeared to be suffering from both
   rising damp and dry rot. One would have thought
   that these two afflictions might meet in the
   middle and cancel each other out, but apparently
   not. Fixing the issue would cost at least
   £80,000.
3. There was no budget available for the work, on
   account of the building allowance having been
   spent on a statue of one of their most generous
   benefactors. Just months after his effigy had been
   unveiled, just outside Mandel Community Center,
   so was his plundering of his company's pension
   fund, which he'd raided to pay for his prolific
   cocaine and gambling habits. He was now
   weaving baskets and cultivating vegetables in
   Ford open prison, but his statue remained until
   the council could afford to replace it.
4. The head of the council was a knob.

Now, to Daphne's horror, they were discussing the benefits of just
demolishing the whole place and selling the land to developers.

Daphne raised her hand. Nobody noticed. Daphne stood up, her hand still raised. They still ignored her.

Daphne did not like being ignored. In the early days of her career, she had been overlooked on account of her sex. Talked over and patronized by a series of self-important, untalented little misogynists. So much had improved in the intervening years and she was glad to see that a couple of the councillors at the meeting were female. But now, she was being ignored because of her age. She appeared to have jumped out of the frying pan of sexism and into the fire of ageism. The final frontier of isms.

Daphne thumped her walking stick several times on the wooden floorboards. She didn't need a walking stick for actual walking. In fact, she prided herself on her mobility and flexibility, aided by twenty minutes of Pilates every morning, and an hour of yoga before bed. How many septuagenarians could do a headstand and sit for hours in the lotus position? She had, however, discovered that her age was a wonderful excuse for carrying around a stout, metal-tipped cane, which could come in handy in all sorts of circumstances. It was perfect for clearing people out of her way, for waving or thumping to attract attention, for giving the appearance of frailty when useful and, in extremis, it could be a dangerous weapon.

Sometimes Daphne deliberately walked down dark alleyways, rather hoping a feckless youth would attempt to steal her handbag, so she could fell him with a blow to the head from her stick, delivered by a powerful swing from her Pilates-honed right arm. Then she could watch him being carted off by an ambulance, while she tearfully claimed self-defense.

Daphne thumped the stick again, and everyone turned to find the source of the disruption. She felt a frisson of excitement, remembering how much she enjoyed commanding the attention of a room, especially one filled with people who'd made the mistake of underestimating her.

"Mandel Community Center is the *beating heart* of our local community," she said, projecting right to the front of the room. She paused to let the words land. "It houses a wonderful nursery, an extremely popular senior citizens' social club"—she hoped the council hadn't bothered to check Lydia's attendance records—"Alcoholics Anonymous, NCT antenatal classes, and a karate club. I can't even imagine the chaos if all those toddlers, bored geriatrics, addicts, heavily pregnant women, and trained killers were left to just wander around the streets! Where, do you propose, are we all going to go?"

"Uh, I'm sure we could use some of the funds raised in the sale to find an alternative venue," said the chief councillor, shifting uncomfortably, like a worm on a hook, under Daphne's hard stare. She tended to have that effect when she was on form—which, tonight, she was.

"Are you, though?" said Daphne. "You've just been talking about the extortionate cost of property in the area. And you've spent the past half hour discussing all the various ways you could divvy up the proceeds of a sale among your various departments, yet not one of you mentioned funding a new community center."

"Let's cross that bridge if we come to it, shall we?" said the councillor. "In the meantime, let's see if we can find the monies required to repair and maintain the current building, while simultaneously requesting proposals from developers. NOTE THAT IN THE MINUTES, PLEASE, VANESSA!"

A large-bosomed, middle-aged blond lady in the corner, who looked suspiciously like she'd been falling asleep for most of the last debate, jumped, dislodging her reading glasses, which slipped off her nose and landed in her cleavage. She fished them out, pushed them back into place, and started scribbling furiously in her notebook.

Daphne was finding it difficult to take the man and his pathetic threats seriously, since he was standing in front of a large, number-themed mural, his head covering the O of the word "COUNT." She pulled out her phone and took a picture. She was sure the local newspaper could have a little fun with that. Daphne was always happy to give karma a helping hand.

Daphne fished a packet of cigarettes from her bag, placed one in her cigarette holder, lit it, and blew a volley of defiant smoke rings over the heads of the audience. Then she shrugged on her coat and picked up her bag. One should always leave a room before one was thrown out.

These irritating paper pushers might have won this particular battle, but she was determined to win the war . . .

Art

S it!" said Art. Maggie stared up at him with rheumy eyes, unmoving. He could have sworn that she raised one of her whiskery eyebrows at him. Then, very slowly, Maggie did a full circuit of his kitchen table, as if to say, *I'll do this in my own time, thank you very much*, then returned to face him and—finally—sat.

"Bravo!" said Art, giving her another piece of sausage. He was quite certain that Maggie knew all the basic commands; she was just trying to work out how much sausage she could snaffle before confessing to the fact. At this rate, she'd be morbidly obese before they even got as far as the audition stage. Still, you had to admire the canny bitch.

"Right, M," he said. "We need to go to the shops."

Art had tried to call his new pet—and future acting partner—"Maggie," as instructed by Lydia, but her surname lurked in the ensuing pause like toxic waste. Art was a proud socialist. He'd marched with the miners, had refused to pay the poll tax, and had cheered when Thatcher had finally been stabbed in the back by her own party. He could not have her namesake actually living in his house. So Art had decided to call his dog "M" for short. Like Judi

Dench in the James Bond movies. They were both old women, but cool and not to be messed with.

Life was more of an adventure with M, he'd discovered. Even a quick trip to the newsagent. She found everything *so fascinating*. They had to stop every two minutes for a good sniff and a wee. She shoved her nose up other dogs' backsides with merry abandon and ate whatever she felt like off the pavement. This joie de vivre and devil-may-care attitude to the world, hygiene, and personal space was inspirational, frankly. And it was catching. Art found himself viewing his familiar surroundings with at least a modicum of renewed interest, and smiling at strangers as they stopped to pat Maggie on the head.

"What breed is she?" asked one woman as they passed by.

"A Jack Russell," he replied. Art was pretty certain this wasn't actually the case, but he'd always thought of himself as a Jack Russell kind of guy. Wily, tenacious, and with a cheeky charm.

Even with her back turned, Art could tell it was Lydia outside the tube station. She usually had an *apologetic* posture, slightly hunched in on herself, as if she were trying to occupy less space in the world. She leaned forward and gave the man she was with a peck on the cheek, an incidental comma nestling up to a bold exclamation mark.

He was not what Art had expected Lydia's husband to look like. He was as self-congratulatory as Lydia was self-effacing, all fancy suit, heavy wristwatch, and polished brogues.

"Don't forget we're going to the Johnsons' for dinner tonight," Art heard the man say, in a voice that was entirely instruction at the expense of affection. "So please can you make a bit of an effort to look presentable? It reflects on me as well, you know."

Art paused for a second, willing Lydia to say something equally insulting back. *That's rich coming from you, you arrogant, over-weight, pompous prick* would do the trick nicely, in his opinion.

"Of course, darling," she responded, making herself even smaller.

Art hid in the bus shelter, so Lydia wouldn't know he'd overheard. A young girl nearby gave him a nervous sideways glance. Did she think he was a flasher? You had to be careful wearing a mac at his age.

As soon as he was sure Lydia had gone, he crossed the road to the newsagent. Art tied Maggie's lead to the lamppost outside the shop, on account of the NO DOGS sign in the window. Although she was hardly a magnet for dognappers, Art made sure he didn't lose sight of her.

"Nice day, isn't it?" said Art to the man behind the counter, who flicked Art a cursory glance, muttered an "uh-huh," and looked back at the phone in his hand.

Art was used to this behavior. He wasn't sure exactly when he'd become irrelevant, or invisible, even—it had crept up on him gradu-ally over the years. He often felt like a ghost. He occupied the same world as ordinary mortals, but most of them appeared to see straight through him. It used to make him angry, but then he'd discovered that invisibility had its advantages.

Art looked down at the brightly colored array of confectionery in front of him, reached out a hand, and picked up a packet of Fruit Gums, which he slipped into the pocket of his voluminous coat.

Art didn't even like Fruit Gums. His teeth hadn't been up to that kind of a challenge for decades.

"Bye!" he called to the shopkeeper. Who didn't reply, obviously.

In the beginning, shoplifting had given Art a real buzz. He'd only started doing it after he turned sixty-five, and it had delivered an adrenaline rush and a thrill of danger that he'd not felt in a long time, and discovered he'd missed. He'd become hyperaware of his surroundings, his heart pumping faster, shot through with energy. It made him feel alive again.

Generally, he only stole from large corporations. He particularly enjoyed ripping off the ones who didn't pay a fair amount of UK tax. He had a whole cupboard full of stuff pilfered from Starbucks, for example, who kept an array of small items in front of the till, right at pocket height. He only ever indulged himself in independent shops when he was badly treated or ignored, or if he knew the owner to be a racist or a misogynist.

Art knew that William had been accused of stealing by the local greengrocer once, just because he was Black. William had, of course, been entirely innocent, but Art had been stealing fruit from that shop every week for years as a form of compensation for the insult. He'd worked his way up from a small handful of cherries to entire pineapples and melons. The shopkeeper never paid him any attention, because he was old, and white.

William was completely unaware of the campaign of retribution Art was waging on his behalf. Art had shared every single secret with William over the years, starting in year two with his secret crush on Belinda, the reigning hopscotch champion with the long blond plaits. But not this one. Art carried the burden of his habitual criminality alone.

The problem with Art's clandestine hobby, however, was that the thrill it gave him was becoming less and less acute, while the hollow, empty feeling which followed that thrill arrived increasingly quickly. The void that grew and grew, swallowing up everything around it like a ravenous black hole, until his next shopping trip.

Art was trying to stop, honestly he was. But it was like building a wall of sand to hold back the tide. However hard he dug to shore up the defenses, the urge would eventually overwhelm him.

Art bent down to untie Maggie from the lamppost. She stared up at him with a look that said, *I know what you did, and I'm disappointed in you.*

"Enough with the judgment, M," said Art. "I didn't say anything when you stole that little boy's sandwich in the park yesterday, did I? You and I are not so very dissimilar."

He knew he was going to have to confront the issue, but he had no idea how. For the time being, he found that keeping busy and just *not thinking about it* was the best way to deal with the problem. Which was why he was determined that the new Senior Citizens' Social Club could not be disbanded. Denial, in his view, was much underrated.

Art and Maggie walked past Mandel Community Center just as the children were being dropped off at the nursery. Within seconds, Maggie was surrounded by small children. She stood patiently while they patted her, pulled her tail, and played with her ears.

Only one boy held back. He stood against the wall, looking at his feet, but Art could see him sneaking sideways glances at the dog. Art had always been drawn to outsiders. It was how he and William had originally become friends.

"Excuse me, kids," he said, easing his way into the crush to rescue Maggie. "M wants to meet someone." He picked Maggie up and placed her gently at the feet of the little boy.

"What's your name?" he asked the boy. He didn't reply or look up.

"He doesn't speak," said the well-rounded lady with dark hair in a swingy ponytail, who was holding the boy's hand. She had a won-derfully warm smile; a credit to modern-day orthodontics. He was sure people hadn't had teeth like that when he was a boy. "The psy-chotherapists call it 'elective mutism,'" she continued. "He's a foster child. His upbringing was a little . . . complicated. His name is Lucky. At least, that's what we call him. I'm Janine. I run the nursery."

"Well, Lucky, this is M, and I'm Art," he said. Lucky leaned over and touched Maggie's head with a tiny, chewed index finger. He waited a few moments, then stroked her with a flat palm. He smiled, and immediately appeared younger, as if his previous pinched ex-pression had been too old for his years.

"Wow. I don't think I've ever seen him smile like that before," said Janine. "Usually he doesn't react to anything around him."

"Does she do tricks?" said another little boy.

If only, thought Art.

"Let's try, shall we?" he said, rising to the challenge. "Sit!"

Maggie sat.

"Lie down!" said Art, more out of hope than expectation.

Maggie lay down.

"Stay!" he said, backing away with his hand out, while Maggie lay patiently watching him.

"Come!" he said, after a few more seconds, and she stood up and walked toward him, wagging her tail.

It turned out that Maggie was very much like him. All she needed was an appreciative audience.

"Anyone fancy a Fruit Gum?" said Art.

Lydia

ydia couldn't remember the last time she'd enjoyed herself so much. She doubted anyone would describe her as "the life and soul," but she was definitely holding her own. For years, she'd felt horribly inadequate at dinner parties. She could always picture the hostess frowning over the seating plan, saying, *Where on earth are we going to put the dull wife?*

Lydia's only topics of conversation revolved around houses and children—morphing over the decades from how to toddler-proof your plug sockets and which were the best primary schools in the area, to the horrors of basement conversions and persuading teenagers to revise for their GCSEs.

She was often sure she could see the eyes of her dinner companions glazing over within minutes of asking her "what she did." On one memorable occasion, she'd been certain she'd heard the man on her left mutter, "Beam me up, Scotty," halfway through her recollections of being a parent helper on a school trip to the zoo.

This evening, however, was proving different. She'd been reading a book called *Feel the Fear and Do It Anyway* for work, and had decided to step outside her comfort zone by telling a few anecdotes about the challenges she faced with her unruly senior citizens. To the entire table.

As she grew in confidence, aided by the rather fine Chablis Jeremy had brought from his extensive wine cellar, which Lydia suspected he loved more than her, her audience had laughed louder and louder. And they were, she was fairly certain, laughing with her, not at her.

Lydia had even been able to forget, for a while, the text that Jeremy had sent her last week. The one that read: I'll be at the restaurant at 7. I've missed you xxx. They hadn't arranged to meet at a restaurant that evening. They hadn't, in fact, been out to a restaurant together for months. Not since her birthday, back in February. Jeremy had told her he'd be working late that evening.

That text had been swiftly followed by a second one: Sorry, darling. Sent you that text by mistake. It was for a colleague. Work dinner.

A colleague? A work dinner? So why *I've missed you*? And the three kisses?

Lydia had managed not to fall apart in front of her senior citizens, who luckily hadn't noticed anything was wrong, but those words had been circulating round her head ever since, while she examined them from every angle, searching for an explanation, a major plot twist, so the story didn't end with her husband being a miserable cheat and a liar.

Jeremy stood up to go to the loo, and as he passed by her seat he leaned down to whisper in her ear. Was he proud of her for feeling the fear and doing it anyway? For entertaining his friends and colleagues with such aplomb?

"WIC," he hissed, his breath heavy with brandy fumes. Lydia

shrank back in her seat, her mood deflating like a sponge cake taken out of the oven too soon. WIC. Jeremy code for "Words in Car." And those words, in her experience, were never good ones.

"What were you thinking, drinking so much?" Jeremy asked her from the darkness in the back of their black cab as they sped along the Embankment, the lights of Albert Bridge reflected in the river beside them like drowning stars. "It was utterly embarrassing."

"*Everyone* was drinking, Jeremy. Including you," she replied. "I was just having fun. Letting my hair down for once. The last couple of weeks have been really stressful, you know, with all this council business. My job's on the line, not to mention the well-being of all my seniors." She could hear herself slurring a little. Perhaps she had had a bit too much to drink.

"Your *job*?" said Jeremy, loading the noun with derision. "It's hardly a job, Lydia. Your wages are lower than my expenses claim each month. They wouldn't even cover the amount we spend on sauvignon blanc. Let alone Châteauneuf-du-Pape."

"Surely that's a reflection on how much you spend on wine, rather than my salary," said Lydia, but Jeremy carried on as if she hadn't spoken. Perhaps she hadn't.

"And you've been so busy with your bunch of parasitic pensioners that you've let everything else go. We had pasta for dinner *three times* last week, and the house is a mess," he said.

"Well, since we're both working now," said Lydia, determined to stand her ground, "perhaps *you* could help out with the cooking and the housework a little bit."

Lydia couldn't make out Jeremy's expression as he stared resolutely ahead in the dark, but she could see his tense jawline and feel the indignation radiating from him in waves.

The cab pulled up outside their house, and Jeremy got out to pay the driver. Lydia waited in the warm, dark cocoon of the back seat, pulling her coat tight around her, putting off the inevitable ratcheting-up of the argument for as long as possible. As Jeremy walked toward the house, not even checking that she was following, she reached for the cab door handle.

"Don't let him push you around, love," said the driver in a comforting cockney accent, winking at her in the rearview mirror.

Buoyed on a sea of white wine and the kindness of a stranger, Lydia followed Jeremy into the cold, unwelcoming house, looked him dead in the eye, and said the words that had been hovering on the tip of her tongue for weeks: "Jeremy. Are you having an affair?"

Jeremy's eyes slid away from hers, and he ran his hand through his hair, the way he always did when he was feeling on edge. Lydia absorbed every small detail of the scene in front of her, thinking perhaps she'd always look back at it as the moment her life had imploded.

Lydia wondered if Jeremy would crumple. Collapse into fits of tears and beg her forgiveness. Urge her not to break up their family. Promise to spend the rest of his life making it up to her.

He didn't.

"Lydia," he said, as he turned away from her and made his way up the stairs. "You're drunk, hormonal, and delusional. Hopefully by the morning you'll have pulled yourself together."

Lydia stared at Jeremy's retreating back, then at the magnetic knife rack on the wall, holding the gleaming steel Japanese kitchen knives Jeremy was so proud of. For a fleeting second, she pictured herself hurling one of those knives up the stairs, where it would lodge, up to the hilt, between Jeremy's vertebrae.

Then she poured herself a glass of water, turned on the dishwasher, and went to bed. Jeremy lay facing away from her, eye mask on and earplugs in to protect himself from any further unwanted communication from his wife.

The "job" that Jeremy had dismissed so cruelly the night before was proving a great distraction. They weren't discussing the elephant in the room—their threatened demolition. Nor were they doing any of Lydia's carefully planned, council-approved activities. Instead, Art had introduced a new game called "Truth or Dare Jenga," which, needless to say, didn't tally at all with the instructions on the Jenga box. Whenever anyone knocked down the Jenga tower—which, given the number of arthritic fingers involved, happened remarkably frequently—they'd have to answer a question or do a forfeit. Some really quite shocking details about her club members had emerged over the past few sessions.

"Bugger! Balls! Bollocks!" said Ruby, as the tower of bricks crashed over the table, one landing in Lydia's not-quite-empty teacup. Ruby looked so demure that it gave her liberal use of swear words much more impact.

"Truth or dare?" shouted Art, gleefully.

"Truth," said Ruby, which was probably wise. Anna had chosen "dare" and they'd given her an orange plastic toy gun and a cowboy hat, pilfered from the nursery next door, then made her charge up to a pedestrian on her mobility scooter shouting, "Hands up! It's daylight robbery!" They'd all watched from the window, giggling like schoolchildren.

"Where's the most daring place you've had sex?" asked Art.

"Mmmm," said Ruby, not showing the slightest embarrassment or reticence. "That would be my mother-in-law's larder."

"That doesn't sound particularly dangerous," said Daphne, dismissively. "Certainly not life-threatening."

"You say that because you've never met my mother-in-law," said Ruby. "For a start, it was filled with dead pheasant and grouse, hanging from the ceiling, covered in feathers and bleeding. And she never believed in use-by dates, so it was riddled with salmonella and E. coli. She was ferocious. She hated me for seducing her perfect only child, and never forgave him for marrying someone brown from Bangladesh, rather than a blonde from the local pony club. That was scandalous in the early nineteen-seventies, in the Home Counties. She was, apparently, the talk of the Women's Institute."

Ruby put her knitting needles down and covered her face with her hands, as if to block out the memory. Her dark, shoulder-length hair, streaked with silver, fell forward like a curtain. Her lap was filled with a nearly finished red-and-white hat. It was beautifully made, with intricate, neat stitches, but the proportions were entirely wrong. It could easily have covered four adult heads. Lydia wondered if she should point this out, but decided that now was not the time. Maybe Ruby just found the act of knitting therapeutic, and the end result hardly mattered at all.

"I'm sorry you had to deal with that, Ruby," said William, reaching over to pat her arm. "Were you happy, though? You and your husband? Despite all the prejudice?"

"Oh, yes," she said. "We were married for nearly fifty years, and

I always felt so loved. You know, every Monday he bought me flowers. Even when he was in the hospice, he asked one of the nurses to pick me a bunch from the garden. I still miss him every day."

Lydia tried to remember the last time Jeremy had bought her flowers. Or made her feel loved. Was he buying flowers for someone else? The thought hit her like a punch in the stomach, making it hard for her to breathe.

"What's the matter, Lydia?" said Art. And, as if he'd pulled her finger from a hole in the dam wall, all the words came gushing out in a confessional torrent.

"I think my husband's having an affair, but he tells me I'm just being paranoid. 'Delusional' was the word he used. He says it's the menopause. I'm hormonal and irrational. But hormones don't send texts with love and kisses and restaurant invitations, do they? Perhaps I am going crazy? I just don't know what to think anymore. I still don't trust him, but now I can't trust myself, either," said Lydia.

The words stopped, replaced by a deluge of tears. This was awful. Humiliating. She was supposed to be in charge. *A leader.* Yet, here she was, falling to pieces in front of her seniors. Pauline had been right; she had no natural authority. She was totally unsuited to this job.

The thought made her cry even harder.

"Mmm. What you need is someone who can find out if he really is up to anything," said Art, putting a scrawny arm around her heaving shoulders. "Someone who's used to following people secretly. Perhaps someone with a few telephoto lenses. Do we know anyone like that?"

Lydia felt a second arm hugging her from the other side, as a voice said, "William Jenkins, retired paparazzo, at your service."

"And me! Don't forget me! I'm coming, too!" said Art. "Where William goes, I go."

Daphne

aphne had never understood dogs. Cats she rather admired. They walked their own path. They were independent and wily, and doled out affection sparingly and only when they had an agenda. Dogs, on the other hand, were entirely too needy and would roll over for a tummy tickle from any random passerby. That was no way to garner respect.

But despite her misgivings, Daphne was actually really enjoying having Maggie Thatcher to stay. The dog was, it transpired, an excellent listener, gave far more back than Daphne's spider plant, and was more trustworthy than the yucca.

"A little more smoked salmon with your scrambled egg, Margaret?" asked Daphne. She refused to call her dog "Maggie." Margaret was far more dignified, and reminded Daphne of one of her role models—Princess Margaret, the late Queen's late sister. Now, there was someone who kicked arse and never took prisoners. And *such style*.

While Margaret ate her breakfast, Daphne checked OurNeighbours.com for any updates. She scrolled down to the post discussing the council meeting about Mandel Community Center, and read again the words that had given her such a thrill. They hadn't used her name, thank goodness, but they were definitely describing her.

Wasn't that old lady brilliant? Who was she? We need her on the council!

She scrolled through the comments, relishing the adjectives used to describe her: "feisty," "eccentric" and—bizarrely—"the bomb." This was the first time she'd been likened to an explosive device. Although, come to think of it, maybe not.

Daphne remembered Jack, in another life, describing her as a firecracker. He'd whispered the word in her ear, with warm, whiskey-infused breath, as he'd pulled her toward him, while they danced in a smoky basement club to the sound of a jazz band. She'd laughed, and he'd wound her auburn hair around his hand, pulling back her head and kissing her in the hollow of her neck. She blinked several times to dislodge the memory, and focused on the screen in front of her.

There were some rather rude adjectives, too, of course, but Daphne was quite used to that. The important thing was that she was being noticed. Back on the map. Yet, still—for the time being, at least—safely incognito.

Daphne wasn't stupid. She knew that all of this could end in disaster. She'd lit a fuse without knowing what it was attached to. Rookie error. But it was such a joy not to be hiding away any longer. And if she was going to go down, she might as well go down in flames. As befitted a firecracker. Or a bomb.

Just as Daphne was about to close her laptop, she spotted something else. A photo of the postbox outside the town hall. It was sporting a giant woolly Santa hat. A hat that looked spookily familiar. MYSTERY YARN BOMBER OF HAMMERSMITH STRIKES AGAIN! read the headline.

Oh, Ruby, you dark horse, she said to herself. *You're the Banksy of the knitting world.* It looked as if Daphne wasn't the only one with secrets.

Daphne closed her laptop and turned to the dog. "Right, when you've finished, we need to go and collect that baby," she said.

Daphne was a little nervous about looking after Ziggy's baby. Kim? Khloe? She was sure it was one of the Kardashians. The Kardashians were Daphne's guilty addiction, on account of her huge admiration for Kris, the matriarch. A modern-day Princess Margaret. She knew that were she and Kris to meet in real life, they'd be the best of friends.

Despite Daphne's assurances to Janine, she had, in fact, managed to reach the grand old age of seventy without having gained any experience with babies whatsoever. Still, it couldn't be that hard to keep a tiny human alive for an hour, could it? Her father, Ziggy, was only a child himself, and he seemed to manage it.

The hallway of the community center was filled with parents and carers picking up their children. On a table, prominently placed in the center, in a display of utterly misplaced optimism, was a collection box labeled *SAVE OUR COMMUNITY CENTER*. How many years of people adding their spare pennies to the box would it take to raise the £80,000 required? It was going to take far more than begging for loose change to solve their problem.

Within seconds, Maggie Thatcher was surrounded by a swarm of children.

"Look! It's M!" said one.

"Don't be silly," said Daphne. "M is just an initial, not a name. Her name is Margaret."

"What breed is she?" asked one of the mothers.

"A toy poodle," said Daphne.

"Really?" said the woman, raising a skeptical, verging on impertinent, eyebrow.

"Yes. She just likes to wear her fur a little differently from the average poodle," said Daphne. "She has flair." Daphne stared pointedly at the old, shapeless polyester tracksuit the rude woman was wearing.

"Kylie!" said Janine to the baby she was carrying on her hip, solving the Kardashian mystery. "You're going home with Daphne today. Isn't that going to be fun?"

Kylie gave Daphne a steady appraising glance, then burst into tears. She was obviously a much better judge of character than Janine.

"Margaret's coming, too!" said Daphne, pointing at the dog. Kylie looked a tiny bit reassured. And, to be fair, Margaret had probably spent more time with babies than Daphne.

Daphne leaned over to buckle Kylie into her pushchair. She'd seen Ziggy do this a number of times, often with one hand. He made it look incredibly easy. It wasn't. Daphne tried rearranging the various bits of plastic and strap in every permutation and combination, but nothing seemed to work. Daphne could solve a Rubik's Cube in under three minutes, and crack a safe almost as quickly, but this was beyond her.

"I imagine the technology's all changed since your day, eh,

Daphne? I bet you used a Silver Cross pram!" said Janine. "Look, you put these two bits together like this, then clip them into here. See?"

"And how do I release her at the other end?" said Daphne.

"You just press this red button here," said Janine.

"Like an ejector seat!" said Daphne. Janine looked at her a little warily, then gave her Ziggy's flat keys and waved them out of the door.

Daphne stared down at the battered *London A–Z* in her hand, trying not to stop moving lest Kylie started yelling again, and someone realized she was totally unqualified and called the police. She was aware that using an actual map in this day and age was an anachronism, that most people used their phones for that sort of thing, but she loved her *A–Z*. Daphne liked to be able to highlight her route, to run her finger along it, and to make little notes in the margins: wonderful flower shop—does creative things with cabbages; café sells good, strong espresso; the alleyway where Jack and I had wild, celebratory sex, after concluding a business deal.

Daphne had had her trusty *A–Z* for decades, so it was no longer entirely accurate. But it was a reminder of paths taken and not taken, and of places still to see. One of which was Ziggy's flat.

Daphne turned into a large, somewhat notorious, council estate, built in the 1960s when low-cost, high-rise housing had become all the rage. While Christmas lights and decorations had started to spring up around the neighborhood streets over the past week or so, the estate remained depressingly gray and bleak, dotted with overflowing rubbish bins. The only festive lights on display were wound around an abandoned, broken fridge-freezer, which at least showed that someone had a good sense of irony.

She felt a prickle at the back of her neck—that strange sixth sense that someone was watching, the one that had saved her life at least once. She turned to see a group of youths in hoodies, leaning against a wall, appraising her. Her practiced eye picked out the heavy designer watches and chunky gold jewelry that looked incongruous against their bleak surroundings. They said nothing, but their eyes followed her, like hyenas tracking a wounded wildebeest.

Daphne was no wildebeest. Certainly not a wounded one. If she had been a wildebeest in a previous life, she'd have been the Kris Jenner of the herd. She studied the group, searching for the leader. She could tell by the body language. The way each of the other boys leaned almost imperceptibly toward him, like sunflowers tracking the sun. She stared him full in the face, chin slightly raised, unblinking. He raised an eyebrow at her, then, a few seconds later, gave a tiny nod.

Still got it.

Daphne pushed the buggy, Maggie Thatcher trotting along beside her, toward a sign reading FLATS 115–159, and backed it through a swing door into a gloomy lift lobby, half lit by a flickering light bulb and covered in graffiti tags. Daphne pressed the button for the lift, which took an age to arrive, and—when it finally did—smelled strongly of urine and cannabis.

The lift doors closed, and Daphne pushed the buggy backward and forward in the confined space, trying to stop Kylie from shrieking. Maggie Thatcher squatted and did a mini wee in the corner.

"If you can't beat 'em, join 'em, eh, Margaret?" said Daphne. She was pretty sure Princess Margaret would never have weed in a lift. Or perhaps she would. That woman had had hidden depths.

The door to Number 143 was immediately to the right of the lift well. Daphne fished around in her handbag for Ziggy's keys, and opened it.

Ziggy's flat, Daphne was hugely relieved to see, was everything the building's common parts were not. Clean, bright, and homely. The tiny entrance hall was filled with coats, boots, and shoes in three sizes—big (Ziggy), medium (his mum, no doubt), and tiny (Kylie). Daphne felt like Goldilocks, and wondered if she might find three bowls of porridge on the kitchen table. Daphne left Kylie wailing and thrashing in the stationary buggy for a few moments while she peered into each of the doors leading off the hallway. This was just like stalking on Rightmove.co.uk, but in real life.

It was the first time Daphne had been in anyone else's home since 2008. It was strangely thrilling being surrounded by possessions that she'd not chosen herself, not knowing what she'd find when she opened a door.

There were two bedrooms—one very neat double and one containing a single bed and a cot, the walls plastered with pictures of Chelsea football team and a couple of scantily dressed reality TV stars on one side, and brightly colored mobiles and glow stars on the other. She found one small bathroom, very clean, but overflowing with a mixture of men's and women's toiletries and a basket of plastic bath toys, nappies, wipes, and creams. Finally, there was a decent-sized living room with a small kitchenette at one end.

Daphne pressed the ejector seat button on the buggy, which released Kylie in a disappointingly muted manner, then picked up the wailing child and sat her in the center of a brightly striped rug on the sitting-room floor.

"What is it you want?" Daphne asked her. "You're going to have to learn to communicate a little better than this, you know, or you'll never get anywhere in life."

Kylie yelled harder, her previously pretty little face all red and scrunched up in an uncannily accurate impression of the angry face emoji. Daphne had recently discovered that one on her new phone and was desperate for a chance to use it.

Maggie Thatcher licked Kylie's face, which was a novel and rather helpful way of removing all the snot and tears. Much better for the environment than wet wipes. Kylie stopped crying for a moment, no doubt in shock. Daphne supposed being licked by a tongue almost as large as your head must be a strange, and not entirely pleasant, experience. For a blissful moment, Daphne enjoyed the silence, before Kylie started up again, even louder.

Daphne sank into the armchair next to Kylie, placing her handbag on the floor. She only had to wait about forty-five minutes until Ziggy got home, but those minutes were going to feel like hours.

Kylie reached out for Daphne's handbag, and clenched her gums around one of the leather straps. Silence.

"You're not supposed to eat it, you know," said Daphne. "Especially since it's vintage Prada. If you insist on eating a handbag, at least choose one from Primark. You carry things in it. Look." She unzipped her bag and showed Kylie the contents.

Kylie grabbed the bracelet around Daphne's wrist.

"Ah, you have great taste, my friend," said Daphne. "Here—you can play with it, if you like."

Daphne unclasped the bracelet and passed it to Kylie, who actually *smiled* at her.

To her immense surprise, Daphne felt something very much like happiness.

Perhaps she and Kylie could, at the very least, reach some sort of understanding.

Ziggy

Ziggy stared at the tableau in front of him in alarm.

Daphne was settled in the armchair, reading his mother's copy of *Hello!* magazine, while Kylie was sitting on the floor, a diamanté bracelet hanging from her mouth, emptying a packet of cigarettes into her lap. And she smelled awful. Where did he even start? At the bottom, he decided.

"I think her nappy needs changing, Daphne," he said.

"Oh, does it?" said Daphne, looking irritatingly vague.

"Couldn't you smell it?" asked Ziggy, trying not to sound too annoyed.

"Don't take this the wrong way, dear boy," said Daphne, "but I don't know what your flat usually smells like. I did wonder why she was crying, but the indiscriminate yelling is a bit hard to decipher. She needs to work on her enunciation and learn about the danger of crying wolf."

"And I'm not sure that playing with cigarettes is a good idea," added Ziggy, congratulating himself on his calm understatement. His mother would be proud of him. Although even she might let loose a few choice swear words at this scenario.

"Oh, no need to worry. I took the lighter away from her," said

Daphne. Was she joking? He was obviously not an expert on old-people humor. "How was your extra lesson?"

Ziggy's annoyance morphed swiftly into guilt. Daphne had been, after all, doing him a favor. And perhaps her generation did childcare very differently.

"It was great, thanks. It's really kind of you to help me out. Look, I'll go change Kylie, then you can tell me what I can do for you," he said.

"Oh, please don't change her. She's perfect just the way she is," said Daphne, turning over the page of her magazine.

"You're kidding, right?" said Ziggy. He really couldn't tell with this woman.

"Of *course* I'm kidding!" said Daphne, with a guffaw that would have suited a rotund middle-aged man more than a tiny old lady. "She's far from perfect, obviously."

Ziggy rolled out the changing mat on the bathroom floor and started peeling off Kylie's clothes. Was it his imagination, or did she look incredibly relieved to have him back? She grinned at him gummily. How could someone so small elicit such huge emotions? A complex tangle of resentment, fear, and confusion, all wrapped up in the most overwhelming, primal love.

Ziggy prized open Kylie's tiny fist to remove Daphne's bracelet, before it went back in her mouth. He shuddered at the thought of all the germs she'd ingested. Still, it could be worse. At least she hadn't been licked by the geriatric dog with chronic halitosis.

"Uh, Daphne!" he called out.

"Yes?"

"Was there a stone missing from your bracelet before you gave it to Kylie?" he said.

"No," said Daphne.

"I'm sorry, but I think she may have swallowed it," said Ziggy. She couldn't get cross, could she? It was, rather, her fault for giving it to Kylie in the first place. "It's not valuable, is it?"

"Darling, if it were a *real* diamond, do you imagine I'd be spending my days at the Mandel Community Center instead of sunning myself on a yacht off the coast of Sardinia? I think not," said Daphne.

"Do you think it'll do any damage?" said Ziggy. "It's not exactly small."

"I'm sure it'll pass through, no problem," said Daphne.

"Do you have any medical expertise, Daphne?" said Ziggy, who'd been taught always to check the small print.

"I haven't killed a baby or small child yet," said Daphne, which sounded less reassuring than she meant it to be.

Ziggy took a sweet-smelling, smiling Kylie back into the living room and put her next to her toy box, as far away from Daphne's handbag and the manky dog as possible.

"So," he said, resolving to get to business as soon as possible so he could get on with his homework and Kylie's tea, "you want help creating an internet dating profile?"

"That's about the nub of it, yes," said Daphne, removing one of the chopsticks that were, bizarrely, sticking out of her bun, and using the end to scratch her nose. Did she keep them there just in case an unexpected opportunity to eat Chinese food cropped up?

"I tried Googling it, but it was all a bit overwhelming," she continued. "And I've been *plagued* by the most ghastly, saccharine lonely hearts advertisements ever since. Still, it makes a change from the usual ads for funeral plans, stairlifts, and incontinence pads. I don't suppose you ever get those, do you?"

"Er, no," said Ziggy, wondering what an incontinence pad was, but with no intention of asking. "Well, I did a bit of research, and found this site, which is free, looks fairly straightforward, and specializes in . . ." he paused, searching for the right terminology ". . . the more mature customer."

"Mature?!?" said Daphne. "Good grief, I'm not a cheese. Or a herbaceous border. Go on, then, show it to me."

Ziggy passed his open laptop over to Daphne, who started fishing around in her bag. What was she going to pull out now? A stash of marijuana? A miniature bottle of vodka? He was hugely relieved when she extracted some reading glasses. Daphne leaned forward and peered at the website on his screen.

"Have you got some good photos?" asked Ziggy. "That's really important. It's sort of like your shop window."

"This is the only relatively recent photo I have," said Daphne, delving into the bag again and passing him a photo. An actual printed-out one with white borders, slightly faded and crumpled. The woman in the picture was rather stunning—auburn hair, streaked with gray, cut in a wavy bob, green eyes, and a teasing expression that seemed to say *I dare you*. And she was at least twenty years younger than the Daphne sitting opposite him. He supposed that at her age, twenty years ago was relatively recent. How was he going to handle this one?

"Uh, it's really beautiful, Daphne," he said, carefully.

"Well, thank you!" said Daphne. "You're more charming than you look."

"But I think you might need something a little more *up to date*," he said. "You don't want to be done under the Trade Descriptions Act. And you need a few more, too. Photos that say something about you—with your friends, family, having fun at parties, on holidays, that kind of thing."

"Well, that poses a bit of a problem," said Daphne. "I haven't let anyone take a photo of me for years, I don't have any friends, I loathe parties, and I haven't been abroad since 1999. Cuba. Fascinating. You must go."

Cuba? In what world would he be able to swan off to *Cuba*? Not this one, anyhow.

"But you know William, at the social club, used to be a paparazzo. Apparently, he spent his life hanging out outside San Lorenzo, trying to get a photo of Princess Diana and her latest beau. Maybe he can take some pictures for me. What do you think?" she said.

"Great idea," said Ziggy, really hoping that this William would play ball, because that was a job he really didn't want to take on—however much free babysitting she offered. "Right, let's start filling out your profile. The first few questions have a drop-down menu, and you can choose the response *I'd rather not say* if you like. Then there are some more fun, open-ended questions. Shall we give it a go?"

Daphne nodded, almost enthusiastically.

"Name?" said Ziggy, hands poised over the keyboard.

"I'd rather not say," said Daphne.

"That's a compulsory field," said Ziggy, attempting to keep his exasperation in check. "What's your surname?"

"Do I need one? Can't I just have one name, like Madonna? Or Prince? Or Plato?" said Daphne.

"The website doesn't allow for that," said Ziggy, trying not to sound as frustrated as he felt.

"Well, that's going to seriously reduce their clientele," said Daphne. "What if Madonna wanted a new toy boy? She seems to go through them quite quickly."

"Surname," said Ziggy, as firmly as he could muster.

"Smith," said Daphne. How could such a common surname belong to someone so . . . uncommon? Ziggy typed *Daphne Smith* into the name field.

"Age?" said Ziggy.

"I'd definitely rather not say," said Daphne.

"Another compulsory one," said Ziggy.

Daphne sighed, then said, "Seventy. Not that it's relevant."

"I grew up in . . . ?" prompted Ziggy.

"I'd rather not say," said Daphne.

"Daphne," said Ziggy, "this is not an FBI interview. You're sounding like a dangerous criminal pleading the Fifth Amendment, not a lovely lady looking for romance."

"Ha!" said Daphne, so loudly that Kylie looked over in alarm, tightening her grip around the head of a Barbie doll which had, like her babysitter, seen better days.

"You need to let your potential matches know as much about you as possible, otherwise this just isn't going to work, OK?" he said.

Daphne rolled her eyes, then nodded.

"Right, let's try one of the more fun ones. My favorite ever date was . . . ?" prompted Ziggy.

"Watching a boxing match then swimming naked in the Serpentine at midnight and smooching in the back of a police car while wearing handcuffs," said Daphne.

"OK," said Ziggy, trying not to picture Daphne naked. An image like that could ruin your week. "That's definitely more detailed. Possibly overly so. How about this one: My pet hate is . . . ?"

"Oh, that's easy," said Daphne, settling back in her chair, interlacing her fingers, and smiling. "Men who wear comedy ties, people who say 'no offense' before being insulting, anyone using the word 'literally' incorrectly, which makes my blood boil. Literally. Being told to 'calm down.' Boris Johnson. Anyone who picks food out of their teeth while driving or leaves toenail clippings lying around. Actual little piles of DNA. Who would do that?"

Daphne took a breath, and Ziggy thought for a moment that she had finished. But no.

"Tiramisu. The words 'moist' and 'gusset.' Especially when next to each other. Drivers of white Transit vans. Meerkats. They look cute, but they're actually terribly devious and borderline evil . . ."

"Daphne," Ziggy interrupted, wondering how on earth anyone could take so violently against a meerkat. Or tiramisu. "You're going to have to narrow it down!"

It was going to be a long evening.

Art

rt couldn't sleep. He'd woken up at three a.m. in the middle of a terrible nightmare involving Anna from the social club. She was riding her souped-up mobility scooter dressed as a cowboy and carrying a bright-orange machine gun, hunting him down as he ran through the aisles of Sainsbury's with stolen goods flying out of his pockets.

Now, as always, the issues that he'd managed to keep shut firmly away during the daylight hours exploded into the silent dark.

Art thought about the children at Mandel Community Center Nursery. All their lives were blank sheets of paper waiting to become stories. Except for Lucky, whose story already had a disturbing prologue. One that only Lucky himself could read.

What had Art wanted his story to be, when he was that age? Not this one, certainly. He'd imagined being a hugely famous actor, surrounded by loving family and friends, mobbed by hysterical fans proffering various body parts to be autographed wherever he went. Not an old man whose family refused to speak to him, whose career was ending before it had ever really taken off, and who couldn't even get noticed when he flagrantly flouted the law.

Something had to change. He wasn't sure what, or how, but he knew that the first step was confronting the issue. He had to open the wardrobe, the physical manifestation of all his shame and loathing.

Art turned on his bedside lamp and sat up slowly, then swung his legs around so that his feet hit the floor. The days when he'd leaped out of bed were long gone. He stood up, stretched out his arms, rolled his shoulders, and shook each of his legs in turn, limbering up for the marathon this task was, then made his way slowly across the landing.

Art opened the door to his spare room, turned on the light, and shuffled in sideways, his eyes trained on his feet. It turned out that dealing with the problem head-on was beyond him. He hated this room. It was a constant reminder of everything he'd lost, and everything he despised about his life and himself.

Kerry's single bed still waited, a threadbare teddy bear by her pillow, in case she ever wanted to come home. He picked up the pillow and buried his face in it. For several years, he'd been able to imagine the faint memory of her scent—Impulse deodorant, minty toothpaste, and Timotei shampoo—but he'd not been able to smell anything other than dust and damp for decades.

The walls were covered with posters—Duran Duran, Spandau Ballet, and Culture Club, all glistening skin, taut muscles, and smoldering eyes. Where were they now, those beautiful boys? Probably languishing on the NHS waiting list for hip replacements. Several corners had peeled down, the Blu Tack holding them in place having long since lost its blue and its tack, revealing a brighter, younger version of the wallpaper behind them.

Art grasped the brass knob on the wardrobe door and took three long, deep breaths, still staring at the floor. *You can do this, Art. You have to.* He flung open the door, so violently that it ricocheted back again before settling in a half-open position. A tsunami of miscellaneous *stuff* fell onto the floor in front of him. A decade's worth of pilfered items, most still with their price labels attached, none of them wanted, none of them used.

Art never used anything he stole. Once the thrill of the acquisition had worn off, the items he'd nicked were simply unwelcome reminders of his shame, and were quickly shoved into the dark recesses of the wardrobe.

Art sat down on the bed, its lumpiness betraying the additional hoard of stolen goods stashed underneath it, and stared at it all.

There were clothes—mostly not even his size—books, boxes of chocolates, toiletries, hardware, software, stationery, games, magazines. He'd picked up anything that caught his eye whenever he'd been unable to resist the urge, like a magpie on amphetamines.

What was he going to do with all this contraband? Where could he even begin?

Some garishly colored plastic caught his eye. A toy truck. Ever since he'd found evidence of his grandchildren on Facebook, Art had been drawn to children's toys and clothes. He had no idea what his grandchildren liked, or how big they were. They must be teenagers by now. Far too old for plastic trucks, in any case.

Kerry's Facebook and Instagram were sensibly, but frustratingly, private. He'd resorted to cyberstalking all her old school friends, in the hope of gleaning some details about Kerry's life. He'd spend hours scouring the internet, and then, when he did manage to find some small detail—a school reunion she'd attended, or a charity event she'd taken part in—it would pierce his heart, lodge itself there and fester. And every answer he found just led to more questions.

Art reached out for the jaunty yellow truck, pulling it free from the pile. For the first time, he knew where he could start.

"OMG, Art, this is *awesome!*" said Janine, pulling soft toys, children's clothes, puzzles, and games out of the bin liner Art had thrust at her. "Where did it all come from?"

"Uh, donations from local shops," Art replied. "It's all new, but out-of-date stock. Stuff they can't sell anymore." That, at least, was true. "I thought they'd be helpful for the kids. And their families."

"You have no idea how much!" said Janine, who was actually looking a little tearful. "Places here are council- and charity-funded, so they're ferociously means-tested. Our kids often come from homes where they have nothing. They're totally reliant on benefits and food banks. This must have taken you so long to collect!" Art nodded, feeling himself blush in a way that he hoped appeared bashful rather than guilty. It had taken longer than Janine could possibly imagine. Ten years, in fact.

"Why don't we let them choose one thing each to take home, then we can share out the clothes among the parents at pickup, and put the rest of the toys in the toy chest, for them to play with while they're here?" said Janine, calling the kids over.

Art watched as each of them sorted through his pile of loot, wide-eyed with wonder, checking again and again that they really could take something home, just for them.

For the first time in years, Art felt something other than shame. A tiny flicker of pride. Perhaps he wasn't just a common thief—he was Robin Hood. Stealing from the rich and giving to the needy. He was a fairer, redistributive taxation system in human form.

"Let's put all the rest of the toys in the toy box, kids," said Janine, "and then we can start working on our nativity play."

"A play?" said Art. Even after five decades of professional disappointment, the word "play" still had the power to make his spine tingle.

"Yes," said Janine, rolling her eyes. "Council edict. I have no idea how we can possibly pull a performance together in the next three weeks with no budget, no costumes or scenery, and no talent. It's going to be a shambles. I even wonder whether that's their intention—so they have another reason to close us down."

"Perhaps I can help?" said Art, whose generosity now knew no bounds. "You see, I am an experienced thespian! Maybe I can get all the social club to muck in. I'll talk to Lydia."

This ideal opportunity had just fallen into Art's lap! He could keep himself busy and out of trouble, and create a part for Maggie. It would give her just the experience she needed in front of a live audience.

Fired up with the excitement and novelty of finding himself on the right side of the moral compass, Art crossed the hallway to the room they used for the social club, putting some spare coppers and leftover Fruit Gums from his pocket into the collecting box on his way.

Lydia

L ydia was handing round slices of her homemade coffee-and-walnut cake, when they were disturbed by a tinny voice coming from the street. Lydia couldn't distinguish the words initially, but as they got louder and closer they became clearer:

"CLEAR THE PAVEMENT! SAVE OUR COMMUNITY CENTER! CLEAR THE PAVEMENT! SAVE OUR COMMUNITY CENTER!"

Everyone rushed—well, insofar as they were physically able to rush—to the windows and peered out. Hoving into view was Anna on her mobility scooter, her hair no longer lilac, but bright, almost fluorescent, orange. She scattered women and children from the pavement in front of her, like a snowplow clearing a drift. A loud-hailer was attached to the handlebars which, in turn, were attached to an old-fashioned tape recorder. Her walking frame was strapped to the back. They watched her dismount slowly, turn off the tape, and switch modes of transportation.

"Nice work, Anna," said Art, as she wheeled into the room pushing the walking frame.

"Just doing my bit," said Anna, peeling off her leather jacket to reveal an AC/DC T-shirt. "Luckily, this ain't my first rodeo." Lydia had no idea what she meant by that.

"You changed your hair color," Lydia said.

"You like?" said Anna, turning her head from side to side. Fortunately, she continued without waiting for a response. "Most folks see gray hair as a sign of age. Not me. I see it as a *blank canvas*. It's a challenge, innit? Hey! Did anyone see the postbox by the town hall? It's wearing a Santa hat! It's causing a right stir. I wonder who could knit a giant red hat like that . . ."

They all swiveled as one to face Ruby.

Ruby said nothing, just stared demurely down at the pale-pink knitting on her lap and murmured, "Knit one, purl one."

"What are you knitting now, Ruby?" asked William.

"Something for my grandchild," said Ruby, with a little smile.

"Sure you are, Banksy," said Daphne.

"So, what's on the agenda for today, Lydia?" asked Ruby, with a deft swerve of subject.

"Well, I brought a huge jigsaw along, which I thought we could do together," said Lydia, slightly nervously. Her club members, she'd learned, did not hold back with their opinions, which were almost invariably negative.

"There's no point doing jigsaws 'cause Daphne cheats!" said Anna.

"I do not!" said Daphne, snapping her head around to deliver a look that would have turned a lesser woman to stone. Anna, however, had spent three decades dealing with truckers, and was not easily intimidated. She held up her right hand, second and third fingers pointed into a V-shape, turned them slowly toward her eyes, then leveled them at Daphne while mouthing, *I see you, Daphne.*

"How is it possible to cheat at a jigsaw?" said Lydia, trying to smooth the waters.

"Last week, she hid the final piece so she could be the one to finish it," said William.

"Prove it, Sherlock," said Daphne, icily.

"That piece, which you pulled miraculously out of thin air, was *still warm* 'cause you'd been *sitting on it* for hours," said Anna. "I know a cheat when I see one. I was married to one for years."

"I didn't know you were married," said Lydia, in a clumsy attempt to move the conversation on before her seniors could start stabbing each other with Ruby's knitting needles.

"Five times," said Anna, rolling up her sleeve and turning over her arm to reveal five names tattooed in cursive script. "Outlived them all. Wimps." The names on Anna's forearm had all been crossed out with neat, black, tattooed diagonal lines.

"Mmm. To lose one husband is unfortunate. But to lose five could be considered careless. If not criminal," said Daphne.

"Look, this is all interesting but irrelevant," interrupted Art. "I have a far more important activity for us all than jigsaw puzzles. The council have asked the nursery next door to put on a nativity performance before we all close for the Christmas holidays, and they desperately need our help."

There was a brief silence while they all digested this information.

"You know what," said Daphne. "You may not be as stupid as I'd thought."

"Well, you are just as rude as I'd suspected," said Art. Daphne ignored him.

"We can skin two cats with one stone. Help the kids next door *and* save our social club," she said.

"Kill two birds, I think you mean?" said Lydia.

"Do you?" said Daphne, with a glare that seemed to pin Lydia to her chair, like a butterfly attached to a corkboard. "The point is, we are never going to save this community center by collecting loose change from people, selling a few cakes, or doing a sponsored walk. What we need is *hearts and minds*. We need to show the council, their constituents, and the local media how important this place is to the community. That way there'll be an uproar if they try to send in the bulldozers. If we can do that, they'll find the money to repair our hall. And a joint nativity production is the perfect vehicle. It's got everything: cooperation, creativity, education, and, to top it all, angels, a donkey, and the baby Jesus. It's bound to succeed because, to quote *The Blues Brothers*, we'd be 'on a mission from God.'" Daphne steepled her hands in front of her on the table and stared at them all.

"I hate to say this, and I very much doubt I'll ever say it again, but I agree with Daphne," said Art. "Which is why it was my idea in the first place. A bunch of geriatrics aren't going to pull the local heartstrings, but if we add some of those cute kids next door into the mix . . ."

"It's genius!" said William. "And I still have contacts in the London press offices: the *Evening Standard*, *Metro*, the *Fulham and Hammersmith Chronicle*. I'll buy them a few pints, and make sure they pick up the story."

"So, William can be in charge of scenery, since he has an artistic eye, and taking publicity shots," said Art. "Ruby, since you're so good with textiles, can you do costumes?"

"On it like a car bonnet," said Ruby, somewhat incongruously. Perhaps she was actually planning to knit a bonnet for a car?

"Lydia, can you organize refreshments? Anna and Daphne can be general helpers, and I'll direct," said Art.

"Of course you will," said Daphne, under her breath, followed by, "General helper, my arse."

"Oh, and don't forget Maggie! I have a role in mind for her, too," said Art.

"Don't they say never work with children or animals?" said William.

"Ha!" said Art. "It'll be fine. I mean, what could possibly go wrong?"

Lydia felt a warm glow of satisfaction, watching her club members collaborating over something that wasn't borderline illegal, or positively dangerous. Or perhaps it was just a hot flash? It was difficult to tell the difference. She was reading a book called *Cracking the Menopause: While Keeping Yourself Together*, but she still felt like she was falling apart. She'd put the book down somewhere and lost it for days, before finding it in the microwave.

"Lydia, about the other project we've been working on," said William.

Lydia's good mood dissipated, replaced by a wave of nausea. She'd given Art and William details of Jeremy's routine, his office address, and so on, but had rather hoped they'd forgotten about the whole surveillance thing. She'd convinced herself that Jeremy was right: she was overreacting. Hysterical. But what if they had found something? Did she really want to know? Wouldn't it be better to keep her head planted firmly in the sand?

"We followed your husband for forty-eight hours, and this is all we got," said William, taking a brown A4 envelope out of his bag and pulling out an array of glossy photographs, which he spread in front of them with the practiced manner of a man who had covered many editors' desks with prints over the years.

"This certainly wouldn't be enough for the legal departments of the *Sun* or the *Daily Express*. Nothing that proves anything *untoward* is going on." Art waggled his gray eyebrows meaningfully at the word "untoward."

Lydia felt her shoulders relax. There were shots of Jeremy entering and leaving his fancy gym. Out for lunch with a client. Shopping in his favorite gentlemen's outfitter's.

"What's this one?" she said, pushing a photo across the table toward William with her index finger. It showed her husband kissing the cheek of a much younger woman on a busy pavement. The sort of woman for whom traffic stopped when she wanted to cross the road. Unlike Lydia, who'd nearly been mowed down by a yellow Fiat Uno the other day, despite being on a pedestrian crossing. It would be just her luck, to suffer the indignity of being killed by an affordable yellow car.

"He was just kissing her goodbye, right outside the office. They walked off in opposite directions," said William.

"I don't think that kiss meant anything," interjected Art. "In my industry—my *ex-industry*—people kiss like that all the time, hundreds of times a day, while calling each other 'darling' and saying *mwah-mwah*."

"It's a great example of how context is everything," said William. "I honestly wouldn't worry about it. We'll keep following him, though. Just for a few more days, if you like?"

"No, no," said Lydia. "I don't want to waste your time." She was feeling utterly stupid and embarrassed. And having Jeremy followed was unethical, if not illegal.

She stared at the pictures again, wondering why she didn't feel more relieved. Something about them unsettled her. There was her husband, chivalrously kissing a woman goodbye, politely pouring wine for his lunch guest, smiling at the doorman as he left the gym.

When had he last treated her like that? Looked at her like that? When had he stopped bothering? When had she stopped noticing him not bothering? When had she stopped feeling worthy of him bothering?

Snap out of it, Lydia, she told herself. Everything was going to be fine. Jeremy wasn't having an affair, they were going to save the community center and her job, and the girls would soon be home for the Christmas holidays. It was all coming together brilliantly.

Lydia helped herself to another celebratory slice of cake. Maybe it would help plump out some of her wrinkles. Like a cosmetic filler, but more tasty.

Art and William were helping Lydia stack the chairs back in the corner of the room, while Daphne was hovering, looking uncharacteristically nervous and awkward, by the door.

"Is there a problem, Daphne?" Lydia asked.

"I have a favor to ask William," she said.

Art and William, who were holding one end of the table each, stopped in their tracks and stared at her in astonishment.

"I was wondering if you could take some photos for me," said Daphne, shifting from one foot to the other, in the manner of someone not used to asking for help.

"What kind of photos?" asked William.

"Of me," said Daphne. "For a website. Ziggy says I need to look happy. Approachable and friendly. The photos should show me doing hobbies, and having fun with friends and family—that kind of thing. Do you think you can do that?"

"Well, of course *I* can do that," said William. "But more to the point, can *you*?"

Ziggy

Ziggy walked out of the classroom and into a world which felt as if it had expanded a little. He'd spent the last hour with Mr. Wingate, playing with coding problems that had made his brain fizz, then looking at some of the online prospectuses of universities he might be able to apply to. Ziggy had scrolled through pictures of worlds filled with ornate, high-ceilinged libraries, huge, high-tech computer labs and groups of smiling kids who looked like they actually *wanted* to learn. Could he insert himself into those scenes? Was there really a place for someone like him? And Kylie?

Ziggy was so wrapped up in this potential shiny new world that he nearly walked straight into Alicia.

"Sorry," he mumbled, expecting her to swerve away from him as quickly as possible.

Ziggy had never fitted neatly into any of the school cliques. He was a strange mixture of geeky—on account of his passion for coding and math—and cool—due to his prowess on a football pitch and, according to the girls, his good looks, a striking combination of conker-brown eyes and blond hair, which frizzed from his head as if he'd stuck his fingers into an electrical socket. But in the past, despite not trying terribly hard to fit in, Ziggy had always had plenty of people wanting to be his friend, or his girlfriend. Even, on one occasion, his boyfriend.

Not now. Baby Kylie had tipped him over the fine, but crucially important, line from being *individual* to *weird*. The only father in year thirteen. In the whole school, even. And the girls, who'd once flocked around him, now avoided getting too close, as if his super-potent spermatozoa might be able to leap the gap between them, like Highland salmon desperately searching for their breeding grounds, and send them hurtling into the same inhospitable uni-verse as him.

But Alicia didn't dash off; she fell into step with him.

"Hey, Ziggy," she said. "Why are you here so late?"

"Extra computer science," he said. "You?"

"Oboe lesson," she said, nodding at the long blue case she had slung over her shoulder.

"Oboe," said Ziggy. "That's so cool. I thought everyone played, like, the violin. Or the guitar or piano."

"That's why I chose the oboe," said Alicia, blowing a red cork-screw curl out of her eyes. Ziggy caught a faint scent of peppermint on her breath, which made him feel strangely lightheaded. "It's a challenge, but it's unique. You could come and watch me at the next orchestra performance, if you like? I'm first oboe. On account of being the only oboe."

"Sure. Thanks," said Ziggy. "I'd like that." And as Alicia headed out of the gates, pausing briefly to wave at him and smile, he edited the picture in his head, of him in the university library, to include a girl who played the oboe and was a challenge, but unique.

Just like him.

Ziggy's phone buzzed in his pocket. He pulled it out and read the text message. Daphne wrote texts, he'd discovered, just the way she spoke: in proper full sentences and with perfect grammar and an undercurrent of condescension. They were the sort of messages more suited to being handwritten on a card and delivered by a butler than appearing on a phone screen.

Ziggy, you can find Kylie and myself at the Fox and Ferret pub on Brook Green. We'll see you shortly, no doubt. Daphne.

Daphne had taken Kylie to a *pub?*

Not for the first time, Ziggy wondered whether Daphne really was the right person to trust with his daughter . . .

W̲ell, it didn't look as if Daphne had taught Kylie to drink vodka straight from the bottle. At least, not yet. In fact, everything appeared—relatively—wholesome.

Kylie was sitting on Daphne's knee, and Daphne was waving a rattle at her and . . . smiling? Actually, it looked more like a grimace, a human facial expression being attempted by a poorly created avatar. Maybe Daphne's smiling muscles had atrophied more rapidly than the rest of her through lack of use. Ah, this was obviously the photo shoot for the dating website. It was all his idea. His fault.

Art, who he recognized from the community center, was sitting on the other side of the table, while another old man—who Ziggy guessed must be the William that Daphne had mentioned—took photos with an extremely expensive-looking camera attached to a huge, scarily phallic lens.

"Are you sure I've not taken your picture before, Daphne?" said

William. "I never forget a face, and I'm pretty certain I recognize yours."

"Highly unlikely," said Daphne. "I'm quite the hermit. I must have one of those bland, interchangeable faces."

Ziggy tried not to laugh. Daphne was about as bland as a chicken vindaloo, and just as likely to blow your head off.

"Try to look like you're at least a little fond of your granddaughter," said William, before taking a few steps back, which was definitely wise.

"Uh, she's not Daphne's granddaughter, actually," said Ziggy. "Do you think it's a good idea to lie like that?"

Everyone turned to stare at him, including Kylie, who—sensing an escape route—stretched her arms toward him and started to cry.

"It's not a lie, dear boy," said William. "We're not going to *say* Kylie's related to Daphne. Photos don't actually *lie*; they just encourage people to see their own version of the truth. And if people *choose* to assume that Daphne has a gorgeous, photogenic, loving family, then so be it. Talking of which, would you mind sitting at the table, just there? You can be Kylie's brother."

William gestured at the empty seat next to Daphne.

"I'm her father, not her brother," said Ziggy.

"Well, I know that's the truth, but it's hardly probable, is it?" said William. "And it doesn't fit the narrative we're creating here."

"Ziggy's been having extra lessons at school, while I've been babysitting his daughter," said Daphne, which Ziggy read correctly as *Don't forget you owe me one.* Daphne was a wily, manipulative old crone. Ziggy sighed, and sat down.

"By the way, I found the stone from your bracelet, Daphne," he said. "Would you like it back?"

"Good God, no," said Daphne, looking rather queasy. "I know where it's been! But you must keep it. Put it somewhere safe. It'll make a great anecdote for when Kylie's older. The diamanté stone that traveled all the way through her digestive tract!"

"Smile, and say, 'Hello, Granny.' Look as if you love each other!" said William. Easier said than done.

After what felt like hours of Ziggy posing as Daphne's fake grandson, William moved Daphne to an armchair by the fireplace.

"We need to make this look like a different place and day," he said. "Daphne, can you take off the jacket and add the silk scarf? Perfect. Right, let's throw Maggie Thatcher into the mix. Everyone trusts people who dogs like, I find."

Art whispered something in Maggie's ear, before placing her reluctantly on Daphne's knee and mouthing, *Sorry*. The dog looked rather put out at being used as a prop. Ziggy knew the feeling.

"Art, you sit on one side of Daphne, and I'll sit on the other. Ziggy, I've set up the shot, so all you need to do is press the button. OK?"

"Sure," said Ziggy, who was, to his surprise, starting to enjoy himself. Kylie was sitting beside him on the carpet (which he really hoped they cleaned regularly), chewing happily on a cardboard beer mat.

"Right, Daphne," said William. "You're going to say something really funny, and Art and I are going to laugh uproariously, while Ziggy takes the shot. Go."

"So you two are my best friends?" said Daphne. William and Art started laughing. What looked like genuine belly laughs.

"That wasn't supposed to be a joke," said Daphne. "I meant, that's the effect we're aiming for, right?"

They laughed even harder.

Ziggy moved to the side to get a better angle.

"By the way, I talked to my old mate, Ned, at the local paper about the nativity," said William, once he'd been able to catch his breath.

"Great!" said Art. "Is he going to come?"

"Yes," said William. "But he didn't think it would make much difference. He has contacts in the local planning department. He says they've already had a proposal for turning the Mandel Community Center site into a luxury apartment complex."

As if he'd turned a telescope around and was peering through the wrong end, Ziggy's world—which had, for just an hour or so, felt as if it were expanding—contracted to a pinprick.

No Mandel Community Center meant no childcare, no school, no university, and no new life.

Art

rt walked toward Hammersmith roundabout—three lanes of constant traffic flowing under the Hammersmith flyover, circling a modern shopping center, St. Paul's church, and the Hammersmith Apollo. He ducked into the dank underpass.

Huddled against the wall was a man tucked into a sleeping bag covered in holes, stains, and burn marks. He either was fast asleep, or had passed out, and was oblivious to the commuters streaming by. They paid him no attention. He was just one of the many sights that Londoners chose to ignore, lest they took the shine off their comfortable existences.

Art pulled three cashmere sweaters out of his bag, each with its price tag still attached. He tucked the sweaters just under the sleeping bag and walked on. With each step he felt a little lighter.

For the first time in decades, Art felt as if his life were on an upward trajectory. He was making inroads into the wardrobe, and he wasn't adding anything new to his stolen loot. He hadn't addressed the root of the problem—he had no idea where to even find it, and suspected he'd have to dig down a very long way—but he was simply *too busy* for a shoplifting spree.

Art had the social club three afternoons a week, plus a few days of intensive dog training whenever he had Maggie to stay. He and William were also secretly continuing their surveillance operation. While they hadn't yet caught Jeremy in flagrante, the man was obviously a tosser, and no doubt up to something. Plus, on top of everything else, Art was writing and directing a drama production which might just win over the hard hearts on the council and save their community center.

Art had a *purpose*. Several of them, in fact.

Art surveyed his audience. The largest, and most attentive, audience he'd had in years, actually. Eighteen children, aged from eight months (Kylie) to nearly five years old (Lucky) were gathered in a semicircle around him. The room smelled of poster paints and Play-Doh, with faint undertones of nappy, transporting him back to his own childhood, in the same neighborhood, but a different century and a completely different world.

"Say hello to Mr. Andrews, children," said Janine.

"Hello, Mr. Andrews," chorused the children in a singsong tone, perfectly in time with each other.

"Mr. Andrews is going to help us with our nativity play, since he is a proper *actor*," said Janine in a gratifyingly reverential tone. A hand shot up. "Yes, Zack?" she said.

"Are you in any of the Marvel movies?" said Zack, staring at him in awe. Art considered lying and claiming to have played Iron Man, but wasn't sure he could get away with it.

"No," he said, and watched the shine drain from Zack's eyes. "But I was in *EastEnders*! Has anyone seen that?" Thirty-four eyes gazed back at him. Lucky, as always, was staring at the floor. Zack started picking his nose, finding the contents far more interesting than Art's unimpressive soap career. And tasty, it appeared.

"Ooh, I *love EastEnders*!" said Janine, taking pity on him. "What part did you play?"

"Well, I was punched once by Phil Mitchell in a bar brawl, I bought two apples and a pear from Arthur's market stall, and I did my washing in the launderette with Dot Cotton a few times," said Art. Janine smiled at him in a politely interested, but also faintly disappointed way. It was an expression Art had become accustomed to over the years.

"Now, the first thing we need to do is decide who plays which parts. It's called 'casting.' Does anyone have a part they especially want to play?" he said.

"Yes, Tallulah?" said Janine to a pretty Black girl with intricately braided hair and an enthusiastically raised hand.

"Can I be the star?" said Tallulah, with an endearing lisp.

"*Everyone* is a star in our production," said Art, wishing that were the case in real life. Every set he'd ever been on had been ferociously hierarchical.

"No, I want to be the actual star!" pouted Tallulah. "The one over the stable. I can be twinkly and shiny and pointy."

"Oh, right. Yes, of course you can," said Art. "And you can double up as the Angel Gabriel as well, if you like." Tallulah beamed.

"Lucky," said Art. Lucky, who was sitting about five feet outside the circle, clinging on to Maggie Thatcher, didn't look up, but he did angle his head slightly in Art's direction. "M is going to be a sheep, and she's going to need a bit of help, since she's never done any acting before. Will you be her shepherd?" It seemed as if the room held its breath, as everyone waited for a response. Lucky's head moved in an almost imperceptible nod. Or perhaps Art was imagining it. "Great," he said, in any case. "Now, does anyone want to be the Virgin Mary?"

A single hand shot up.

"Mary is a girl's part, Noah," said Janine. Noah was wearing the Elsa costume which Art had stolen from Tesco and which now lived in the communal dressing-up box. The blue polyester skirt pooled over his crossed legs. He looked crestfallen.

"I don't see why our production can't be gender-neutral," said Art. "It's all the rage these days. Did anyone see Glenda Jackson as King Lear? A seminal performance! No, I guess not. Anyhow, the Angel Gabriel was male, but is being played by Tallulah, and Kylie's going to be the baby Jesus, since she's the smallest, and technically Jesus was a boy."

"And a newborn," said Janine. "Kylie's way too big."

"This is a play, dear girl," said Art. "It's make-believe. We can be size-neutral as well as gender-neutral. I'm sure you'll make a fine Virgin Mary, Noah!" Noah grinned at him and clapped his plump hands together, and Art thought this might be the best day he'd had in years.

Art and William sat at opposite ends of the bench, just as they'd sat at the bus stop as children, leather satchels at their feet, on the way to school. They had a perfect view of Lydia's husband's office, right across the street.

The vast glass skyscrapers towering above them made Art feel incredibly small. Why hadn't he traveled into the center of town for so long? He'd forgotten how magnificent the capital he lived in was. Here, in the city, these giant modern offices butted up against each other, each trying to look down—both physically and metaphorically—on its neighbor. And, right next to them, the ancient Tower of London and the majestic, winding Thames, which had seen the city evolve over centuries, through the Great Fire and the Black Death, outlasting millions of its inhabitants who had, for their short time on this earth, fooled themselves into feeling significant.

They drank the coffee they'd brought in a Thermos flask, raising their two tin cups in perfect synchronicity. William kept a practiced eye trained on the glass revolving doors, while one hand rested on his camera, hidden beneath his large overcoat. A never-ending, fast-flowing stream of cars, taxis, cyclists, and pedestrians passed in front of them.

"I had such fun with those kids today, William," said Art to his friend.

"That's great, Art," said William. "But doesn't it make you wonder whether you should maybe get to know your grandchildren? I bet you don't even know their names. You should look up Kerry. Apologize. Build bridges."

"I have apologized. Over and over," said Art, trying not to sound as sulky as he felt. For once, he'd been feeling positive about his life, and William had just rained on his parade. He felt a drop of water on his forearm. Oh, great. Now it was actually raining.

"I know you have," said William. "But you need to try again. You're the parent. Enough time has passed. Give it another go, before it's too late. I don't want you being lonely." William reached across the gap between them to grab Art's hand. Art snatched it away, then immediately felt guilty.

"I'm not lonely. I have you," he said, punching his friend on the arm in a well-worn gesture.

William was one of the Windrush kids, arriving by boat from Grenada as a baby in 1948. His dad had worked for British Rail, and they'd lived just around the corner from Art, in one of the only boarding houses not displaying a sign in the window reading NO DOGS, NO BLACKS, NO IRISH. They'd met at primary school, when Art had decked the boy in the lunch queue who was waving a banana at William and making monkey noises, and they'd had each other's backs every day of the subsequent seventy years.

"I might not be here forever, Art," said William. "And I worry about what will happen to you."

"Don't be ridiculous, William! You're younger than me!" said Art.

"By three months," said William.

"Car crash or train crash?" said Art, desperate to change the subject.

"Train crash. More dramatic. Car crashes are so common," said William. This game had started in 1958, with debating who was the best footballer; had morphed, once the hormones hit, into who was the hottest girl; and had now become the more morbid "Best Way to Die." The only way, they'd found, to deal with approaching death was to stare it right between the eyes.

"Train crash or plane crash?" said William.

"Still train," said Art. "Definitely. A plane crash is *way* too drawn out. Imagine that plunging-to-earth thing, with oxygen masks dangling from the ceiling, and everybody screaming while the air stewardesses shout, 'BRACE! BRACE!' because there's nothing else they can do. No, thank you."

"Hey, do you remember that time you were desperate to impress some kind of big-shot casting director, and you'd turn up at the same events as him while I followed you around with a camera, shouting, 'Art Andrews! I love your work!'?" said William.

"Yes!" said Art. "Days of effort, and all it got me was the 'before' man in a TV advertisement for dandruff shampoo." Art mimicked brushing flakes of dandruff off his shoulders.

"Look, isn't that Lydia's husband?" said William, nodding toward the man being propelled from the revolving doors onto the pavement opposite. "He's with that girl again."

They watched as Jeremy unchained a silver metal scooter from the bike rack outside his office. What kind of a grown man rode a *scooter*? What a pillock.

Jeremy pushed the scooter slowly along the pavement, keeping time with the girl walking beside him. The same girl he'd been kissing in the photo they'd shown Lydia. The kiss they'd insisted had been entirely innocent. Art could hear the rapid shutter-click of William's camera.

"I'm going after them," said William. "You stay here. It'll be less obvious if I tail him alone. I'll message you when they get to wherever they're going." William stood up and rushed off, more fluid and mobile than Art had seen him in years, which just went to prove that gainful employment was good for a man.

Art drained the last of his coffee, which had turned cold and bitter, and rested the cup on the bench beside him. He sat in the drizzle, his head deeply in the past, in the days when he'd had lines and call sheets, a runner who fetched him scones and jam between takes and a family waiting for him at home with the table laid and a stew in the oven.

Art watched two teenage girls walk past, heads together, laughing at a shared joke, and felt the familiar wave of grief that time's passing had dulled, but could never eradicate.

A rattle brought him back to the present with a jolt. He looked down at the source of the noise. Someone had thrown a handful of copper coins into his cup.

Ziggy

Ziggy just happened to leave his extra lesson with Mr. Wingate at the exact time that the orchestra were packing up their instruments. He just happened to take the front stairs, rather than the usual shorter route out via the back stairwell, and to notice that his shoelace had come undone, just as he reached the open door to the hall. He wasn't *intending* to bump into Alicia, but she just happened to come out, swinging her oboe case, as he was still standing there, since his lace was proving more tricky than usual.

What were the chances of that?

"Oh, hi, Alicia!" he said. "I wasn't expecting to see you here." Ziggy gave himself a mental kicking. *I wasn't expecting to see you here!* Where else would you expect a girl who played first oboe in the orchestra to be, other than at a rehearsal of the orchestra? *Idiot.*

"Oh, hi, Ziggy!" said Alicia, beaming at him as if she didn't mind his total ineptitude in the slightest. "Where are you heading? We're going to the café on the Grove. You want to come with us?"

"Uh, I need to get home, for Kylie's babysitter—sorry," said Ziggy.

"No worries," said Alicia, in a tone that was just a little less warm than it had been.

"She's not a regular babysitter, actually," said Ziggy, desperate to keep Alicia talking, so she wouldn't leave with the impression that he was making excuses for not spending time with her. "She's really a mad geriatric with an amazing collection of costume jewelry, who smokes cigarettes in this cigarette-holder thing like an old film star, uses her hair bun as an extra pocket, and has taken up internet dating."

"She sounds kind of cool," said Alicia. "Like Evelyn Hugo!"

"Totally!" said Ziggy, not willing to admit to having no idea who Evelyn Hugo was. A fashion designer? Politician? Aristocrat? Who knew?

"I'd love to meet her, and Kylie. Do you have a picture?"

"Of Daphne?" said Ziggy.

"No, you idiot. Of Kylie."

Ziggy hesitated. He really should be avoiding the subject of his daughter, if he were to have any hope at all of ever having another relationship. After all, what normal teenage girl wanted to be lumbered with a boyfriend who had to worry about babysitters and saving his pocket money to buy nappies? Not that he was thinking of having another relationship, obviously. His days of shagging in stationery cupboards—or anywhere, actually—were behind him. And if he did ever have sex in the future, he was wearing a full-body condom. He'd make damned sure none of those suckers ever got loose again.

"Here she is," said Ziggy, showing Alicia his favorite picture on his phone's home screen.

"Oh, she's *gorgeous*," said Alicia. She handed Ziggy's phone back to him, and he noticed that her bare arm was covered in a constellation of tiny freckles. How long, he found himself wondering, would it take to kiss every single one of them? *Stop it, Ziggy!*

They reached the door of the café where the orchestra had commandeered a few tables. "Well, I guess this is where we say goodbye," she said.

Before he could stop to analyze the idea that formed in his head, the words were out of Ziggy's mouth.

"You know, they're doing a nativity performance at Kylie's nursery. Mandel Community Center, in a couple of weeks' time. Do you think you and some of the orchestra might be able to play some Christmas carols or something? The kids would really love it. We all would," he said.

There was a silence, which seemed to stretch for minutes. Then Alicia said, "Sure. Why don't you take my number, then you can message me the details?"

Boom.

Ziggy barely noticed his journey home. He didn't see the drizzle falling from the bleak December sky, the rubbish scattered on the pavement, or the urban foxes scavenging in the bins outside the Chinese takeaway. Ziggy's head was in a sun-drenched lecture theater, his files spread out on the desk in front of him, and a whiteboard on the wall covered with complex code. Then collecting Kylie from the university crèche, which was filled with thriving, smiling babies and toddlers, and in his student digs, where he was making his mum's chicken-stir-fry recipe for a girl with red corkscrew hair, freckles, and an oboe. Which was just a coincidence, honestly.

Ziggy was so immersed in his future life that he didn't even notice the gang lookout—stationed, as always, by the entrance to the estate—until a loud whistle pierced his dreams.

A large, shadowy figure blocked his path. Floyd.

"Where's the baby, bro?" said Floyd, his voice a low growl.

"Uh, with the babysitter," said Ziggy. "I need to get back, actually."

"You need to look after her, man. She's precious," said Floyd, managing to turn a compliment into a threat.

"I know," said Ziggy.

"We'll keep an eye on her, too," said Floyd. "Since you're one of us. You *are* one of us, right?" He stamped on an empty Coke can, which crumpled immediately, without any semblance of a fight, then kicked it into the gutter. It landed with a clatter.

Ziggy felt sick. There was no right answer to this question. A "no" would see him and his family targeted, but a "yes" could land him in a whole heap of trouble.

"You're taking your time," said Floyd, with a smile that wasn't a smile. "I thought you was supposed to be clever. Is it a difficult question?"

Ziggy teetered on the edge of the ravine, weighing up which bottomless crevasse to leap into. There was only one option—the one least likely to endanger his daughter or his mother.

"Yeah, I'm one of you. 'Course," he said, staring down at his feet and playing with the zip fastener of his coat.

"Right answer," said Floyd, walloping Ziggy on the back so hard he nearly lost his balance. "So, why have I not seen you much recently? You've not been pulling your weight, bro. Come find me tomorrow. I've got some jobs for you."

Daphne

aphne was doing rather well, if she said so herself. Baby Kylie was all clean and fragrant, since Daphne had learned how to change a nappy with the help of a YouTube video.

You could, Daphne had discovered, learn how to do *anything* with the help of YouTube. She'd also successfully unblocked a sink in her apartment that hadn't drained properly since 2013, and taught herself how to use makeup to achieve something called a "foxy, smoky eye." If she could only get YouTube to snuggle on the sofa with her, drinking martinis and watching reality TV, she'd be able to abandon this whole dating malarkey.

Now, Daphne and Kylie were happily sitting in Ziggy's armchair with Margaret, watching *Love Island* on Daphne's iPhone.

Kylie, it transpired, was even more of a fan of *Love Island* than Daphne. Daphne suspected this was on account of all the breasts. She wasn't entirely au fait with Ziggy's domestic arrangements, but it was clear that Kylie's mother wasn't on the scene, so Kylie had no doubt missed out on mammaries. And now there were tens of perfect, if milkless, specimens parading right in front of her squishy little nose.

"These aren't representative bosoms, you know, Kylie," said Daphne, who was taking her role as educator and protector most seriously. "Genuine breasts come in all manner of shapes and sizes. As do noses, and eyebrows and teeth. That is the beauty of real women. They're unique! These women have all spent an absolute fortune having painful, often downright dangerous procedures to make themselves look identical and forgettable. You, my friend, must always remember you are perfect just as you are. Do you understand?"

Kylie turned to her and smiled a huge, virtually toothless smile, and Daphne felt an almost physical tug. A *connection*. She couldn't remember the last time she'd felt a physical or emotional connection to another human being. Would she have made a good mother? She'd always assumed not, on account of being way too selfish and—of course—her demanding career, but perhaps she'd been wrong. Maybe having a baby would have changed all that. Changed *her*.

All this introspection made Daphne desperate for a cigarette.

"Let's go out on the balcony, honey, and I'll show you my smoke rings," said Daphne, deciding that Ziggy would probably be a bit antsy about her smoking indoors. Young people today were so precious.

Daphne strapped Kylie into her buggy—with one hand! Not bad, given the arthritis. She tucked a blanket around her, then pushed her onto the tiny balcony.

"Right, Kylie," she said, as she blew a volley of perfectly formed smoke rings over the edge. "We should probably talk about how to deal with *unwelcome advances*. A lit cigarette, I always found, was terribly useful for removing an unwanted hand from the buttocks, but I expect you'll be far too sensible to smoke, and those silly vape things don't have the same effect. A stiletto heel makes a really good weapon. Picture your enemy. Let's call him, just for the sake of illustration, Art Andrews. Now, take your heel and press down on the exposed fleshy bit of his ankle until he squeals like a stuck pig. Then, give it a little twist." Daphne mimicked a twisting action, and Kylie grinned at her.

"Do Gen Z wear stilettos? Or just trainers?" said Daphne. "And what comes after Gen Z, do you think? Do they start all over again at A? It also helps to carry a hairpin. I'll show you what to do with one of those once I can trust you not to swallow it. You have form in that area, you know. Ooh, look! There's Daddy!"

Daphne watched Ziggy chatting with the youths she'd eyeballed previously, who always seemed to be hanging out by the entrance to the estate. She was glad he still had a social life, despite his challenging circumstances. Although those boys weren't the friends she'd have chosen for him. She knew the type, only too well. They were trouble.

"Quick, Kylie! Retreat!" she said as she saw Ziggy walking toward them. She stubbed out her cigarette and tossed it into the bushes several floors below. The bushes already contained a couple of plastic bags, a football boot, and a broken microwave oven, so adding a cigarette butt to the mix wouldn't make much of an impact.

Daphne sprayed herself with the perfume she kept in her handbag, sat Kylie on her knee, and picked up the worn copy of *The Very Hungry Caterpillar* she'd had prepared for exactly this eventuality.

"'In the light of the moon, a little egg lay on a leaf,'" she read. Why on earth, when there were so many more important things they could be teaching their children, would parents waste their time reading stories about an insect with a dysfunctional relationship with food? And she objected to the use of a butterfly as an aspirational ending. Butterflies were fragile, and had extremely short life expectancies and the tiniest imaginable brains. What sort of a role model was that? A unicorn would be far more appropriate. At least they carried a built-in weapon on their heads.

Daphne heard the front door open. She continued reading, in that overly enthusiastic voice she'd heard Janine use with the kids in the nursery. It was exactly the same singsong tone people used to address retirees. *How are you feeling today, dear? Lovely weather we're having . . .* Nobody ever spoke to Daphne like that more than once, thankfully.

"Hi, Daphne!" said Ziggy. "Everything OK?"

"We've been having a lovely time, haven't we, Kylie?" said Daphne. Ziggy, she noted, did not look his usual, sunny self. He seemed stressed. Maybe these extra lessons weren't a good idea at all.

"How's the internet dating going?" said Ziggy, hanging up his coat and schoolbag on the pegs in the hall and kicking off his trainers, without undoing the laces.

"Good. Those photos seem to have done the trick. I have three dates lined up over the next three days, actually," said Daphne. "I did have four, but one sent me what I think you young people would call a 'prick picture,' so I had to cancel him."

"You mean a dick pic, I think," said Ziggy.

"Well, whatever you choose to call it, it looked like the scrawny neck of the last turkey in the chiller cabinet. I can't imagine why he thought that would help his cause. Here's the chap I'm meeting this evening." Daphne passed Ziggy her phone, displaying Tony's picture.

"He looks nice. I like his dog," said Ziggy. Why was it that people assumed dogs were some form of positive character reference? "Cool phone, by the way."

"It's an iPhone Fourteen Plus, with a dual-camera system, face ID, and five hundred and twelve gigabytes of storage," said Daphne, which—judging by the expression on Ziggy's face—was an unnecessary amount of detail.

"Now, you do know the internet dating rules, don't you?" said Ziggy, handing her back the phone.

"What rules?" said Daphne, with a shudder. The only good rules—with the exception of grammar—were broken ones.

"Always tell someone where you're going, and who with."

"With whom," corrected Daphne.

"Don't correct their grammar. They'll find it intensely irritating," said Ziggy. Daphne suspected he'd added that one on the spur of the moment, but she let it go. "Meet in a public place, like a café. Keep the initial meeting brief. Oh, and have a friend lined up, in case you need to get out of there quickly. Tell them you'll text them if you need an exit, so they can call you and you can say, 'Oh no, my friend Marge has had a fall and needs help. Must go,'" said Ziggy.

"Why do you assume that I only have friends called something like Marge who have no sense of balance?" said Daphne.

"Sorry, Daphne. I'm sure you have lots of cool friends," said Ziggy.

"Actually, I don't," said Daphne. "I'm sure I told you that. I don't have any friends at all. Apart from Kylie." Where had that come from? Then, even more humiliatingly, she heard herself say: "Will you be my emergency contact, Ziggy?"

"Sure I will, Daphne," said Ziggy.

Daphne felt unaccountably warm, despite her menopausal days being well behind her. She'd rather missed having an accomplice.

"And just so I know, what name would you like your imaginary friend to have?" asked Ziggy.

"Taylor," said Daphne. "Like Swift."

She admired a self-made woman.

The man sitting opposite Daphne, wearing a paisley-patterned cravat around his jowly neck and a silk handkerchief poking imperiously out of his jacket pocket, was at least ten years older than in the photo on his profile. He had far less hair on top, and far more sprouting from his nose and his ears, and the dog Ziggy had been so enthusiastic about had been buried under the apple tree in his garden for some time.

Tony had long since retired from the job he'd mentioned, and it turned out that when he'd said he worked in the Foreign Office, he'd not been a spy, as she'd hoped. He'd actually spent his whole career processing passport applications, about which Daphne now knew more than any normal human being could ever need or want to know.

Daphne was able to see the irony in being cross about other people's false narratives, but even so.

Daphne had spent the first half hour of their date wondering how she was going to avoid answering any searching questions, and the last half hour wondering if Tony was going to ask her any questions at all. So far, she'd just been treated to an incredibly dreary monologue.

The waitress picked up the bottle of red wine in front of them and poured some into Tony's glass.

"Stop! Stop!" he said, shoving his hand over the top of his glass. "You complete idiot. You should never fill a wine glass more than one third, so it has room to aerate. Have you had no training *at all?*"

The waitress pulled the bottle away to avoid covering Tony's fingers with wine, causing a few drops of bloodred wine to splash onto the white linen tablecloth. She stammered an apology.

Enough was enough. Daphne reached into her pocket and surreptitiously sent the text message she'd had prepared for this eventuality. Within seconds, her phone rang.

"Who is it?" she said, feigning surprise rather well, she thought.

"Daphne, it's Taylor!" said Ziggy, in a ridiculous falsetto voice. "I've had a terrible fall. Can you please leave your date immediately and come and help?"

"Oh no," said Daphne into the phone. "How awful. I'll be there as soon as I can."

"Is there a problem?" said Tony.

"Yes," said Daphne, the prepared lie poised on her lips, before the truth barged right past it. "The problem is you're a rude, self-centered, patronizing prig." She picked up Tony's wine glass and poured half of the extremely expensive red wine into his lap. "There. It's only one-third full now, and aerating away." Then, she winked at the waitress and left.

What a waste of her foxy, smoky eyes.

As Daphne turned the corner, she spotted two familiar figures, bundled in fur throws and sitting under a patio heater outside the pub. Usually, she'd have avoided them like the plague, but she didn't want to go straight home. She needed time to decompress, so the memory of that oaf didn't infect the atmosphere of her lovely apartment. Her safe place.

"Art, William," she said. "What are you doing sitting out here in the cold and damp?"

"Lydia's husband is in there, with another woman," said Art, who was wearing a trilby and a turned-up collar, in a poor approximation of a John le Carré spy. "We're keeping an eye out."

"How very good of you," said Daphne, trying not to let her irritation leech into her voice. Why was it that every good deed Art insisted on doing just made her feel more . . . grubby? She could be thoughtful and kind, too, if she wanted. She just didn't. Life was too short to spend it worrying about other people.

"Although Lydia doesn't know we're still tailing him, so keep it under your hat," said Art, tipping his hat to accentuate his point. "You want to join us?"

"Thanks," said Daphne, pulling up a chair and wiping it down with the end of William's throw before sitting on it. "I will, actually."

"Talking of eyes," said Art, "what on earth happened to yours? Did someone punch you?"

"You obviously know nothing about the latest makeup trends," said Daphne.

"Ebola or dengue fever?" said William.

"What?" said Daphne.

"We're playing 'Best Way to Die.' Endless fun," said William.

"Oh, I see. Ebola," said Daphne. "So dramatic. All that bleeding from the eyeballs."

"Interesting viewpoint. Not what I expected," said William. "Your turn."

"OK. Being patronized to death or bored to death?" she said.

"Bored to death," said Art.

"Well, quite," said Daphne. "Which is why I'm sitting here with you two and not with my date."

"Charmed, I'm sure," said Art.

"Poor Lydia," said Daphne. "She doesn't deserve that scumbag."

"How on earth are we going to tell her?" said William.

"Let's at least wait until after Christmas," said Art. "Nobody wants that sort of news at Christmas."

"It looks like Lydia may not have a job soon, either," said William. "If the council accept that proposal from the developers, to replace the hall with luxury apartments." He said "luxury apartments" in the tone most people would use to say "rat-infested slum." "Unless we can completely blow their socks off with the nativity, and make a big splash in the media, we're all out on our ears. There's a council vote at the end of January."

"Mmmm. Let's burn that bridge when we come to it, shall we?" said Daphne.

"Cross that bridge, you mean?" said William.

"No, dear boy. I'm all about burning my bridges. There's never any point in going back," said Daphne, who was, despite herself, actually having fun. She couldn't remember the last time she'd indulged in a bit of banter.

"Daphne, I've been meaning to talk to you, actually," said Art tentatively, as if he expected her to shout at him. Which was ridiculous, since NO SHOUTING OR GLARING was on the whiteboard. "You see, I could do with spending more time with Maggie, and I'm sure you could do without the extra hassle of having her to stay. Why don't I take on your shifts for you?"

Daphne stared at Art in horror. *How dare he?* The utter gall of the man, trying to usurp her relationship with her dog.

"That's an outrageous suggestion!" shouted Daphne, rising to her feet so she could, just about, glare down at Art. "It is quite clear that Maggie loves me best. Frankly, I feel terrible every time I send her away. The poor thing is obviously distraught. If anyone were to become her primary carer, it would be me."

"Ha!" said Art. "That dog has far more fun with me, actually. We're more than just pet and owner. We're friends, colleagues, *comrades*. We have a purpose."

William snorted with laughter.

"What?" said Art.

"You two. You're far more similar than you think," he said.

"We are not," said Daphne and Art simultaneously.

Daphne wasn't going to listen to this nonsense any longer. She turned her back on the both of them and stalked off into the night.

"Let me know if you change your mind!" she heard Art call after her.

As if.

Lydia

Lydia had a full house, and a full heart, again. Sophia and Ellie were back from university, and it was her turn to take care of Maggie. She looked around the breakfast table and felt a wave of contentment. Jeremy sat at the head, laughing over one of Sophia's stories of student antics, the perfect picture of the fond, benevolent father. How could she possibly have suspected him of betraying her? It was the empty nest, the menopause, and the acres of time on her hands that had made her temporarily lose the plot.

"Sit," she said to Maggie. Maggie sat. "Lie down," she said, more out of interest than expectation. Maggie lay down. "Roll over," she said, just for fun. Maggie rolled over.

"Wow, Mum!" said Sophia. "You've trained her really well!"

"Have I?" said Lydia. Perhaps the effect of being in such a happy, well-run home was having a positive impact on Maggie's behavior? If only Lydia could get her to eat properly. Maggie seemed to have completely gone off her dried kibble. Whenever Lydia poured it into her bowl, she just stared at her, as if she'd been badly let down. Yet, strangely, she seemed to be getting fatter. Lydia made a mental note to ask Art and Daphne if they'd had the same problem. Maybe a trip to the vet was in order.

Lydia's job had transformed, as well as her home life. The social club had joined the nursery next door for the afternoon, so they could help with the final nativity rehearsals, scenery painting, and wardrobe fittings. It was a hive of happy activity, interspersed with the occasional temper tantrum. Mainly, but not entirely, by one of the children.

Art was sitting in a canvas chair with *DIRECTOR* written on the back. He was taking his role frightfully seriously.

"OK, Joseph, you need to go up to the door of the inn, leading Mary on the donkey!" said Art through a megaphone, despite the children being only feet away from him. Zack, dressed as Joseph, with one of Lydia's checked tea towels on his head, was holding a short rope which was tied to Anna's mobility scooter. The scooter was covered in a donkey costume knitted by Ruby, and on it sat Noah as Mary, in an adapted Snow White outfit.

"Stop, Noah! Before you run over Kylie!" shouted Art. "Then we'd have no baby Jesus. And who would save mankind then?"

Janine had her head in her hands and was muttering something about Health and Safety and P45s.

"Right, knock on the door, Zack, and say your words. Can you remember them?" said Art.

"Uh. Hi. Can I have a room?" said Zack, which must have been more or less what Art had in mind.

"Brilliantly done, Zack! Do you want to be an actor when you grow up?" said Art.

"No, I'm going to be a bay leaf," said Zack, confidently.

"A bay leaf?" said Lydia. "That's more an ingredient than a career, surely? Why?"

"Bay leafs get to go into other people's houses and take all their best things home with them," said Zack.

"Ah, I think you mean a *bailiff*, Zack," said Lydia.

"Why not go the whole hog and be a Tory politician?" mumbled Art. "Now, innkeeper—Tabby, it's your line!"

"No, sorry. We're full up, up, up, to the tippedy-top," said Tabby, who Lydia suspected was improvising a little.

"OK, Zack, now you need to say: 'If Thatcher hadn't sold off all the council housing in the eighties, we wouldn't be in this sorry mess,'" said Art.

"Art!" interrupted Lydia. "I think your own agenda is less hidden than it might be, here. Anyhow, that line is *way* too challenging for Zack. He's only four."

"Four and a quarter," said Zack, with righteous indignation.

How lovely it must be to be an age at which you wanted to add quarters rather than subtract decades.

"Lydia," said Art. "What other opportunity will we have to influence a captive audience of council members?"

"I don't think anyone from the council is coming, Art," said Lydia. "I've invited them all, obviously, but they're busy."

"Busy!" shouted Daphne, who Lydia hadn't even realized was listening. Despite her age, Daphne seemed to have the hearing of an adolescent bat. "What do you mean, *busy*?"

"Uh, as in they have something else on?" said Lydia, wondering if she'd misunderstood the question.

"And you just accepted that, did you?" said Daphne, narrowing her already narrow eyes.

"Well, yes. What else was I supposed to do?" stuttered Lydia. The rehearsal seemed to have ground to a halt, the whole room had gone silent, and everyone was staring at her.

"Lydia, you need to stop taking what irritating, self-important men tell you as the gospel truth," said Daphne. Lydia wondered whether she was referring to the council or Jeremy. Possibly both. "You are not a doormat for them to wipe their feet on. You are a grown woman, at the height of her powers. You just need to channel them."

"Uh, how?" said Lydia, feeling a hot flush coming on. She could probably power a kettle, even if she couldn't stand up to the council.

"You and I are going to the town hall. Right now, with Mary, Joseph, the baby Jesus, and the donkey," said Daphne. "No, no, don't get changed, Zack! We need you and Noah in costume!"

They caused quite a stir, progressing down the high street, handing out copies of the flyer William had made, using the children's drawings, to advertise the nativity. Lydia and Zack (Joseph) walked alongside the mobility scooter, which was still decked out as a donkey, while Daphne and Noah (Mary) rode on top. Kylie (baby Jesus) was strapped to Lydia's chest in a baby carrier, facing outward, grinning enthusiastically at everyone they passed.

"Zack and Noah," said Daphne. "You know how good you both are at acting?" Mary and Joseph nodded enthusiastically, sending both of their headdresses slightly awry. "Well, I thought we could give a little demonstration to the council. So, if I tap you on the shoulder, I need you to cry. As if someone's just kidnapped your siblings at gunpoint and set fire to your house."

Zack and Noah looked as stunned as Lydia felt, but rallied quickly.

"Can you do that?" prompted Daphne.

"Yes," said Zack, looking at Daphne slightly nervously. Lydia felt a huge affinity with this small child.

"Should I show them my pirouettes, too?" said Noah.

"Not this time," said Daphne. "Best to keep something back for a possible encore, don't you think?"

The receptionists at the town hall, who were usually ferocious gatekeepers, were so taken aback by the sudden arrival of Joseph, Mary, and Jesus in their lobby that they waved them through the barriers, directed them to the right office, and even offered to keep an eye on the donkey.

Mr. Dixon, Lydia's council representative, was—for the first time since she'd met him—entirely lost for words. After several seconds of staring at them, open-mouthed, he said, "I'm afraid I'm all out of stables till the next financial year." Then he laughed so hard at his own joke that his chins flowed like a wave, up and down his neck.

Lydia felt Daphne poke her in the back, and realized that she was, at this moment, more scared of the septuagenarian standing beside her than she was of standing up to Mr. Dixon.

"We don't need a stable, Mr. Dixon," said Lydia. "We just need to ask you to reconsider coming to the Mandel Community Center nativity on Friday, with the rest of the council."

"Hold on a minute," said Mr. Dixon, one hand rifling through a huge leather desk diary.

"We must insist you come, actually," said Daphne. She kept looking over at the industrial-sized stapler on Mr. Dixon's desk. If Lydia hadn't known her better, she'd have assumed that Daphne's subtext was: *Do as I say, or I'll staple your hand to that desk.* "It's an important community event. The local media will be covering it," she continued, staring from Mr. Dixon to the stapler and back again.

"Well, I'm afraid I can't make it then. None of us can," said Mr. Dixon, prodding at the date in his diary with a corpulent index finger. "It's our Christmas lunch, you see." He rested his hands on his heaving belly, as if preparing it for the task. If any belly was primed to receive a plateful of cholesterol-busting food, it was this one.

"How lovely for you all," said Daphne. "Where is it?"

"At the Taverna Portabella, on Brook Green," said Mr. Dixon.

Daphne pulled out her phone. Her fingers flew over the screen in a manner more like Lydia's daughters than a regular pensioner. Then she passed it to Lydia. Lydia knew exactly what she was suggesting, and something about Daphne's presence made her feel courageous, as if she were leeching off Daphne's invisible force field. She pushed back her shoulders and inhaled slowly.

"Hello. I'm calling from Mr. Dixon's office," she said, hearing her initially shaky voice building in confidence. "Our booking for Friday . . . yes, that's right, eighteen people in the function room . . . Is it possible to start a little later? At one thirty p.m.? We have an extremely important appointment beforehand . . . Thank you. See you then."

She handed the phone back to Daphne, who gave her an

approving nod. She'd never done that to Lydia before. Lydia felt like she'd been nominated for a Nobel Prize. Or, at least, a *Blue Peter* badge.

"But . . . but . . ." spluttered Mr. Dixon.

"You're not going to let these children down, are you, Mr. Dixon?" said Daphne. "They'd be so terribly upset if none of our most special guests came to their show." She tapped Mary and Joseph surreptitiously on the back of their shoulders, and both of them started weeping, exactly as if someone had just kidnapped their siblings at gunpoint and set fire to their house. Baby Jesus, whose tiny face—peering out from the baby carrier on Lydia's chest—was precisely at the level of Mr. Dixon's head, began wailing in sympathy.

"Argh! OK, OK! Just get everyone out of here and we'll see you on Friday!" said Mr. Dixon.

They left before he could change his mind, or Daphne could do any serious damage with the stapler.

"Daphne," said Lydia, as they processed with the donkey on their triumphant return journey down the high street. "You were spectacular! Thank you."

"As were you, my dear," said Daphne. "I wasn't sure you had it in you, to be honest. But it's not so hard, is it? You just need to take a deep breath, and channel your power."

Lydia stood just a little taller, feeling a tingling in her fingertips. Was that the power Daphne was referring to, or just poor circulation?

Art

Art hadn't been so excited about a performance since he'd played one of Prince Vultan's more minor Hawkmen in *Flash Gordon* back in 1980 and, for a few heady days, had been Brian Blessed's New Best Friend.

He'd borrowed a Christmas tree, complete with decorations, from the local garden center, and it was now placed at the entrance to the hall. In this instance, he and two of the children had actually *asked* if they could take it for free, and to his immense surprise they'd said yes!

Perhaps he should take small children dressed as innkeepers with him everywhere he went. He wasn't invisible when he was with the kids. *Everyone* noticed them, smiled at them, asked how they could help. The children were a magic portal back into his old world.

Arranged around the Christmas tree was a gorgeous group of teenage musicians from Ziggy's school, draped in tinsel and belting out an enthusiastic rendition of "Rudolph, the Red-Nosed Reindeer." The past few decades seemed to have passed in a flash, yet

Art couldn't imagine being that impossibly young and unbattered by life.

Art wondered if he'd jump at an offer to live it all again. Then he spotted Ziggy mooning around after the redheaded oboe player, reminding him of the exquisite torture of young love. Perhaps not.

The tired, neglected old hall was as warm, inviting, and primped up as the madam of a high-class brothel. It had a whole new lease of life, much like himself and the other senior citizens.

At the back of the hall, a table groaned with tea, coffee, and a huge array of cupcakes baked by Anna and the children (with varying degrees of success), along with a small mountain of confectionery he'd liberated from Starbucks over the years. Some of the regular attendees at the Alcoholics Anonymous meetings were manning the stand. They needed the community center to survive, too, and were, they'd told Lydia, experts when it came to tea and cake.

At the front, the stage was set for the performance, with the scenery enthusiastically created by the kids. A projector screen hung from the ceiling, onto which William's carefully curated photographs of happy, collaborating children and seniors, painting backdrops and rehearsing the play, were being beamed.

"Art!" said Lydia. "Doesn't it look amazing? They're never going to be able to close us down once they see all this! By the way, I dropped into Starbucks to thank them for sponsoring the play. The manager looked a bit nonplussed, to be honest. I suspect he was overstressed, what with Christmas being their busiest trading period. Anyhow, he said he'd try to come along. Isn't that great?"

"So great!" said Art. Although it wasn't great at all, obviously.

"Must go and check on the cast. They'll be needing a preperformance pep talk."

"Better to die of stage fright or anaphylactic shock?" said William, who was sitting behind the stage dressed as one of the Three Kings in a velvet cloak and crown.

"Definitely stage fright," said Art. "Imagine the drama of dying in front of a captive audience! A magnificent, noble way to go! Far more interesting than a peanut allergy. Not that that's going to happen today, hey? It's going to be a triumph!"

"My friend from the local rag turned up with a photographer in tow," said William. "He says we're the perfect festive feel-good story. He's hoping one of the nationals might even pick it up, if it's a quiet news day. And there's a cub reporter here from the *Evening Standard*!"

"Amazing! And it's a full house! Did you see, the whole council is sitting in the front two rows?" said Art.

"I'm starting to think we might just pull this off," said William. "If we get lots of glowing press coverage, they'll find it really hard to sell our hall from under us. There's nothing the council loves more than positive PR."

"How's my cast feeling? You're all going to be absolutely fabulous, darlings!" said Art to the assembled children, who were sitting in a nervous and hyperactive huddle on the floor, bubbling away like a volcano about to erupt.

"Jamal and Jessica, the kings were good friends, and didn't hit each other over the head with their gifts for baby Jesus. Please can you get in character? And I think the sheep is eating someone's rice cakes! Drop, M! Right, we have ten minutes till curtain up. Does anyone need the toilet?"

A hush fell over the audience, with the exception of Noah's dad, who was complaining to anyone who would listen about his son wearing a dress. A spotlight veered wildly across the stage before illuminating Art, the narrator. Anna's hand-eye coordination was a little hit and miss. Just as well she was no longer in charge of an articulated lorry. At least she'd got into the Christmassy spirit of the whole thing, and had dyed her hair half red, half green, with giant glittery Christmas baubles hanging from her ears.

"Welcome to the Mandel Community Center nativity!" said Art. "Today we are telling the Christian story of the birth of Jesus, but our nursery and senior citizens' group represent people of all faiths, and celebrate all their major religious and cultural events." Art paused for the smattering of applause and "Hear! Hear!"s from the council—a group of mainly white, middle-aged men who prided themselves on their inclusivity.

"Mary and Joseph lived in Nazareth, an awfully long time ago," said Art. "Before even I was born. And one night, something incredible happened."

Right on cue, Tallulah appeared in the spotlight, magnificent in wings and halo. She pointed her wand at Noah—Art had tried to explain that angels didn't have wands, but Tallulah, for whom the line between angel and fairy was somewhat blurred, had insisted—and said, "Mary, you're going to have a baby! He's the son of God and his name will be Jesus!"

"Mary was pretty surprised to hear this," said Art, and paused for Noah to do his surprised face, which looked a little like Munch's *The Scream.* "And due to decades of Tory government austerity and the inadequacy of Universal Credit, Mary and Joseph had to travel to Bethlehem to visit the food bank."

Art hadn't actually cleared this slight deviation from the script with Lydia and Janine, but hoped they would forgive him. He surreptitiously checked the front two rows to see if his subtle message had landed.

Noah climbed onto the donkey mobility scooter and, led by Zack, processed around the full perimeter of the hall, following the signs—painted by one of the older children—reading bEtHLEhEM THiS WaY.

"Meanwhile," said Art, "in the fields, the shepherd watched his sheep by night." Art held his breath, wondering if Lucky would make it onto the stage. Janine came on leading Maggie, dressed in her sheep costume knitted by Ruby.

"Come on, Lucky! You can do it!" she said, crouching down and gesturing to the small boy standing in the wings, hugging his stomach.

Anna swung the light onto Maggie, and finally, shuffling silently forward, looking at his feet, Lucky appeared next to her, dressed as a shepherd. Art blew a whistle, and Maggie stood on her back legs and turned a full circle, before bowing to the audience, who cheered wildly at them both.

"You did it, M!" said Art under his breath. All those hours of training and mountains of sausages had not gone to waste.

Lucky stood, stoically, by his sheep, his fists clenched by his sides, and his eyes flicking once or twice toward his audience. The clear, reedy sound of a single oboe played "Silent Night," and Art felt a lump forming in his throat.

"The shepherd saw something amazing in the night sky!" said

Art, once the oboe had fallen silent. Anna swung the light toward the wings, lighting up a twinkly Tallulah, who was sitting on William's shoulders, her hands clutching tightly on to his ears, as if they were the handlebars of an out-of-control bicycle.

"I'm a star! I'm a star!" she shouted, causing a ripple of laughter from the audience. Then she added, "I really, really need a wee."

William put her back down onto the floor remarkably quickly.

Daphne

Daphne had got so carried away with the performance that she even found herself joining in with the enthusiastic rendition of "We Wish You a Merry Christmas" at the finale. She hadn't sung in public since an Elton John concert in 1989. Her voice had sounded thin and tremulous at the beginning, but was positively lusty by the end.

The nativity had been a triumph, and watching the excitement and joy on the children's faces as the audience applauded had made her feel surprisingly proud, despite the fact that neither they nor the play had anything much to do with her.

"Thank you for coming to the Mandel Community Center nursery and seniors' show!" said Lydia, with an uncharacteristic level of gumption. The woman was making progress! When Daphne had first met her, she wouldn't have said boo to a goose. Let alone to a group of councillors.

"We'd like to thank the local council for their support for this fabulous hall, where all members of the community can come together, and we look forward to many more wonderful, collaborative and creative performances in the years to come!" Lydia continued.

She had, Daphne thought, laid it on a little thick. She might as well have worn a T-shirt printed with the words *WE'RE ALL REALLY NICE. PLEASE DON'T EVICT US.* But she'd forgive the heavy-handedness and overuse of flowery adjectives if it did the job.

"Let's have a round of applause for our director—the famous actor Art Andrews, without whom none of this would have been possible!" said Lydia.

Art, flushed with success, stood up and bowed, so low that it looked for a moment as if he might never be able to come up again.

Famous actor? Art certainly wasn't famous. It wasn't even entirely clear he was an actor.

"Please go and help yourselves to refreshments, supplied by our lovely, clever children and our generous sponsor—Starbucks!" Lydia continued. It seemed that once she'd started there was no stopping her. Had Daphne created a monster? *For pity's sake, sit down, woman!*

The audience surged en masse toward the refreshment table. Daphne could see Art through the crowd. He was surrounded by people, and had that smug, mock-humble look of someone who was being showered with congratulations, as if he'd pulled off the whole event single-handedly. Had he even stopped to consider the fact that all his planning and hard work would have gone entirely to waste had Daphne not made sure the council turned up to witness his "triumph"? She very much doubted it.

Daphne watched Art laugh at something one of the fawning crowd said to him, then he gave a little bow, his hands in prayer position, signifying gratitude. Daphne felt a knot of irritation forming in her guts. *For God's sake.* Was there anything more annoyingly vomit-inducing than a goody-two-shoes?

Daphne sighed. She really should go over herself, to congratulate him. She had to practice all these social niceties, however much they stuck in her throat, if she was going to be able to tick off all the items on her whiteboard. She needed to turn over a *new leaf*. Become an entirely new plant, even.

Daphne pulled back her shoulders, lifted her chin, and elbowed her way expertly through the throng. Whenever she encountered a blockage, she employed a sharp prod with her walking stick, which she'd brought along for exactly this eventuality. But just as she managed to reach Art, still hoovering up all the compliments like a self-satisfied aardvark, a man dressed in a badly fitting suit, with a slightly greasy comb-over, bashed a spoon against a coffee cup.

"Everybody, STOP RIGHT NOW!" he said, showering the people in his immediate vicinity with a fine spray of spittle, as if they were a car windscreen he was attempting to wash. "DO NOT TOUCH THE PACKAGED GOODS. THEY ARE WAY PAST THEIR SELL-BY DATES. SOME OF THESE ITEMS WERE DISCONTINUED YEARS AGO!"

All around her, people were staring at the food they were holding. Some were even spitting whole mouthfuls into napkins, or their bare hands. Just as she'd thought her day couldn't get any better.

"But these were given to us by the local Starbucks, our sponsor," said Janine, indignantly.

"Well, I'm the manager of Starbucks, and I can assure you I did no such thing," said the man, who was, indeed, still wearing his *STORE MANAGER* badge on his lapel. Did he wear it to bed, too? wondered Daphne. His name was helpfully printed under his title: GAVIN GRAVELY. This figured. He looked exactly like you'd expect a Gavin Gravely to look: pompous and unhappy.

"Art," said Lydia, pointing at him with one of the suspect fingers of shortbread. "You told me Starbucks were sponsoring us."

Daphne turned to stare at Art, along with everyone else.

"Uh, I didn't, actually," said Art, who'd certainly been brought back down to earth with a remarkably satisfying bump. "I said Starbucks were *supporting* us. They just weren't entirely aware of the fact."

"It's precisely these front-of-till items that keep going missing from my store," said Gavin Gravely, fixing Art with a steely gaze. "We've been aware for years that we've had a prolific thief operating in the area. In fact, I'm quite sure I recognize you from my CCTV."

"You didn't steal all that stuff, did you?" said Lydia, in a whisper.

"I prefer to use the word 'liberated,'" said Art, whose face had flushed a deep red. For a supposed actor, he was completely inept at appearing innocent.

"Oh, Art," said Daphne, who was suddenly feeling much more cheerful. "Haven't you been naughty?"

This was a marvelous turn of events. Perhaps Art wasn't quite so irritatingly perfect, after all. Maybe they did actually have something in common.

Art turned to her, his face all creased and blotchy. He seemed to have aged five years, which at their time of life one couldn't afford to do, frankly. "I'm fed up with you thinking you're so much better than everyone else, Daphne. I'm sure you've never put a foot wrong in your entire life but, unlike you, some of us are HUMAN!"

Daphne was a little taken aback, and slightly disappointed. Just as she'd started to rather like Art, he'd stamped on any notions she might have had about a fledgling friendship. She should have known better.

"Unless you can produce receipts for these items, I'm going to the authorities!" shouted Gavin Gravely, leaning over Art aggressively.

There was a blur of movement as a small, wiry figure wove her way through the legs of the crowd and launched herself at Gavin Gravely's buttocks.

"SOMETHING BIT ME!" he yelled.

"Let him go, Maggie Thatcher!" shrieked Lydia.

"Go for it, Margaret!" said Daphne.

"Ooh, she's a wolf in a knitted sheep jumper," said Ruby.

"Why's the sheep eating the nasty shouty man?" asked one of the innkeepers.

This was the most fun Daphne had had since Pauline had died.

Lydia

Within the space of a few minutes, Lydia's great triumph had morphed into disaster.

The hall, which had been a hubbub of celebratory, festive conversation, had fallen silent. Lydia had managed to push her way through the throng to grab Maggie by the collar and stop her doing any more damage to the generous posterior of the man from Starbucks.

"THAT DOG SHOULD BE DESTROYED!" shouted Gavin Gravely, all buggy eyes, flared nostrils, and quivering belly.

Within seconds, Maggie was surrounded by small children, creating a miniature human shield around her and crying hysterically.

"She was just protecting an old man who was being bullied," said Lydia. "I bet she didn't even break the skin."

There was a sharp intake of breath from the crowd as Gavin Gravely undid his zip and pulled down his trousers to expose his graying Y-fronts, and two tiny red marks underneath his right buttock. Janine placed her hands over the eyes of the small child standing in front of her.

"Well, now she's got a taste for human flesh, there's no knowing what she'll do next," said Gavin Gravely, who seemed disappointed not to find a more dramatic wound.

"I would have thought that after tasting that particular flesh it would put her off for life," said a voice that was unmistakably Daphne's.

Art was sitting in his director's chair, curled in on himself like an "@" sign, his head in his hands.

"I'll have you know, I'm calling the police with regard to your collection of stolen goods," said Gavin Gravely, sucking in his stomach and doing his belt back up.

"Get out of here, you odious little man!" shouted Daphne, levering Gavin Gravely away from Art with her walking stick. Lydia wasn't at all sure why Daphne carried a stick. She certainly didn't need it for walking. She was, in fact, almost unnaturally sprightly.

"You have no proof *whatsoever* that any of those items were stolen or, if they were, that Art is the culprit. So, you can take your baseless insinuations and stick them where the sun. Don't. Shine." With each of those last three words, Daphne poked Gavin in his retreating, protesting arse.

"And don't you dare threaten my dog!" she shouted after him.

She was *magnificent*. And, as always when she was with Daphne, Lydia found herself feeling braver. More determined. More resourceful.

She had to get the day back on track.

Lydia headed over to William's laptop. If she could get those happy photographs of all the play preparations and rehearsals beaming onto the projector screen again, at least they would be the final images the council members saw before leaving for their lunch. Better, by far, than memories of feral dogs and rotten stolen goods.

Lydia clicked the touch pad, and saw a folder pinned to the home screen labeled *PHOTOS*. Thank goodness William had made it easy. She clicked on that and saw a handful of files, one helpfully labeled *LYDIA*. She clicked it and selected *Slideshow*. See! She may be past fifty, but she was no Luddite.

Lydia picked up Maggie, in her sheep jacket, just in case the horrid Starbucks man decided to come back with the dog police, and pushed her way through the crowd to the group of musicians from Ziggy's school.

"I know you'll be needing to get back to school soon," she said. "But I'd be super grateful if you could just play a couple more carols. Something really cheerful!"

As the sounds of "Ding Dong! Merrily on High" filled the hall, Lydia stepped back and looked up at the screen. It took her a while to adjust to what she was seeing. There was a photo of her, but not at the community center. She was saying goodbye to Jeremy, who was leaning against his scooter on their doorstep. What was that picture doing in there?

Then there was Jeremy again, this time with a blond woman at least twenty years younger than Lydia. The one who could stop traffic. First, getting out of a taxi, then entering a pub. Then the two of them sitting at a table, heads so close to each other that they were almost touching. Hands clasped over the tabletop. Then kissing. More kissing. Proper kissing. The sort of desperate, hungry kissing she'd seen teenagers do when she'd helped organize the junior prom at Ellie and Sophia's school. Not at all like the half-hearted middle-aged kissing she and Jeremy indulged in. When he kissed her at all.

It wasn't just her, staring at these images of her husband virtually *devouring* a woman barely older than their daughters. Almost the entire hall was watching. And the ones not looking at the screen were looking right at her, aghast, as tears streamed down her face and her world collapsed around her.

Ziggy

Ziggy dashed toward the laptop and slammed down the lid, stopping the slideshow dead in its tracks. But not in time. Not before Lydia had run out of the hall, clutching a startled Maggie to her chest and sobbing.

Ziggy had only met Lydia a few times. Just briefly, as he was dropping off or collecting Kylie. She seemed like a lovely lady, if a little quiet and unsure of herself. Those old people appeared to run circles around her. Given her reaction, he presumed it must be her husband in the photos, kissing a woman closer to Ziggy's own age than Lydia's.

Lydia deserved much better than that. As did the girl being kissed, to be honest. The man rode a scooter, for God's sake.

Ziggy considered, for a moment, running after her. Somebody should check if she was OK, and he'd be faster than any of her senior citizens, apart from that dangerous one with the psychedelic hair and wheels. But he couldn't leave Kylie. And he really had to see Alicia. Just to say thank you, nothing more. She, along with her musician friends, had given up her whole lunch hour to do him a favor, after all.

Ziggy slung his backpack over the handlebars of Kylie's push-chair. All the excitement of the show had allowed him, just for an hour, to forget that it contained one of Floyd's packages. He should have dropped it off before the performance started, but there hadn't been time. If he didn't deliver it soon, he'd be in huge trouble. Floyd's customers were not renowned for their patience.

Ziggy hadn't ever opened any of the packages he'd delivered or collected for Floyd and his gang. He didn't want to know what was inside, although he could obviously guess. You couldn't spend your whole life on his estate without having a general idea of what went on in the dark, pungent shadows of the alleyways and stairwells.

Ziggy certainly didn't want to hang on to this one any longer than was necessary. It felt like traveling with a hand grenade that could explode, taking out his entire life, at any minute. Last week, he'd Googled "plausible deniability" but didn't think it would hold up in court. Then he'd spent all night worrying that even his search history was compromised.

Kylie was sitting safely strapped into her pushchair. Glad to be released from the "swaddling clothes" she'd been wrapped in as baby Jesus, and playing with the superhero key ring attached to the zip on Ziggy's backpack.

Ziggy pushed Kylie over toward the musicians, who were pack-ing up their instruments, music stands, and sheet music.

"That was totally amazing!" he said to them all, although it was Alicia he just happened to be looking at directly. Alicia, with the normal, uncomplicated life, whose greatest challenge was translat-ing all those lines, dots, and squiggles into such glorious music. How did she do that? It was a mystery.

"Thank you so much. You really made the performance. You were awesome," he said.

"We enjoyed it!" said Alicia, looking like she actually meant it. "I hope the kids weren't too freaked out by all that drama and shouting at the end."

"I bet they've forgotten about it already," said Ziggy, thinking how pretty Alicia looked with her dimpled, freckled cheeks and silver tinsel wound around her swinging ponytail.

"Are you going back to school?" asked Alicia.

"No, I have to get Kylie home. The nursery's closed for the rest of the day, on account of all this," said Ziggy, gesturing at the rows of abandoned chairs and the empty stage.

"Your daughter's so gorgeous!" said Alicia, crouching down and smiling at Kylie in the pushchair.

"I know!" said Ziggy, trying not to mind that it wasn't him Alicia was describing as gorgeous. He couldn't let himself be jealous of his own baby. That would be weird.

"I hope that envelope isn't important," Alicia said, laughing. "Kylie seems to be eating it. Is she teething? My little sister used to chew *everything* when she was teething."

Ziggy's mouth ran dry. He leaned forward so he could see over the top of the pushchair. Kylie had opened his backpack and pulled out the package. The one he'd not dared look inside. And she had the corner of it clamped between her gums.

Ziggy grabbed the other end of the package and pulled it, but the paper, weakened by Kylie's chewing and drooling, tore, spitting its contents onto Kylie's lap.

Alicia stared down at Kylie, her mouth open. Ziggy did the same. Kylie reached her plump little hands forward, clutching several of the tiny little see-through baggies filled with fine white powder. Ziggy was completely frozen. His mind was screaming, *Do something!*, but his limbs were unable to move.

Alicia stared at Ziggy, her hazel eyes flitting through several emotions: shock, disgust, and confusion, before settling on something along the lines of deep disappointment.

"We need to get back for lessons," she said, and the whole tone of her voice had morphed from warm and musical to an icy cold monotone.

Without saying another word, Alicia stood up straight, turned her back, picked up her oboe, and left, followed by the rest of the musicians.

As Ziggy stared helplessly at Kylie's lap, liver-spotted hands started collecting the little bags together, shoving them back into the brown paper package. Peeling open Kylie's fingers to release the ones she was holding in her tiny fists.

"Pull yourself together, Ziggy, for God's sake. We need to get out of here, before someone spots what's going on and calls Social Services," said Daphne, who seemed to have apparated from nowhere.

Ziggy pushed Kylie toward the door as Daphne cleared the crowd in front of them with her walking stick. He didn't dare look around to check if anyone else had seen what had just happened.

"It's not what you think, Daphne. They're not mine," he said as they left the hall.

"Any fool can see that, Ziggy. You're obviously a complete amateur. But what on earth did you think you were doing? You're a father. You have responsibilities," said Daphne.

"That's exactly why I had no choice," he replied, not expecting her, or anyone, to believe him.

"Look, give me your keys. I'll take Kylie home. You'd better deliver that package to whoever is expecting it, or I imagine you'll be in even more trouble," said Daphne, displaying a remarkable level of understanding, and total lack of shock.

Maybe it would be better if he did lose custody of Kylie. Perhaps she could be adopted by parents who actually knew what they were doing. Ones who could keep her safe and give her everything she needed. Then Ziggy could go back to just being a schoolboy.

Ziggy looked down at his daughter and felt a physical squeeze around his heart, making his head swim.

There was no going back. Ziggy wasn't the same person he'd been eight months ago. Kylie had burrowed into his soul and, without her, there would forever be a giant hole right at his center. One that could never be filled.

As Ziggy trudged toward the address he'd memorized that morning, the contents of the exploded hand grenade in his rucksack, two questions kept spinning around his head:

Would Alicia ever speak to him again? And who on earth was Daphne?

Art

It took Art three attempts to unlock his front door, as his hands kept shaking. It was almost as cold and unwelcoming inside as out. Due to the outrageous cost of fuel and his lack of any savings or income, other than his state pension, the only radiator turned on in Art's house was in his bedroom.

Art climbed the stairs. The staircase he'd crawled up as a baby, tobogganed down in a sleeping bag as a child, then bounded up with his first girlfriend as a teenager, shedding articles of clothing on the way, then quickly retrieving them so they wouldn't be spotted by his mother. The staircase he could still picture his young wife climbing, with a mound of washing under one arm and a baby on her hip. Recently, climbing these stairs felt like ascending a small mountain. Today, more than ever.

Without even removing his shoes, Art got into bed, pulling the musty-smelling duvet over his head.

A noise penetrated Art's dreamless sleep. His room was dark, with only the dull light of a streetlamp leeching around the edges of his tatty curtains. The digital alarm clock—the height of sophistication back in 1986—on his bedside table read 8:02. Could it really be so early still?

He heard the noise again. A rattle against glass. William had been throwing stones at this window to attract Art's attention since the 1950s. This house, built just after the last war, had belonged to the council back then and had been rented by his parents. Art had bought it in the 1980s, under Thatcher's Right to Buy scheme.

Yet another thing to feel guilty about: profiting personally from a policy that had completely depleted the stock of available, affordable local housing. It was selfish of Art to live here all by himself when so many large families were squashed into tiny apartments. If he had any decency, he'd give it up for a family of Afghan or Ukrainian refugees and shuffle off into an old people's home.

"Art! I know you're there!" said William, ringing the doorbell several times. "Will you let me in?"

Art pulled the duvet back over his head.

"Amy's made you a casserole. I'm leaving it on your doorstep," said William.

Amy was one of William's daughters-in-law, a reminder of how very different his life was from Art's. William's sizable family all lived within a few miles of William, and were continually in and out of each other's houses. They'd very kindly adopted Art as one of their own. They made huge efforts to ensure he felt loved and included, not knowing that, much as he adored them, they were a constant, painful reminder to him of everything he'd lost.

Would they really want Art around them and their children now they knew who he really was? A liar. A leech. A parasite. A common thief. And how could he ever return to the social club—if indeed there was one to return to, after today's debacle—loaded with such shame and humiliation?

For a while he'd been flying so high! He'd been busy, admired, thanked. He remembered the thrill of the audience's applause as he'd taken his bow, his pride in his cast, in himself for having done the right thing, his conviction that they'd saved the community center.

Then, just seconds later, as if a trapdoor in the stage had opened, he'd been plunged into a whole different reality. It was clear to him now that he hadn't solved any of his problems—all he'd done was cover them with sticking plaster and a handful of glitter. And now they were exposed to the air again: his lack of money, the end of a career that had never even begun, his addiction to stealing, and, underlying all of it, his overwhelming shame at what he'd done to his family so many years ago.

But even they couldn't possibly hate him more than he hated himself.

Better to die of shame or humiliation? he considered shouting down to William, but he couldn't summon the strength.

Art thought that William must have gone, but then there was another long ring on the doorbell. He heard William shout up at the window, "I'll be back tomorrow, Art. You're not doing this to me again."

Lydia

Lydia could hear them talking outside her bedroom.

"What's up with Mum?" asked Ellie, sounding more irritated than concerned.

"Hormones, probably," replied Jeremy. Lydia was sure she could hear his eyes swivel up to the ceiling. She wished she could storm out of the room and confront her lying, philandering, patronizing husband with proof of what was actually up with Mum, but how could she detonate her daughters' lives like that? At Christmas?

And a truth niggled away at her: it wasn't just altruism that prevented her dealing with the situation, it was also fear. Lydia had been a wife and mother for so long. She'd only just started coming to terms with the fact that her role as mother was no longer so necessary. If she wasn't a wife anymore, either, then what on earth was she? What was the point of her? She was just a badly paid part-time organizer of a social club which was also on its way out. Both she and Mandel Community Center were about to be replaced by newer, shinier, more attractive models. Both of them surplus to requirements and gradually falling to pieces.

Lydia turned back to the book she'd been trying to distract herself with for hours. She'd bought *The Seven Principles for Making Marriage Work*, thinking it might help her discover where it had all gone wrong, but she'd read the same paragraph over and over, and she still had no idea what it said. Her vision kept being interrupted by snapshots of those awful pictures of Jeremy and that nameless woman, that *child*, as if the Mandel Community Center slideshow were still running in an endless merry-go-round of humiliation. Kissing. Holding. Groping. Laughing. Again and again and again.

Gradually, Lydia's anger with Jeremy began to morph into a different, more familiar, set of emotions: guilt and shame. She was beginning to wonder whether she'd actually brought this all on herself. Had she used up all her energies over the past decade trying to be the perfect mother, at the expense of being a good-enough wife? Perhaps if she'd spent more time creating some romance in their marriage—organizing more date nights, buying lacy underwear, having more sex, or, at least, having sex more enthusiastically— Jeremy wouldn't have felt the need to look elsewhere? There were always two sides to a story like this, weren't there?

Lydia heard a scratch at the door and opened it to let Maggie Thatcher in.

"You know you're not allowed in here. It's against the rules," she said, her voice feeling unfamiliar and awkward after days of near hibernation. "But I guess it's OK just this once, so long as you don't get onto the bed."

Lydia climbed back under the duvet and picked up her book. Within minutes, she felt a small, warm body snuggle up next to her, and a damp nose against her cheek. She pulled Maggie in closer, buried her head in her wiry curls, and began to cry. Again.

"What is that awful dog doing in here?" shouted Jeremy, startling Lydia out of her half doze. "It's bad enough having her in the house at all, but I am definitely NOT sharing my bed with her."

It's a bit rich, you being fussy now about who you share a bed with, said Lydia in her head.

"Sorry," she said out loud. "She's going today, in any case." She didn't add that she'd be back again in a week's time.

"Thank God for that," said Jeremy. "Look, I'm just going out for a quick pint with the lads. I'll be back in a couple of hours."

Of course you are, thought Lydia, the slideshow playing in double time onto the back of her retinas.

Lydia watched as Jeremy changed into his favorite shirt, then stood in front of the mirror, slapping his expensive new aftershave onto his neck. The expression on his face was one he only used when looking at his reflection and involved sucking in his cheeks to give him more chiseled cheekbones and lifting his chin to reduce the puffiness around his jawline.

She heard the front door close, and peered out of the bedroom window, watching Jeremy zip down the road on his stupid scooter.

Lydia picked up her phone. Still no response from her message to Art, who was next on Maggie's rota. Maybe he was ignoring her because her utter humiliation at the nativity made the thought of a conversation with her too awkward. Thank God the social club was closed for a couple of weeks for the holidays. Was it too much to hope that they'd all have forgotten by January? Was it too much to hope that she'd *ever* forget?

She pulled up Daphne's number and typed, **Can't get hold of Art. Don't suppose you could take Maggie instead?**

Within seconds there was a reply: **No problem.**

Thanks. I'll drop her round now, typed Lydia.

Lydia was going to miss Maggie Thatcher. Over the last few days, the need to walk Maggie had at least forced her out of the house, and interactions with other dog owners and random passersby had ensured that she hadn't completely cut herself off from other people. And it felt so good to be appreciated. Adored, perhaps. Even if only by a geriatric dog.

Lydia was concerned for Maggie, too. As her primary carer, Maggie obviously loved Lydia the best. And, not to be boastful, just realistic, Lydia's home was probably far larger than Art's or Daphne's, with a sizable garden for Maggie to run around in.

This enforced separation was going to be as hard on Maggie as it was on Lydia.

She stared down at the address on the scrap of paper in her hand. It was only when she looked up at the building in front of her that she realized she'd been expecting a small, run-down Victorian terraced house, complete with net curtains and floral-printed interiors. Not this industrial-style warehouse conversion overlooking the Thames, which would have looked more at home in the Meatpacking District of New York than in Hammersmith. Not that Lydia had been to the Meatpacking District or, indeed, anywhere in New York. And now she probably never would, since she was going to be a sad, lonely, and penniless divorcée, saving up for an annual Saga outing for over-fifties, to the seaside at Margate.

There was a row of buzzers by the steel and glass-paneled double doors. She couldn't see Daphne's name against any of them. One had been left unhelpfully blank. By process of elimination, she pressed that one.

"Hello?" said a familiar voice through the intercom.

"Daphne, it's Lydia," she said. "And Maggie."

"Come on in, and take the lift to the third floor," came the reply.

The entrance hall was lined with pigeonholes, presumably to hold post for the various apartments. She could see the local newspaper stuffed into several of them. She knew exactly what the headline on the front page read, since a copy had landed on her own doorstep just yesterday: DRAMA AND DISGRACE AT COUNCIL NATIVITY, along with a photograph of the crowd staring open-mouthed as they witnessed Gavin Gravely attacking Art, and Maggie attacking Gavin Gravely. If they hadn't already been doomed, then that article would certainly be the final nail in their coffin.

Lydia pulled all the newspapers out of the pigeonholes and thrust them into her shopping bag. Then she panicked that she might have been caught on some hidden CCTV, so she put them all back again.

"I'm sorry to do this to you," said Lydia to Maggie as she pressed the button for the third floor. "But you'll be back with me in a week. It'll go in a flash." Maggie wagged her tail, obviously putting a brave face on the situation, for the sake of Lydia. Bless her. Dogs were so empathetic.

The lift door opened, and Lydia could see Daphne standing at the entrance to her apartment. She was dressed in what the magazines would probably call "stylish athleisure." Nothing at all like the aged, baggy Lycra which Lydia wore to her weekly Zumba class. Had Daphne been doing yoga? Was that even safe at her age?

Maggie pulled so hard at her lead that Lydia dropped it, and she charged toward the open door, without a moment's hesitation or a backward glance.

Even her dog was in love with someone else, it seemed.

The tears which Lydia had managed to hold back for the last couple of hours erupted again, right in front of a startled Daphne. For several minutes, Lydia just cried, and Daphne just stared.

"I think you'd better come in," said Daphne, finally.

Daphne

aphne stared at the woman on her doorstep in horror. This was exactly why she should never have let herself get involved. A friend in need was a friend to be avoided.

She hadn't invited *anyone* over her threshold since she'd moved in, in 2008. Except for the occasional, necessary workman. And in those instances, she'd spent several hours removing all of her more personal memorabilia from display beforehand.

But she could hardly leave a grown woman weeping on her doorstep. Apart from anything else, what would the neighbors think? Before long, she'd be the subject of all the building gossip, which she'd so carefully swerved for all this time.

Daphne sighed. She'd broken so many of her rules recently that one more would hardly make a great deal of difference. And besides, she'd grown almost to like Lydia, despite her being such a wimp, as all this crying clearly demonstrated.

She ushered Lydia into her open-plan apartment, with its floor-to-ceiling Crittall windows, exposed brick walls, polished oak parquet floor, concrete pillars, and vast crystal chandeliers which refracted hundreds of tiny shards of light around the huge space, like giant disco balls. Maggie Thatcher had already settled herself into her favorite spot on the huge, battered leather Chesterfield sofa, covered in jewel-colored velvet cushions, in the middle of the living area.

"Down, Margaret!" she said. "You know you're not allowed on the furniture. It's in the rules, remember."

Maggie Thatcher got down slowly, shooting Daphne a baleful look which Daphne read as, *You and I both know that's not the case, but I'll go along with the ridiculous charade anyway, since I love you the most.*

"Did you just call her Margaret?" said Lydia as she sniffed and wiped her face with her sleeve.

"Slip of the tongue," said Daphne, wondering how she could surreptitiously remove the organic, grilled, and sliced duck breast she'd left in Margaret's bowl as a coming-home present, before Lydia spotted it.

"Wow, this is amazing," said Lydia, staring around Daphne's treasures with her mouth open, like a goldfish exploring a new tank. "It's like a museum of the sixties and seventies. No, it's too cool for that. More like an art gallery. Or an installation."

"What were you expecting? Lace doilies, swirly wall-to-wall carpets and a dusty collection of china figurines on a mantelpiece?" said Daphne. "It's incredible how everyone always typecasts the elderly."

"No, no, that's not what I meant," said Lydia. She was blushing furiously, which rather suggested Daphne had hit the nail on the head, but at least gave her haggard face some color. "It's just I've never seen anything like this."

Actually, Daphne was more than a little chuffed with Lydia's art gallery analogy. She had spent an enormous amount of time curating her home—displaying her favorite fashions from her favorite decades on artfully arranged mannequins, photographs of personal friends and admired icons, who were sometimes one and the same, and memorabilia from extraordinary places she'd been to. She'd figured that if she was going to spend her life under what felt much like voluntary house arrest, she might as well ensure that that house was spectacular. And if her future looked entirely bleak, she could at least immerse herself in a past which had been so extraordinarily colorful.

Lydia was staring at the huge, framed sepia photograph of Hopesbury House, with its circular drive, beautiful Georgian proportions, wings, and stables.

"Is this where you grew up?" she asked.

"Yes," said Daphne.

"Wow," said Lydia.

"It's not what you think," said Daphne. Lydia laying all her emotions out on display so overtly seemed to have triggered an unfamiliar urge to be honest. "I was the illegitimate daughter of the housekeeper. My mother died when I was just seven years old, and the family fostered me."

Daphne reached over to the photo of her childhood home and tilted it upward slightly on one side, then stood back to check if it was straight. She then moved on to the surrounding pictures, adjusting them by a millimeter here and there—not because they looked crooked to any regular viewer, but in order to avoid eye contact. Her confessions could only slide out unobserved.

"I think they assumed that my father must have been one of the family, or one of their house guests," she continued. "My role was to be the physical proof of their boundless benevolence. So I grew up surrounded by all of that wealth and breeding, but being constantly reminded that I was an interloper. The charity case."

"That must have been hard," said Lydia, reaching for Daphne's hand. Daphne fought the urge to snatch it away, and discovered that she found the unaccustomed warmth of skin against skin comforting.

"I grew up in an ordinary middle-class semi, but with a happy, supportive, safe nuclear family. We even had the requisite Labrador. All I ever wanted was to re-create all of that," said Lydia. "My favorite board game was The Game of Life. I loved adding a little blue peg next to my pink peg in the front of my miniature plastic car, then pegs in the back seat for two children. And until recently, that's what I thought I had: the perfect family."

"I was far more demanding than you. I wanted everything I'd been taught to admire but never allowed to own," said Daphne. "The clothes, the jewelry, the art, the respect, the notoriety. All of it."

As Daphne spoke the truth out loud, a question nudged at her, becoming increasingly insistent on being heard, like one of the nursery children with their hand raised, saying, *Me! Me! Over here! Listen to me!*

The thing she'd really been missing as a child wasn't all the material belongings and social standing; it was what Lydia had had. Genuine friends and a loving family. Yet she'd spent most of her adult life focusing on a career which, while thrilling and demanding, had rather precluded forming close relationships, and the last fifteen years in almost total isolation. Had she got her priorities entirely wrong? Would she have been happier with a life like Lydia's? An ordinary life.

Daphne stared at Lydia, blotchy from all the weeping, and diminished from years of playing second fiddle, and thought not. But there must be a happy medium—a perfect life, somewhere between hers and Lydia's.

Daphne left Lydia exploring her apartment while she made a pot of tea. She replaced Margaret's duck with the dried kibble authorized by Lydia. She'd make it up to her later. They were having fillet steak for dinner, with a béarnaise sauce and dauphinoise potatoes. After years of eating alone, Daphne was making the most of having a regular dinner guest.

Knowing that Lydia was picking her way through Daphne's past made her feel like the skin was being stripped from her bones, layer by layer. And, at her age, skin was thin and fragile, the bones close to the surface. At least she'd had the presence of mind to clear the whiteboard before she'd opened the door, just in case. Old habits died hard.

Daphne tried to ignore the discomfort but was hugely relieved when she could pull Lydia away from her treasure trove and onto the sofa with a mug of tea. Margaret watched them both from her barely used bed on the floor, a mutinous expression on her face.

"So, I presume all these . . ." Daphne waved her hand around vaguely while searching for the correct expression. *Histrionics? Melodramatics?* She eventually settled on "waterworks." Less judgmental.

"So, I presume all these waterworks are the result of those unfortunate photographs at the nativity the other day?" she said.

"Oh, Daphne," said Lydia, weeping again. It made Daphne feel extremely awkward. Was she supposed to *hug her*? Daphne wasn't a hugger. She passed her a dusty box of tissues. "She's so *young* and beautiful. How am I ever supposed to compete? I'm sure Jeremy's going to leave me, and my daughters will be devastated. I don't know what to do."

"You're hardly *old* yourself, dear. You can't be a day over sixty," said Daphne.

"I'M FIFTY-THREE!" wailed Lydia, weeping harder than ever.

Honestly! When Daphne was Lydia's age, not long before she'd moved here, she was . . . Best not to think about that but, needless to say, she wasn't pretending to run a doomed social club and letting her husband treat her like a doormat.

"Maybe some sugar might help? It usually does, I find," said Daphne. She walked over to the kitchen area and opened the lid of the rice cooker, which she'd bought on a whim and now used to store her emergency chocolate. Was this a Twix kind of situation, or a Curly Wurly? No, this particular emergency required a Cadbury Flake, she decided.

"You're looking at this whole situation from the wrong angle, Lydia," she said, handing her the chocolate. "You're only thinking about what Jeremy wants and what your daughters need. How old are they, anyway?"

"Nineteen and twenty-one," said Lydia with a sniff, pulling the wrapper off the Flake and eating half of it in one bite.

"Well, exactly. They're adults. The question you should really be asking is: What do *you* want? And as for the husband, do you love him? Like him, even?"

Lydia looked nonplussed and, for a moment, even stopped crying. "I guess so," she said, without sounding entirely convinced.

"Well, I·have no idea why," said Daphne. "He's clearly utterly vain and foolish. Whereas you are one of the loveliest, kindest women I've met in years."

This set Lydia off again. Daphne, of course, had met only a handful of women over the past fifteen years but, regardless, the compliment was entirely genuine, even if it had taken her until right this minute to realize it. You couldn't not like Lydia. It would be like taking against a homeless, helpless puppy.

"Anyhow," said Daphne, "as far as your daughters are concerned, you need to make sure they learn that you should never let a man treat you the way Jeremy does. You wouldn't want them to have a relationship like yours, would you?"

"But it's not all his fault, Daphne. It's just as much mine. I've been a terrible wife. I've not prioritized our marriage. I've spent years focusing almost entirely on the girls. It's no wonder he ended up looking elsewhere," said Lydia.

"Good God, what utter tosh," said Daphne. "That's all just more evidence that you're a much nicer person than he is. Do you think he feels any guilt? Do you think Jeremy prioritized your marriage? Even if there were a modicum of truth to your reading of the situation, he could have *talked to you* about it, rather than deciding to shag an adolescent."

Lydia blanched. *Rein it in a little, Daphne,* she told herself.

"The problem as I see it, Lydia," continued Daphne, more gently, "is that you don't actually like yourself. You've spent so long worrying about everyone else that you've completely lost sight of who you are and what you need. Am I right?"

Lydia sniffed and nodded, then tipped the remaining Flake crumbs into her mouth.

"The perfect place to start, I generally find, is with a makeover. Just wait until you see my wardrobes and my spectacular costume jewelry collection," said Daphne, feeling a prickle of excitement. This might actually be fun. Giving a girlfriend a makeover was exactly the kind of thing the Kardashians did.

"William tells me you've been dating," said Lydia as they walked toward Daphne's dressing area. "How's it going?"

"It was a complete disaster," said Daphne, employing a generous dose of understatement. "But I met a chap yesterday. Sidney. He was definitely the best of the bunch. And he seems quite keen."

Sidney had, in fact, been bombarding Daphne with messages, which, despite herself, she found rather flattering. He'd even invited her to spend Christmas Day with him in a local bistro. Daphne hadn't shared Christmas with anyone since she'd moved here. Was it all going too fast? She supposed that, at her age, it had to. Taking one's time was a luxury they couldn't afford.

"I met my husband on the internet," said Lydia. "Internet dating was really new back then, and my friends dared me to give it a go. The very first date I went on was with Jeremy."

"Well, that didn't turn out too well, did it?" said Daphne, regretting the words the second they fell out of her mouth. Not because she didn't mean them, but because Lydia, predictably, started wailing again.

"What do I do about Jeremy?" she said, between sobs. "Do you think a makeover might make him love me again?"

"I couldn't give two hoots about what that man thinks or doesn't think. The thing that matters is whether we can make you love *yourself* again," said Daphne.

Lydia sighed, then carried on weeping, making it quite clear what an uphill struggle *that* was going to be.

"Are you familiar with the lovely Michelle Obama?" said Daphne.

"Oh, yes! *Becoming* is one of my all-time favorite books," said Lydia. "So inspiring."

"Well, then, you'll know what Michelle says about what to do when 'they go low'?" said Daphne. Lydia nodded.

"When they go low . . . we get revenge," said Daphne, with a flourish.

Lydia frowned. "I don't think that's what she said at all, Daphne," she said. "In fact, I know it's not."

"Well, she should have done," said Daphne. "See, not even Michelle Obama is infallible. Now, let's explore these wardrobes and discuss strategies."

Ziggy

Ziggy had spent the past ten days on high alert. It was Kylie's very first Christmas, and his mum had tried so hard to make it memorable and special, working double shifts so they could buy Kylie a small mountain of presents. Even Jenna had made a flying visit to see her daughter. She'd bought her a T-shirt bearing the slogan *MY MUMMY IS THE BEST.* Given that Jenna was horribly hungover from a Christmas Eve party, had nearly knocked Kylie out with stale vodka fumes and hadn't bothered to wrap the present, which was already too small for Kylie, Ziggy highly doubted that this was the case.

Even on Christmas Day, Ziggy couldn't relax. He kept expecting the doorbell to ring at any moment as the police, or Social Services, or both, turned up to remove Kylie from his completely inadequate care. Or to find one of Floyd's men on his doorstep, thrusting another toxic package and address at him.

Over and over again, he ran through that scene at Mandel Community Center. How many seconds—or minutes, even—had Kylie sat there covered in class A drugs, looking like a miniature Pablo Escobar? Was it possible that nobody other than Alicia and Daphne had noticed? Was there a chance that Alicia had decided not to tell anyone else?

Even if he had, by some miracle, got away with it this time, he really couldn't risk being in the same situation again. But how could he avoid it? Since his school and the community center were both closed for the holidays, he'd been able to steer clear of Floyd and the gang by staying holed up in his flat. But he couldn't keep doing that forever. Besides, both he and Kylie were going stir-crazy. There were only so many times you could build a tower of bricks then knock it over with a plastic truck, and his threshold was considerably lower than Kylie's. How many years did he have to wait before he could teach her to play *Grand Theft Auto*?

Ziggy wrapped Kylie up against the cold, strapped her into the buggy, grabbed the shopping list his mum had left on the kitchen table, and headed toward the supermarket.

"We're going on a mission, Kylie! Engage weapons and activate force field!" he said, hoping that his comically gung ho and upbeat tone might infect his actual mood, and wishing that the weapons and force field were real.

He couldn't see Floyd as he approached the exit, but he spotted a lookout, younger than him, sitting on the wall. The boy put two fingers into his mouth and whistled. Just a couple of minutes later, he saw Floyd sauntering toward them with his trademark swagger. He'd probably come out of the womb walking like that.

"Hey, bro," he said. "I've been looking out for you. Here. Merry Christmas." He offered Ziggy a handful of folded notes. Five well-used twenty-pound notes.

"What's that for?" Ziggy said, his hands gripping the buggy handlebars tightly, so he wouldn't be tempted to reach out and grab it, trying not to think what that cash would mean for him, and for Kylie.

"Those errands you done for me. You've earned it," said Floyd, waving the money at him. "I always look after my people, don't I?"

"Thanks, but I don't want it," lied Ziggy. Then he took a deep breath and grabbed at the opportunity being offered. "Actually, I can't do any more of those errands. It's not safe for Kylie. You get it, right?"

The ensuing pause lurked like a physical entity between them, as Ziggy held Floyd's unblinking, reptilian gaze and tried not to flinch.

Still not looking away, Floyd put the notes he was holding back into his jeans pocket.

"OK," he said, finally. "You do one more run for me, then we'll call it quits. Deal?"

"Deal," said Ziggy, letting out a long exhalation.

Floyd nodded to the guy standing a few steps behind him, who handed him a package, much larger than the previous ones, and a slip of paper with an address.

Could this all really be nearly over? Why hadn't he plucked up the courage to do this before? He hadn't expected it to be so easy. Had he been putting himself and Kylie through all this stress for nothing?

Ziggy almost skipped to the address he'd been given, about fifteen minutes' walk away, the beam of light at the end of the tunnel he'd been crawling through for weeks. He could see his bright future shimmering in front of him like a mirage in the desert. All he had to do was this one job, then he'd be able to reach out and touch it.

It was obvious from a distance which door he was headed for. It was the one with the peeling paint, covered in graffiti tags. Junk mail and bills spewed from the letterbox. He slowed as he approached, trying to appear casual, while surreptitiously checking for any sign of police or—even worse—Floyd's rivals. Once he was as certain as he could be that he wasn't being watched, he knocked on the door. As always, it was quickly answered, the package snatched from his hand and replaced by another one, which Ziggy shoved into his backpack. The less time he spent with his fingers actually touching it, the better.

"Mission accomplished, Kylie," he said. "Let's take this back to Floyd, then we can get to the shops. We could buy a Colin the Caterpillar cake to celebrate! What do you say?" Kylie grinned at him, his mood infectious.

Ziggy turned the buggy into a narrow side street which the sun was unable to penetrate. It smelled of rotting food and piss, so Ziggy picked up the pace, trying to get back onto a main road as quickly as possible.

The moped came from behind. He could hear the engine getting louder as it approached, the roar reverberating off the sides of the alleyway, and tucked the buggy as close to the wall as he could to give it space to get by.

Ziggy never knew what hit his head. A baseball bat, perhaps. All he saw, as he lay in the gutter, his cheek pressed against the grill of a drain and a high-pitched ringing in his ears, was a man in black leathers and helmet gunning the moped's engine, with Ziggy's backpack flung over his shoulder. The backpack containing Floyd's package. The final package. His escape route.

"It's OK, Kylie," he said to the crying baby in the pushchair next to him, as he pulled himself to his knees and tried to make his eyes focus. The freezing water from the gutter seeped into his jeans. He reached round to the back of his head, which was sticky to the touch. "It's all going to be OK," he repeated, his voice thick and slurry, before vomiting into the drain.

But it wasn't going to be OK, was it? It was very, very far from OK. How was he going to tell Floyd that his package had been stolen? Even if Floyd believed it wasn't his fault, he'd make Ziggy pay. Someone always had to pay. The bash on the head he'd just received would be nothing compared to the beating he was likely to get from Floyd and his lackeys when he returned empty handed.

The light at the end of the tunnel flickered, dimmed, then went out.

Daphne

S o, this must be the famous Margaret I've heard so much about," said Sidney, a few days after Christmas. He crouched down to pat Maggie Thatcher's head. Daphne was reluctantly impressed. At their age, achieving an actual crouch, and standing up again without clutching on to something or wobbling, was no mean feat. Although Sidney was only sixty-five, so it was no wonder he was so sprightly. A toy boy! She'd never had a toy boy before.

Margaret looked at Sidney a little warily. Wise woman. Daphne had looked at Sidney much the same when she'd first met him. It didn't do to let one's guard down too quickly.

"You're looking gorgeous, as always, Daphne," said Sidney, moving in to kiss her. To her surprise, his lips landed on hers rather than on her cheek.

It was the first time another mouth had touched hers since Jack's, and she found she liked it. Or, at least, didn't dislike it. His lips were dry, but warm and welcoming, and it felt like exchanging a secret, or a promise. It wasn't anything like the first time she'd kissed

Jack, of course. That kiss had set her alight. It had affected her so fundamentally that she'd been surprised when she'd looked in the mirror later that she'd appeared just the same, apart from the flush in her cheeks and the glitter in her eye.

It would take more than a kiss to set her alight these days. It would take a can of gasoline and some matches, and even that was unlikely to achieve more than a slow smolder.

Dating Sidney kept bringing back memories of Jack. Memories which she'd spent so long suppressing.

She'd met Jack when she was just eighteen. She'd finally left Hopesbury House behind, with all its stifling formality and rules, and the constant expectation of gratitude, and moved to London, where she'd found a job as a waitress in a West End club.

The table Jack and his friends had been sitting at hadn't been making a huge amount of noise, but they had been sucking up all the attention, all the energy. Jack always did that. When he walked into a room, it was as if every molecule in the atmosphere shifted, coalescing around him.

She'd gone over with a tray of drinks, and a hand had brushed across her bum. An electric shock had shot up her spine and down her legs, making her tremble. She'd had to focus hard to keep the tray level, and had cursed her treacherous body for reacting so en-thusiastically to such an impertinent violation.

"Touch my arse again and you'll get the next drink in your lap," she'd said.

He'd laughed, hard. "I love a girl who stands up for herself," he'd said. And within a few minutes her manager had called her aside, telling her that Jack had requested that she spent the rest of her shift sitting at their table. She still didn't know how much Jack had paid him, or whether he'd just owed Jack a favor. She'd soon learned that everyone seemed to owe Jack something.

That evening was just the beginning. Before long, she was Jack's "girl," and then his wife. And for the first time in her life, she found herself not at the bottom of the pecking order, but at the very top. And all the things she'd lusted after from afar her entire childhood, she could have. All the clothes, the jewelry, the furnishings, the art, the respect, and the admiration.

But it was lonely at the top, she'd discovered. And everything had its price.

Sidney was no Jack. He didn't make her heart hammer in her chest, but nor did he scare her. He was safe. Dependable. And good-looking, despite the inevitable ravages of age.

Sidney took his hand in hers, and they started walking along the towpath, past all the cheerfully colored moored houseboats, covered in potted plants, from Hammersmith Bridge toward Barnes Bridge, gulls swooping above their heads. The low winter light had turned the murky river into a ribbon of shimmering silver.

"Thanks again for spending Christmas Day with me," he said. "I haven't enjoyed Christmas that much for years. And it stopped me worrying too much about Sonny."

"I loved it, too," said Daphne. Which was true. She usually spent Christmas Day pretending it wasn't happening, which meant staying in bed all day with a good book featuring a high kill rate, and avoiding the TV, radio, or newspapers until at least Boxing Day.

Daphne and Sidney had eaten a huge traditional Christmas dinner in the local bistro, while exchanging endless details about their lives. Some of which Daphne hadn't even fabricated.

"Sonny sent me a new photo," said Sidney, passing her his phone.

The photo was of a ruggedly handsome young man wearing khaki, crouched down and smiling at a group of grubby, grinning kids, one of whom wore his arm in a sling. Sonny was, Daphne knew, an aid worker, helping refugees on the Polish-Ukrainian border.

"You must be so proud of him," said Daphne, handing back the phone.

They sat on a bench, overlooking the river.

"You're so beautiful, Daphne," said Sidney.

"Huh!" she replied. "I'm older and more wrinkled than Art's underpants."

"Who's Art, and why are you looking at his pants?" said Sidney, in mock indignation.

"He's an extremely irritating man at my social club, and I haven't seen his underwear, but you can just *tell* it would be manky," said Daphne.

"Anyhow, it's those wrinkles that *make* you beautiful," said Sidney. "They're signs of laughter, and wisdom and experience."

"What utter bollocks," said Daphne, resisting a childish urge to make retching noises. "I was far more beautiful when I had skin like a peach. Does that line usually work with the women you date?"

Sidney laughed. "Yes, it does, actually," he said. "And they've never referred to other men's undergarments. You're not like other women at all, Daphne, are you?"

"God forbid," said Daphne as she pulled her cigarettes out of her bag and lit one, enjoying the first catch of nicotine in the back of her throat. Then she felt something against her head, and she lashed out at it instinctively. Beside her, Sidney screamed.

"You burned me!" he said, jumping to his feet and showing her the round, raw cigarette burn on the back of his hand.

"I'm sorry," said Daphne. "But you really shouldn't touch someone's head like that without warning."

"I was just stroking your hair!" he replied.

Daphne was going to have to get used to this whole intimacy thing, or she'd scare him off completely. And, she realized, she didn't want to do that. Not at all.

Art

rt hadn't left the house for more than two weeks. The world, however, had carried on turning despite him, and it was yet another bloody new year. He'd heard the fireworks and the celebrations in the street outside, but they seemed to come from a different life. A parallel universe. New year, but same old Art, with the same old problems.

He'd been surviving on food left on his doorstep by William and knew that, by replacing the full casserole dishes with the empty ones, he was providing proof of life and preventing William from breaking his door down. The last delivery had come with a note, however, reading: You've got two more days to sulk, Art. Then you're either letting me in or I'm calling the authorities. Your friend, William xxx.

At the bottom was a postscript which had made him smile, despite himself: PS. Better to die of stubbornness or being strangled in frustration by your best friend?

It was time to venture outdoors. He needed to buy some supplies. Just the major food groups: tea, milk, chocolate Hobnobs, and whiskey. Art shrugged on his voluminous winter coat, a woolen hat, and some lace-up boots. He caught sight of his reflection in the hall mirror. He looked pale and haggard, and had grown more hair on his chin than he had remaining on his head. He was also sure he must smell, since he'd turned the hot water off to save money, and hadn't washed for so long that he'd grown immune to his own body odor. It didn't matter. He was only going out for a few minutes, and he would avoid engaging with anyone.

Art walked past the community center, the scene of his latest humiliation. He didn't care now that it was likely to be demolished within the next few weeks. In fact, he'd love never to see it again. If he had more courage, he'd hide inside it and let them take him with it. Mashed by a wrecking ball. William would approve of that dramatic and unusual way to die. Better than slowly rotting away with self-neglect and self-hatred.

The door was open, and it looked as if the nursery and social club had started up again. He pulled his collar up, stared down at his feet, and kept walking. Not even stopping to look at the extraordinary sight on the plinth by the hall, which was surrounded by people taking photos on their phones. He was just glad they weren't looking at him. How strange to think he'd once craved an audience so badly. Now he would happily walk through the rest of his life entirely unnoticed.

The supermarket was busy. Art didn't bother with a trolley or a basket, since he only had a few items to buy. He made his way straight to the biscuit aisle. Art picked up a packet of chocolate Hobnobs then, out of habit, checked the location of the CCTV cameras. No cameras, nobody else in the aisle, except for a young mother who was distracted by a toddler throwing a tantrum.

Art opened his coat and slipped the biscuits into his inside pocket. He felt a sudden jolt of adrenaline, making his heart beat faster. For the first time since the nativity, he felt alive. Invigorated. He picked up a pack of Kit Kats and put them into the pocket on the other side.

Art walked round to the next aisle, his pace getting faster and faster. Chocolate went into a pocket, Haribo, spot cream, a scented candle, a tube of mascara, a spatula. He stopped checking the cameras, stopped looking out for other shoppers; he just kept filling his pockets until he looked twice the size he'd been when he'd come in.

Art knew what was coming. He wanted it to happen. He'd pressed the big red self-destruct button, and it felt wonderful. It was the same feeling he'd had as a teenager, at the top of a roller coaster, hands in the air, as the carriage teetered on the edge. That moment when, after a long, slow climb, you're anticipating the giddy, terrifying, inevitable, and unstoppable rush of descent.

It only took a few seconds after walking through the exit for that plummet to happen, in the form of two uniformed security guards, one on either side, and a gathering crowd of rubbernecking onlookers. But there was no thrill in the plunge, just stomach-churning nausea and a sudden, grinding, shocking application of the brakes.

They steered him back into the shop and through a plain white door he'd never noticed before. Then they took off his coat and sat him on a hard, plastic chair in a brightly lit, sterile room as they emptied all his pockets onto the table in front of him, a catalog of shame. The carriage of the roller coaster ground to a shuddering halt, leaving him shaking and sweating.

"What's all this about, then?" said one, waving the packet of Hobnobs at him.

"Where am I? I thought we were going to the seaside. Have you come to take me home?" he replied, employing a line he'd been given the last time he'd played a grandfather with dementia.

The security guards exchanged puzzled glances, but before they could say anything the theme tune from *Jaws* filled the room. They looked down at the glowing phone on the table—the one they'd removed from Art's pocket.

"Look who's calling!" said one, staring at the name on the screen.

"I think we'd better answer that, don't you?" said the other.

"I've never seen that phone before in my life," said Art.

Lydia

ydia walked toward Mandel Community Center, thinking that it looked even more run-down and neglected than it had before Christmas, as if it had already given up the will to survive. Unlike Lydia herself, who was wearing a midnight-blue 1960s Christian Dior jacket, which cinched at her waist and flared out over her hips, along with a double strand of pearls, so lush and luminous that they'd almost have looked real, if they hadn't been so huge.

"You *drown* yourself in all these tent-like clothes," Daphne had told her. "Like you're hiding from the world. You should *emphasize* those marvelous curves! Isn't it funny that we never appreciate how attractive we are until we look at photos of ourselves in five years' time? Believe me, from where I'm sitting, you're a complete knock-out. Now, let's try Dior. He was a master of the fuller silhouette. Fashion isn't frivolous, my dear. It's *armor*. Dressed in Dior, you can take on the world. See?"

And Daphne had turned Lydia to face the full-length mirror. The woman who had stared back at her was a different Lydia—confident, successful, attractive. Wearing Daphne's clothes made her walk differently, talk differently, feel differently. She might not stop traffic, but she at least looked like the sort of person who'd never be mowed down on a pedestrian crossing by a yellow Fiat Uno.

Then Daphne had added, "We just need to do something about that ghastly hair," which had ruined the moment a little.

Despite Lydia's protests, Daphne had insisted she took the pearls and four or five outfits home with her. "They deserve more outings than I can possibly give them, even in the most optimistic of scenarios," she'd said.

When Lydia had appeared at the breakfast table this morning, Jeremy had choked on his croissant.

"Is that new?" he'd said.

"No. Very old," she'd replied. Which was the truth.

"You should wear it more often," he'd said, before returning to his newspaper. Even Jeremy's compliments came in the form of instructions, Lydia realized. Nevertheless, it was the first compliment Jeremy had paid her for as long as she could remember, and she'd waited to feel the thrill of that, only to find that she didn't care. Well, not much, in any case.

Lydia frowned. Why was there a crowd outside the hall? There must have been around thirty people, many of whom were holding phones aloft, crowded around the statue of the benefactor with the prolific cocaine habit.

Lydia pushed her way through the melee. It was easier to do that when one wore Dior, she found. And to use words like "melee." And to cope with sitting across the table from your philandering louse of a spouse without plunging the butter knife into his carotid artery. Good grief, was wearing Daphne's old clothes actually turning her into Daphne?

The sight in front of her made her laugh out loud. The pompous brass figure of the disgraced businessman on the plinth was sporting a fabulous pair of large and perky pink knitted breasts with prominent knitted nipples, a flouncy, flowery knitted skirt, and flowing knitted blond tresses. And he—or she?—was holding a placard reading SAVE MANDEL COMMUNITY CENTER FOR THE COMMUNITY!

A florid, cross-looking man pushed through the throng beside her. He was carrying a huge pair of scissors.

"Move out of the way!" he shouted. "Clear the area!"

He grabbed the knitted skirt in one hand and opened the scissors with the other.

"STOP RIGHT THERE, EDWARD FUCKING SCISSOR-HANDS!" came a shout. Daphne. Obviously. She was brandishing her walking stick above the heads of the crowd like a sword.

"This needs removing," said the man, as the crowd began to protest. "It's disrespectful."

"This is CREATIVITY! YOU UTTER PHILISTINE!" said Daphne. "It's the work of the infamous Hammersmith Banksy of yarn bombing. Yarnsy, if you like. Do you want to be the official who's all over the internet for destroying a unique work of art?!?"

Daphne gestured at all the phones surrounding them, trained on the altercation.

"Argh!" said the man, closing his scissors, turning on his heel and beating a retreat, jacket pulled up around his head to avoid the cameras.

The crowd cheered. Lydia wiped a tear from her eye. The good kind of tear, this time. It was a miracle she had any tears left. She'd cried so many buckets recently that surely she must have lost weight?

"You were wonderful, Daphne," she said as she unlocked the

hall. But Daphne didn't look buoyed with success. She looked troubled, playing nervously with the emerald bracelet around her delicate wrist. Seeing Daphne disconcerted was hugely disconcerting.

"What's the matter?" asked Lydia.

"Do you think there's any chance that video footage of me won't end up on the internet?" she asked.

"I'm afraid not," said Lydia. "Did you see how many people were filming? You might even go viral. I know how you feel, though. Ever since I hit fifty, I've hated seeing myself on film."

"If only it were that simple," murmured Daphne. Lydia wasn't sure if Daphne was talking to her, or to herself. "Time is running out."

"Hey, you're the youngest seventy-year-old I've ever met! You have oodles of time left!" said Lydia. But Daphne just looked at her blankly, as if she'd been speaking in a totally different language.

"CLEAR THE PAVEMENT! SAVE OUR COMMUNITY CENTER!" came the recorded voice from Anna's loudspeaker outside. Followed shortly afterward by Anna herself, hair dyed a neon pink, and Ruby. Ruby looked a little tired, as if she'd had a busy night.

"Did you see the wonderful statue outside, ladies?" said Lydia.

"Yes! Isn't it amazing?" said Anna.

"They're calling the mystery yarn bomber Yarnsy, you know," said Lydia.

"Are they?" said Ruby, with a little smile. "I rather like that." She sat down and, as always, took her needles and wool out of her bag. The exact same shade as the naked, knitted breasts adorning the statue outside.

"I wonder who he, or she, could be?" said Lydia, staring at Ruby, who was staring at her knitting.

"I expect they want to remain incognito," said Ruby. "It's all about the mystique, isn't it?"

"Happy New Year, everyone!" said William, walking into the room with a woman who looked younger than Lydia. "This is Amy."

"You're much more youthful than our regular membership," said Anna.

"Either that or she has a miraculous skin-care regime. Do give me your secret," said Ruby.

"I'll have whatever she's having!" said Anna, with a cackle.

"Leave the poor girl alone," said Daphne. "Amy is William's daughter-in-law. I invited her."

"Hi," said Amy, with a meek, cautious little wave, reminding Lydia of how terrifying she'd found all her social club members when she'd first met them. How terrifying she still found them, actually. Despite having read *You Are a Badass: How to Stop Doubting Your Greatness and Start Living an Awesome Life.* Twice.

"I'm sure Lydia has a thrilling, age-appropriate activity planned, like basket weaving or needlepoint, but Amy is a hairstylist, and has very kindly offered to create a salon for us all, right here. And she's starting with Lydia," said Daphne. "It's a *new year, new you* session."

"I'm doing the washing and cutting," said Amy, "and my two daughters are coming to do color and blow-dries."

"I'm really sorry, but I don't think my entertainment budget will stretch to all that," said Lydia.

"I'm paying, Lydia," said Daphne. "And Amy's very kindly agreed to give us a hefty discount. Don't argue. It's my money. At least, I earned it, in a manner of speaking, and I'll spend it how I like."

Before she could open her mouth, Lydia was thrust into a chair and draped in a gown while three women washed, colored, cut, and blow-dried her hair. From time to time one of her seniors would stand in front of her and go "oooh" or "aahhh." She had no mirror, so was entirely unsure what was going on with her head, but the amount of hair gathering in piles on the floor was a little worrying. This was definitely not the "light trim" she usually asked for.

"How did your husbands die, if you don't mind me asking?" said Daphne to Anna, who was sitting next to Lydia having her pink hair blow-dried.

"The first ate poisonous mushrooms on toast, silly man," said Anna, pointing at the first of the tattooed, crossed-out names on her underarm. She then progressed down the list, pointing at each name in turn. "The second had a terrible allergy to bees and managed to disturb a hive when he was in our attic laying down some insulation. Number three fell overboard from a cruise liner. Drunk, obviously. Number four was a trucker, like me, and his brakes failed on the M62. And number five went missing. They found a neatly folded pile of his clothes on Bournemouth Beach, but his body was never recovered."

"Gosh. What a very unusual collection of accidental deaths," said Daphne. "Did they have life insurance, by any chance?"

"What are you trying to say, Daphne?" said Anna.

"Nothing," lied Daphne. "Just how terribly unfortunate for you. More so for them, obviously."

Finally, Amy pronounced Lydia finished.

"Wait!" said William, as he tied his scarf over her eyes.

"Don't mess up the blow-dry, William!" said Amy.

They led her, blindfolded, into the entrance hall and placed her in front of the large, floor-length mirror on the wall, then all gathered around her before William removed his scarf.

"Ta-da!" he said.

The woman standing in front of Lydia, in the beautifully cut jacket and pearls, had her mouth wide open in shock. She looked like Lydia, but several years younger, far more confident, and . . . yes, just a little sexy. She had light-brown hair, highlighted with silvery-blond streaks, cut in a choppy bob that framed her face, gave her actual cheekbones for the first time in years, and accentuated her green eyes.

The woman in the mirror started to cry. Again.

"Aahh. I think she likes it," said Ruby, whose head was covered in pieces of tinfoil, clapping her hands together. Anna had persuaded her to add some blue streaks to her black-and-silver hair.

"For goodness' sake, pull yourself together," said Daphne. "Women in Dior never cry in public. Or at all. The only emotion they show is disdain, with a touch of boredom."

"Excuse me," boomed a man in a suit, who they hadn't even noticed come in. "I'm from the council planning department. You must be the architect from the developer's." He was looking right at Lydia.

"No," she said. "I'm afraid not. The office asked me to tell you she's had to cancel. So sorry. I'm sure she'll contact you to refix."

The man turned on his heel and left, cursing under his breath. Lydia was rather thrilled with her quick thinking, but even more by the fact that she'd been mistaken for an architect.

"Nice improvisation, Lydia," said William. "Art would be impressed."

"It sounds like they're not hanging around for the official vote at the end of the month," said Ruby. "They're drawing up plans already. It's obviously a foregone conclusion."

Everyone fell silent.

"Where is Art, anyway?" said Lydia, keen to change the subject that had dampened everyone's high spirits. "I've not been able to get hold of him. Is he away?"

"No, he's very much not away," said William. "He's holed himself up in his house and won't come out. He does that whenever he can't deal with life. It took me nearly a month to prize him out the last time this happened."

"I'll try calling him," said Daphne. "I was planning to hand Margar—Maggie over to him today." She gestured at the dog, who was looking rather pleased with herself after her shampoo and blow-dry.

Daphne took out her phone and pulled up her contacts. Everyone watched as she listened to the ringing tone.

"Hello," she said, after three or four rings. "You're not Art."

There was a long pause, before she said, "Oh, I see. Yes, I'm his wife. The silly man's obviously forgotten to take his meds again. Which supermarket? OK, I'll be right there."

"What's happened?" said Lydia.

"Art's in a spot of bother," said Daphne, pulling her coat from the hook. "But nothing we can't fix."

"I'll come with you," said William.

"No, you stay here, William. I know what part he's playing, and luckily I'm a better actor than he is," said Daphne, as she pushed open the door to the street, nearly knocking over a woman who looked very much like an architect who'd been stood up by the council planning department.

Daphne

A rt, darling. How many times have I told you not to go shopping on your own?" Daphne said to the hunched-up man on the seat in the corner of the room. "Did he forget to pay again?" she asked the security guards, trying not to laugh at the bizarre collection of items on the table. A spatula? Acne cream? Mascara?

"Maggie Thatcher!" said Art, as the dog bounded up to him.

"Oh dear, it's one of those days," said Daphne. "He sometimes doesn't even recognize his own wife, as you can see. It's the first time he's called me after a former prime minister, though."

"We thought it might be his wife calling, on account of the ring-tone!" said one of the security guards.

"Yes, if I changed my wife's ringtone to the *Jaws* theme tune and her name to Cruella de Vil, she'd kill me," said the second.

Daphne, who could see Art smirking from the corner of her eye, tried very hard not to look annoyed.

"Yes, well, my husband always had a unique sense of humor," she said. "Sadly, that's gone. Replaced with dementia—as you can tell—

double incontinence, flatulence, and erectile dysfunction." *Take that, Art, you old goat.*

"Well, you'd better get him home," said the security guard, eyeing Art a little warily, probably wondering where they kept the emergency cleaning fluids. "We're obviously not going to charge him, given the circumstances, but please don't let him in here on his own again."

"Don't worry, gentlemen. I shall be keeping a very close eye on him," Daphne said, holding out her hand to Art.

"I'm so ashamed," said Art in a whisper, as she led him out of the supermarket.

"I'm not surprised," said Daphne. "You smell terrible."

"Not about the smell," said Art. "Or, at least, not just about the smell. The whole arrest thing. All that stuff I stole. Things I didn't even need. You must despise me."

"Well, that's where you're quite, quite wrong, old chap," said Daphne. "To be honest, I like you way more than I did before. Which isn't to say that I actually like you. I just dislike you a lot less, now you're not quite so perfect. I've always loved a man with a fatal flaw, as well as a penchant for mascara. Was the spatula intended for icing cakes, or is it some kind of fetish?"

"Well, I like you more, too, since you saved my bacon. So, we're even," said Art. "Will you let me make you a cup of tea? To say thank you?"

"Sure," said Daphne. "Why not?" There were many reasons why not, obviously, but she was not going to turn down another opportunity to see inside somebody else's home.

"We'll just need to stop off at a shop to buy milk, tea bags, and Hobnobs," said Art.

"Don't take this the wrong way," said Daphne, "but why don't you wait on the pavement with Margaret, and I'll do the shopping?"

Art's home—if you could call it that—was the polar opposite of Daphne's. His furnishings weren't so much curated as merely accumulated. Decades' worth of ugly, often broken, things just shoved together randomly. And then covered in dirt and grime. Did men not *see* cobwebs and dust? Or did they see them, but simply not care? A ghastly array of socks and underpants were draped over the radiators. Daphne was both gratified and disgusted to note that she had not been wrong about the state of Art's underwear.

"Good God, when I said I loved a man with a fatal floor, this is not what I meant," said Daphne, staring at the stained and cracked kitchen tiles. "Art, if you want me to sit in your kitchen, you're going to have to let me clean a bit of it first."

"Sure," said Art. "That's a little strange—rude, even—but go ahead while I make the tea."

Daphne found some old cleaning products under the sink and spent fifteen minutes cleaning one tiny corner of the kitchen, so she had somewhere to drink her tea without worrying about botulism.

Art passed her a cup of tea and a plate of Hobnobs.

"Right," said Daphne. "You'd better tell me what's been going on."

Art sighed. "I think I got to the point where I hated myself and my life so much that I just wanted to blow the whole thing up," he said.

That was a sentiment Daphne could understand. After all, wasn't it exactly what she'd done fifteen years ago? Although in a very different way. It wasn't herself that she'd got arrested.

"I don't understand this self-loathing thing you have going on," she said. "I've always found you irritatingly *good*, to be honest. I mean, look what you've done for all those children—giving them toys and clothes, directing their nativity. And you've been trying so hard to save the community center, as well as looking after Margaret. You should be proud of yourself, surely? Smug, even. I'd certainly assumed you were."

"But I've been doing it all for the wrong reasons, Daphne. It's all been completely and utterly selfish." Daphne just raised an eyebrow at him and let him continue. There was nothing better than listening to someone else's guilty conscience being off-loaded.

"The toys and clothes were all stolen, obviously. I have a whole wardrobe rammed with things I've nicked over the years, and just knowing it's all lurking there keeps me awake at night, but I can't bring myself to throw away all that valuable, unused stuff. Finding a good home for some of it gave me back a tiny bit of my pride." Art paused while he took a large bite of Hobnob, which seemed to give him the strength to continue.

"And the nativity was just a form of distraction, to take my mind off the end of my career, and to keep me out of the shops. Plus, it was good practice for M," he said, through a mouthful of biscuit.

"M?" said Daphne.

"Maggie," said Art. "The only reason I agreed to help with Maggie was because I had this ridiculous idea of entering her into a TV talent competition. There's a one-hundred-thousand-pound prize, you see. And the visibility, as my agent pointed out."

"A hundred grand?" said Daphne. "That money would repair the community center and keep the developers away! It's a genius plan! Why on earth didn't you say?"

"Because it wasn't for the community center, Daphne," said Art. "It was for me. For my retirement. So I could afford to heat my house and maybe even go on holiday. Anyhow, it won't work."

"Why not?" said Daphne.

"Because the auditions are tomorrow, and I've not done any practice with M for the past two weeks," said Art.

"Nonsense," said Daphne. "Right. We are going to take Margaret to that audition. We are going to win that money. You are going to give it to the council to save our hall, and that way you will be able to completely wipe clean your conscience and stop all this frightfully boring, self-pitying nonsense. You could keep a little back for your gas bill. It's bloody freezing in here. Now, take me to the wardrobe of shame."

Art opened his mouth, paused, then closed it again. Daphne often had that effect, she found. Then he led her up his stairs and into a room which was like a 1980s time capsule. A teenage girl's room perfectly preserved under inches of dust.

"Whose room was this?" she asked.

"My daughter's," said Art. "Kerry. She and her mum left in 1987. I never saw either of them again, and I've never met my grandchildren. My wife, Jill, died about ten years ago, still hating me. Cancer, apparently."

"I'm so sorry," said Daphne. And she genuinely was. She really wanted to know why Art's family had walked away from him, and to ask about the second bed in the room. This was a bedroom for two children, surely? But she'd pushed hard enough for one day. Slowly, slowly, catchy the rolling stone, as they said.

"Let me see inside this wardrobe," she said.

Art walked over to the large cupboard in the corner of the bedroom and, screwing his eyes tight shut, opened the door.

"I see," said Daphne, who did very much see. "We need someone to help us move all this stuff. I bet you Lydia has a Volvo."

"Why do you say that?" said Art.

"She's obviously the sort of woman who drives a Volvo," said Daphne.

"You make some ridiculous assumptions," said Art. "But with such admirable conviction."

"Do you have a spare set of house keys?" asked Daphne. Art nodded. "Do you trust me?"

"Yes," said Art.

Which was remarkably stupid of him. When people trusted Daphne, it tended to end badly. As Jack had discovered.

Daphne's phone rang. This very rarely happened, so it took her a while to realize it was hers, then to locate it.

"Yes?" she said, suspiciously.

"Daphne. Sorry for bothering you. It's Janine. You're on my emergency contact list for Kylie. I need your help. It's Ziggy. Can you meet me at the nursery, as soon as possible?"

"I'll be right there," said Daphne.

Good grief. How on earth had all these people managed up until now without her? And how had she turned into the sort of woman one called in an emergency?

Ziggy

Ziggy! Get out of bed! You should have left ages ago!" shouted Ziggy's mum.

"I'm coming!" lied Ziggy, pulling the duvet over his head and wishing that one day he could just wake up and find himself somewhere else. Anywhere else.

"Look, I'll take Kylie into the nursery on my way to work—that way you might just get to school on time," she said. "But you owe me one, because it'll make me late for work. Again."

"Thanks," said Ziggy, who hadn't actually been to school once since the new term had started, nearly two weeks ago. It had taken a week for the worst of his bruises to fade, and for him to be able to walk without wincing, and by then he hadn't been able to see the point of returning. It would only remind him of everything he'd lost. And just the thought of bumping into Alicia made him dizzy with anxiety.

Ziggy had managed to stagger back to the estate, following his mugging in the alleyway, only to find himself being beaten up by Floyd, as punishment for not bringing back the package that had been stolen from him. It had, it transpired, contained a huge amount of cash. Ziggy had curled himself into a ball while Floyd kicked him over and over with steel-capped boots, hoping that Kylie's push-chair was angled away from the sight of her father being pulverized. Or, at least, that she was too young to understand or to remember what she was witnessing.

In between the kicks, Floyd had explained that Ziggy now owed him £10,000, which he would have to pay off by being at Floyd's beck and call for the foreseeable future.

"You're lucky I choose to believe you," he'd said, with a sharp kick to Ziggy's ribs. "I don't think you're stupid enough to steal from me. But your life is mine now, you hear? Until every penny you owe me is paid back." Deft kick to the abdomen. "Get it?" And one in the back of the head, still raw from the mugging. "Raise your arm if you get it!"

Ziggy had managed to lift his trembling arm a few inches and the kicking, mercifully, had stopped. One of Floyd's lackeys had deposited him and Kylie on his doorstep, and he'd had to explain to his horrified mother that he'd been the victim of a random robbery. He'd refused to let her call the police, or take him to hospital, so she'd patched him up with antiseptic and plasters as best she could, reassuring him that it was all over now.

But the nightmare was just beginning.

There was no point in going to school, and taking his mocks, or submitting his UCAS form for universities that he'd never be able to attend. Because if he disappeared without paying back his debt, it just passed over to his mother. And Ziggy couldn't let that happen.

So, he was fucked. Right, royally fucked.

Ziggy went back to sleep. But even that wasn't an escape, as his dreams just taunted him with replays of the past few days until he was woken by a flurry of notifications on his phone.

Floyd needed him to do a delivery.

By the time Ziggy had completed that delivery for Floyd, followed by another two, it was early afternoon. He still had three hours before he was due to collect Kylie, so he put the twenty-pound note and the shopping list his mum had left on the kitchen table in his pocket, and headed for the supermarket. But then he walked past a pub and saw the promise of temporary escape. The only way to forget, just for a while, the car crash of his life.

Ziggy found some mates at the bar. Well, not mates so much as boys he had once known vaguely, who had dropped out of school after spectacularly bombing their GCSEs. But when you're seeking oblivion, anyone else doing the same is automatically your best friend. Especially ones who'll lend you cash to buy more vodka shots. And then offer you a line or two of coke, just to straighten you out a little.

"Your phone's ringing, man," said one of Ziggy's new best friends. "Who uses actual voice calls? Must be a scammer."

Ziggy squinted at his phone. The letters on the display danced in front of his eyes. He put a hand over one side of his face, flinching at the smell of wee and weed on his fingers. The name on the screen came temporarily into focus: *JANINE.*

Fuck.

Ziggy looked at his watch. He was already fifteen minutes late to collect Kylie.

"Hi, Janine. I'm on my way. So sorry," he said, amazing himself at how incredibly sober he'd managed to sound.

"Ziggy. You're paralytic. You can't turn up here in that condition. Where are you?" said Janine.

"The Nag's Head," slurred Ziggy. Too drunk to lie.

"I'll call your mum," said Janine.

Even in his current state, Ziggy knew this was not a good idea. If his mum found him like this, it would lead to a whole string of questions. Like why he hadn't been at school, taking his mock A-level exams. Like why he was throwing his entire future away. Like whether he was fit to be responsible for her grandchild.

"No, don't do that. Call Daphne," he said. A decision he would come to regret.

"OK," she replied, and hung up.

"WHERE IS ZIGGY?" came a shout from the doorway, just a few minutes or so later. Or maybe longer. Ziggy's perception of time was doing very strange things.

"Oooh, who's in trouble?" said one of Ziggy's new friends.

"Your mum ain't aging well, Ziggy," said another.

Ziggy stood up. Then fell over.

Daphne walked up to the barman. "Right, you!" she said, leaning across the bar and prodding him in the chest with her metal-tipped walking stick. "The one who lets teenaged boys get legless on a school day in the afternoon." He looked terrified, as well he might. He wasn't the only one. "Look after this baby while I deal with her father. Try not to get her drunk."

Daphne walked over and grabbed Ziggy by the scruff of his neck. Ziggy's new friends just stared, mouths open, like a row of targets in a fairground game, waiting for someone to throw a ping-pong ball at them.

"Fuck, you're strong," he said, the words garbled by the force of her grip.

"I do weights. Helps prevent osteoporosis," said Daphne, through gritted teeth. "This way."

She steered him toward the toilets. The ladies' toilets. Then she propped him against a sink while she filled it with cold water. She took a handful of his hair and plunged his face into the basin.

He gasped and spluttered as she pulled his head out. Then she did it again.

He should have called his mum.

"How DARE you?" she said, pulling his head up and shoving his face toward the mirror, so he could see what a mess he looked. "You have been given the gift of youth, of health, of a beautiful CHILD and you are pissing it all away." Head back in the sink. "One day you will get to my age, if you don't get murdered before then, and you'll realize what an honor and a privilege you had, and how spectacularly you wasted it all."

Ziggy took a deep breath and wiped the water from his face with his sleeve, thinking his punishment was over. Wrong.

"You STUPID"—sharp slap to the right cheek—"STUPID"—and one to the left—"FUCKER!"—back in the sink.

"Right," she said, toweling off her hands, reverting to a normal, relaxed tone, as if they'd just been discussing the weather over tea and cake. "Let's rescue Kylie from the negligent barman, go back to your place, have a strong cup of coffee, and work out what we're going to do to fix the mess you're obviously in. OK?"

"OK," said Ziggy, weakly.

"Hey," said the barman as he handed over Kylie. "I knew I'd seen you somewhere before. You're on TikTok."

"Don't be ridiculous," said Daphne.

"You definitely are," said the man, thrusting his phone toward them. "You're a meme."

Lydia

"What do I do about Jeremy?" Lydia had asked Daphne.

"Don't worry. He's on the whiteboard. I'll make sure I get to him before the bomb goes off," Daphne had replied.

This response had raised far more questions than it had answered. Where was this whiteboard? What else was on it? Was the bomb actual or metaphorical? She assumed the latter, but one could never tell with Daphne. And was anyone going to get hurt when it went off? Literally or metaphorically?

Not knowing which issue to start with, Lydia had just said, "OK."

Luckily, she was too busy to fret about it. Having had a phone call from Daphne yesterday, with a list of precise instructions, she'd spent all morning going backward and forward from Art's house to Mandel Community Center, transporting bin bags full of the most extraordinarily random collection of stuff from Art's wardrobe. Daphne hadn't said where it had all come from, just that Art wanted to simultaneously declutter and do some good for the community.

Given all the shenanigans at the nativity, Lydia thought it best not to delve any deeper. It might make her an accessory.

Thank goodness she drove a Volvo. Such a practical car, and perfect for this kind of job.

Lydia's planned activities for the social club had, yet again, been hijacked. She wondered if she would ever be able to unveil the macramé plant-holder kits she'd stashed in the storage room.

She pulled back her shoulders and took a deep breath. It was time to rally the troops.

The room was more crowded than Lydia had ever seen it. William was there, of course, along with Anna and Ruby, but they'd been joined by around eight heavily pregnant women. Lydia had ambushed them on their way out of their antenatal class and persuaded them to come along to help.

Lydia had also bumped into Tim, who'd manned the tea stand at the nativity, on his way to set up the Alcoholics Anonymous meeting.

"Can you help?" she'd asked him.

"Of course! I'll rally the friends of Bill. The opposite of addiction is connection!" he'd replied, smothering her in a bear hug. Lydia was getting a little fed up with people talking in riddles. Who on earth was Bill, and was he coming to help, too?

Luckily, although Daphne wasn't there in person, Lydia was channeling her energy by wearing another one of her outfits: a military-style jacket from Alexander McQueen which, she suspected, had far more experience at this kind of thing than Lydia herself did.

Lydia had been reading a book called *Make Your Bed: Little Things That Can Change Your Life . . . and Maybe the World* by a former navy SEAL, so was picturing herself standing on the deck of her warship on the morning of battle, her marines assembled before her, waiting for her to unveil the plan of attack.

"Thank you all for coming today. I really am so grateful," she said, out of habit. Then kicked herself. Lord Nelson wouldn't have started his Battle of Trafalgar briefing like that, would he?

"We have two simultaneous battles to fight today," she said, dropping her voice an octave. Was it her imagination, or had her audience all sat up a little straighter? "First, on the home front. These bags of items"—she gestured to the bulging bin bags which contained the contents of Art's wardrobe—"need to be divided into three separate piles. One, things for the nursery on the other side of the hall. Two, things for the local charity shops. Three, things to be thrown away or recycled. The antenatal class will do the sorting with the help of Ruby. Anna will do runs on her scooter to the local charity shops."

"Yes, ma'am!" said Anna, with an actual salute. "I have a trailer attached especially for the job, ma'am."

"Good job, captain," said Lydia. Then, worried she might have gone too far: "Also, if you find anything you'd particularly like to keep, please help yourselves, as a thank-you. Call it the spoils of war, if you will.

"The rest of you," said Lydia, gesturing to the Alcoholics Anonymous group, "are going with William to Art's house, to fight the second battle. It needs to be decluttered and cleaned thoroughly. At the end of the day, I'll collect all the rubbish and recycling in the Volvo. Any questions?"

"Yes!" said Ruby, her hand in the air. "Where is Daphne?"

"Off somewhere spinning her web, no doubt," said William. "But where's Art?"

"He's with Daphne," said Lydia. "They said they had an important mission to complete and would be away all day."

"Both of them? Alone? Together?" said William, looking alarmed.

"Isn't that like putting a squirrel in a cage with a tiger?" said Ruby.

"Best way to die: Eaten by a tiger or being harangued to death by Daphne?" said William.

"I'd take the tiger any day," said Anna.

"Poor, poor Art," said William, shaking his head. "Hasn't he been through enough?"

Lydia spent the afternoon shuttling between the two sites, checking on progress and providing direction, encouragement, and refreshments. She hadn't felt such a sense of achievement in years.

At the end of the day, she bid everyone farewell—which wasn't very professionally done, on account of her having become a little emotional and weepy—and loaded up the Volvo for a trip to the dump.

Was there anywhere quite as satisfying and cathartic as the council recycling center? Lydia removed each item from her boot and took it to the relevant skip, dividing everything into card, wood, metal, plastic, and so on. As she chucked the final item into its skip, with a little run-up and a vigorous overarm throw, she felt lighter, less encumbered. She imagined that she could just lift her arms and float home. But that would mean abandoning the Volvo.

It felt good to rid yourself of things you no longer needed, things that were weighing you down.

And, for the first time that day, Lydia thought of Jeremy.

Daphne

aphne scrolled through TikTok, which she'd made Ziggy install on her phone. Sure enough, there she was, just as the barman had said, brandishing her walking stick like a sword and shouting, "STOP RIGHT THERE, EDWARD FUCKING SCISSORHANDS!" That clip had popped up everywhere, Ziggy said. Set to music, cut together with footage of celebrities and politicians, covered in emojis. She was the new Jackie Weaver.

Daphne loaded up OurNeighbours.com. She was all over that as well. *I think she lives in my building*, someone had written. It was only a matter of time before her image was linked to her name, and then to her address.

She could hear the relentless ticking of the clock, the countdown gathering pace. If only she knew exactly how long she had left, so she could plan more efficiently.

Daphne stared at the new list on her whiteboard, pen in hand.

There were just too many things to do.

1. Deal with Ziggy's gang
2. Find Art's daughter (Do I care? Genuine question)
3. Save the community center
4. Revenge on Jeremy (Kneecapping? Too much?)
5. Buy more loo roll

Item five was an easy one, admittedly. But the others would take time.

And then, there was Sidney. Daphne had been rather too busy to spend much time with her new beau, which was quite possibly why he was so keen. People always want what they can't have. Daphne's whole life had been driven by that truth.

Daphne and Sidney had now had four or five dates. They hadn't been to each other's homes, or done more than fairly chaste kissing. Sidney had been a little wary after the cigarette burn incident, although it seemed to have healed fairly quickly, so Daphne suspected him of overreacting a little.

Daphne was starting to think that maybe, just maybe, she could take Sidney with her. Having spent the last few months experiencing the thrill of having friends, and a life outside her apartment, the thought of leaving it all behind made her unbearably sad. Perhaps she should never have opened the Pandora's box, because she couldn't see how she'd have the strength to close it again.

Daphne picked up a pen, pulled off its lid with her teeth, and wrote:

6. Ask Sidney to come with me?

But that was a decision for another day. Today she had to get cracking on item three, part one. The auditions for the dog talent show.

Daphne, Art and Maggie took the tube out to Ealing, where the auditions were being held in a large TV studio. Apart from a couple of brief forays into neighboring Barnes, Fulham, and Putney, Daphne hadn't left Hammersmith for fifteen years, and found it almost as thrilling as she'd found flying to Tokyo, New York, or Berlin in the old days. She wasn't letting on to Art, of course, and was managing to maintain a look of bored disdain.

"Isn't this fun?" said Art as the tube rattled through Turnham Green, toward Chiswick Park. "It's like we're on a date!"

"A date?" said Daphne, horrified. "Good God, I'd never go on a date with someone like you."

"Why not?" said Art, looking intrigued rather than upset. Where did she even begin?

"You're too old, for starters. I only date toy boys," said Daphne. "You're badly dressed, probably insolvent, and you have dubious personal hygiene."

"You haven't mentioned the stealing, the deception, and my recent near-arrest," said Art.

"No. Those are the things I like about you," said Daphne.

"You're a very strange woman, Daffy," said Art.

"It has been said before," said Daphne, rather thrilled at having acquired a nickname. She'd never been the sort of person who'd been given a nickname. At least, not to her face.

"Anyhow, I think you protest too much. I know you secretly fancy me," said Art, winking at her.

"I'll add total lack of emotional intelligence and extreme narcissism to the long list of reasons why I dislike you," said Daphne. Although the truth was, she was actually starting to dislike him just a little less.

It was obvious when they'd reached the right place, as the queue of people and dogs stretched all the way down the street. And the *dogs*. They were all dressed in the most extraordinary outfits. There were superhero dogs, cowboy dogs, butch-looking dogs in leathers, and slutty little dogs in rah-rah skirts with huge pink bows on their heads. Good grief, were they wearing *false eyelashes*?!?

Maggie, who up until now had been so proud of her recent shampoo and blow-dry, was looking seriously intimidated, reminding Daphne just a little of Lydia.

"Don't let those bitches freak you out, Margaret," said Daphne. "We're going to wipe the floor with them all." The problem was, she was beginning to doubt that this would be the case. They might have underestimated the task at hand.

First things first. They had to deal with this ridiculous queue. There were certain things one grew out of with age, like tube tubes, threesomes, and, most definitely, queuing.

"Excuse me! Excuse me!" she yelled, waving her walking stick at a barely postpubescent child with jeans that hovered precariously around the bottom of his bum, and a clipboard. He was wearing a headset that he seemed inordinately proud of, as if he were part of the presidential security detail, as opposed to monitoring a motley queue of dog owners. He sighed theatrically, then came over.

"Yes?" he said, looking as apathetic as only the very young can.

"My companion has mobility and"—she leaned over to hiss in his ear, and barely resisted the urge to pull up his trousers—"incontinence issues. It's his prostate, you see. I don't suppose you could bump us up the queue, could you? I mean, we could wait, but I'm really not sure what might happen . . ." She threw in a grimace and waved her hand in the direction of Art's crotch.

"But . . . but . . ." squawked Art beside her. She pressed her walking stick down hard on his foot.

"Aaarrghhh!" he said.

The boy looked alarmed, and promptly pulled them both out of the queue.

"Oi! What's going on? That's not fair!" yelled the man in front of them, who had four Chihuahuas on leads, dressed in matching turquoise sequined leotards and feathered headdresses.

"INCONTINENCE ISSUES! IT'S HIS PROSTATE!" shouted Clipboard Child, pointing at Art, who flushed bright red and glared at Daphne. "Go join that queue there," he said, gesturing at a line just one tenth the length of the main one, labeled *VIPS ONLY.* That was more like it.

Even in this line, Daphne had to cope with nearly half an hour of Art's sulky resentment before they reached the front. Two or three fights had broken out, and it wasn't entirely clear who'd started them—the dogs or their handlers.

"Right, you're on," said Clipboard Child finally, ushering Art, Daphne, and Maggie forward. Daphne was suddenly rather nervous. Her comfort zone was exceedingly spacious, but this experience lay well outside of it.

"Is it OK if I smoke?" she said, fishing her cigarettes out of her bag.

"Uh, no," said Clipboard Child, looking shocked. "This isn't the, like, eighties."

Daphne replaced the cigarettes reluctantly. It was ridiculous that these people were, no doubt, all doing cocaine in the greenroom, or popping prescription opioids in the lavatories, yet she wasn't allowed a tiny cigarette.

"Hello!" said the man in the middle of the panel of three people behind a trestle table. "Name of handler?"

"Art Andrews. Actor," said Art.

"And your dog?" he said.

"M," said Art, at the same time as Daphne said, "Margaret."

Clipboard Child, who was patting Maggie, swiveled her collar around and looked at her tag. "Uh, it says here *Maggie Thatcher*," he said.

"Ha ha!" said Left-Hand Judge. "What's her act? Canceling free school milk? Declaring war on Argentina? Or smashing the trades unions?"

Daphne gave him one of her finest withering looks. He paled and went silent.

"Right, off you go," said Right-Hand Judge. "Just give your music to Jez, over there."

"No music," said Art.

"Oh, well, no matter," said Middle Judge, in a tone that implied it obviously mattered a lot.

Art and Maggie walked to the center of the stage, while Daphne stood next to the judges, so she could surreptitiously read any notes they were making.

Art blew his whistle, and Maggie did the trick he'd taught her for the nativity, turning full circle on her hind legs, then bowing for the audience. There was a desultory clap or two from Left-Hand Judge. Right-Hand Judge appeared to be compiling a shopping list, as Daphne was sure he'd just written *large bunch coriander.*

"High five, M!" said Art. Maggie raised her paw to Art's outstretched hand. "Bang!" he said, pulling a toy gun out of his back pocket. Maggie collapsed to the floor and rolled onto her back, paws in the air.

She was *magnificent.* Living proof that you could indeed teach an old dog new tricks.

"Is that it?" asked Middle Judge, sounding bored.

"Uh, yes," said Art.

"OK, *next!*" said Middle Judge.

"WAIT!" said Daphne, seeing a hundred grand just slipping away from her. She walked onto the stage, standing next to a defeated-looking Art, facing the panel. "When you film your show, don't you need some fairly useless competitors for the audience to feel sorry for? To make the others look good? Especially if the handler is from a disadvantaged group. Like someone who's nearly ninety years old?"

"But I'm not . . ." spluttered Art. Daphne prodded him with her stick again.

"Mmm, well, maybe. What do you think? Worth going for the sympathy vote?" said Middle Judge, turning to Left-Hand Judge with a raised eyebrow.

"It might work, if he has an emotional backstory," said Left-Hand Judge.

"Do you have an emotional backstory?" said Middle Judge to Art.

"He does! He does!" said Daphne. "He's lost touch with his only child. He hasn't seen her for about thirty years, and has never met his grandchildren."

"Actually, that might do it," said Right-Hand Judge.

"OK. You're in," said Middle Judge. "Don't make me regret it. Give your details to Jez. We'll be in touch. NEXT!"

Art

"I had rather expected you to be a little more grateful, since I saved the day," said Daphne as they sat next to each other on the crowded tube. Daphne had intimidated a middle-aged couple into relinquishing their seats. The minute she'd trained her beady eyes on them, they'd wisely given up all hope. Maggie sat on Art's knee, looking extremely proud of herself, as well she might.

"Daphne. Since I've known you, you've shouted at me in the street, threatened to have me arrested, then accused me, publicly, of having dementia, incontinence, a dodgy prostate, flatulence, mobility issues, and erectile dysfunction," he said, then wished he'd spoken more quietly as he noticed the woman to his left edging away from him nervously. "You've added nearly fifteen years to my already not inconsiderable age, and then, to top it all, you take the most painful part of my life, something I revealed to you in confidence, and use it for your own ends, without thought of the potential ramifications. So no, I'm not fucking grateful, actually. I'm livid."

Art had never met anyone more infuriating. He waited for the apology, which any normal person could have seen was required at this point, but Daphne was obviously far from being a normal person, so there was just silence. Or as close as you can get to silence when you have a hundred people squashed into a metal carriage underground, many of them listening to your conversation.

Finally, Daphne spoke.

"Haven't you worked out by now that if they're going to stereotype us, we might as well use their lazy preconceptions to our advantage? It's thanks to your imaginary dementia, advanced age, and incontinence that you weren't arrested for shoplifting and we got to the front of the queue and a place in the TV show," said Daphne.

Annoyingly, Art could see her point, but he wasn't going to let on. He was far too angry to concede any ground.

He refused to look at Daphne, staring resolutely ahead, but found her reflection in the dark window opposite eyeballing him instead. He glared at the Daphne in the glass, who bared her teeth back at him.

"Anyhow, what are we going to do about Jeremy?" said Daphne, with such a rapid change of subject that it gave him whiplash.

"Why on earth do you think it's your place to fix Lydia's marriage?" said Art. "It's none of your business and, besides, you've never struck me as the type that likes to do a good deed."

"That's not what I was planning at all," said Daphne. "I have no intention of fixing her marriage. She'd be far better off out of it, in my humble opinion." Art snorted at the use of the adjective "humble." "I just want to make that duplicitous weasel of a husband suffer."

"You're not a very nice person, Daphne," said Art.

"Well, luckily, I've never aimed for *nice*," said Daphne. "That sort of wishy-washy adjective is much more your bag. You can wallow in *nice* as much as you like, just don't expect me to be a part of it."

There was another long silence, and Art was just starting to think that he might get all the way to Hammersmith without having to speak to her again. Then she said, "I'm thinking that Jeremy has no idea how lucky he is to have Lydia. And I bet that if he was faced with the reality of shacking up with that flibbertigibbet of his, he might get a bit of a shock. He'd find himself hoist to his own bollard."

"You mean 'petard,'" said Art. "'Hoist by his own petard.'"

"No, I don't," said Daphne, glaring at him. "What the hell is a petard when it's at home, anyhow? I want to hoist that fucker to a bollard. Then, ideally, chuck him over a bridge into the Thames so he can swim with the fishes."

"As I said, not a very nice person," said Art.

Art noticed a group of youths in hoodies, nudging each other, staring at their phones and then at him. Had he been recognized? In the fifty years of his "career," this had only happened a handful of times, and it was always a thrill. Perhaps they'd want an auto-graph, or a selfie. Art gave them a sly sideways look, as if to say, *Yes, it is me. But don't make a fuss about it in public . . .*

He waited for them to make a fuss about it.

The train pulled into Hammersmith station, and he and Daphne stood up to leave. One of the young men elbowed his friend.

"STOP RIGHT THERE, EDWARD FUCKING SCISSOR-HANDS!" he shouted, brandishing an imaginary sword.

Had he been mistaken for Johnny Depp? Well, that was a first. He must be aging better than he'd thought. Or maybe Depp had gone seriously downhill recently. He smiled, brandished an imagi-nary sword back at them, bowed gracefully, and got off the train. Daphne had to be impressed by that, surely? Not that he wanted to impress her, obviously. Why on earth would he want to do that? He couldn't give a toss what she thought of him or, indeed, of anything.

"Tick tock, tick tock," muttered Daphne, under her breath. He had no idea what she was going on about, but had no intention of asking. The safest strategy with Daphne, he'd decided, was to engage as little as possible.

As they emerged back at street level, Art wondered whether he should escort Daphne home. Just in case she attacked any local muggers. But before he could even suggest it, she'd taken off without a backward glance, her walking stick thrown over her shoulder.

Art's buoyant mood dissipated as he and Maggie approached his house. The lights were on. Had he been burgled? He pushed open his front door, dreading what he might find inside. Something was definitely not right. The house reeked of fresh pine and lemons. What kind of burglar leaves your house smelling of cleaning products?

"Welcome home, Art!" said William, appearing from his kitchen holding two tumblers of whiskey.

"What's going on?" said Art.

"Have a look around," said William.

William led an incredulous Art from room to room of his house, which was not his house. It felt as if he'd been catapulted back through time, to the days before Jill and Kerry had left, and it had been a home, rather than just a building filled with stuff that he happened to live in. It was clean, and warm, uncluttered and welcoming.

"Shall we go upstairs?" said William, and Art felt his insides clench. As if William could read his mind—which, after all these years, he actually could—he said, "Don't worry. I've not thrown away any of Kerry's things. I've just stored them carefully."

William threw open the door to Kerry's old room, which was clean, fresh, and empty. The memory of her was still there, but it was no longer overwhelming, suffocating. Art walked slowly toward the wardrobe, then looked back at William, who nodded and gave him an encouraging smile. He clutched the doorknob and pulled it open as quickly as possible, like ripping a plaster off a wound.

He stared, unable to take in what he was seeing. The wound had been excised and cauterized. All his years' worth of accumulated loot, of festering shame, had *gone*. Replaced by neatly stored teenage possessions. Carefully cataloged memories.

Art sat down on the bed—no longer lumpy, now there was nothing hiding underneath it. He felt lighter. As if a huge weight he'd been carrying for so long had been removed from his shoulders. And he began to cry. For the first time since Jill and Kerry had gone. Huge, bone-shaking sobs, while William sat next to him and rubbed his back.

"You're not going to start filling that cupboard again, are you, old chap?" said William, once the sobs had subsided to hiccups.

Art shook his head.

"You know it was just a displacement activity, don't you? To take your mind off Jill and Kerry. And . . . well, you know."

Art did know, but it was the last thing in the world he wanted to talk about right now.

"It's too late to find Jill, but you can still track down Kerry. Please, Art. I'll help you. Can we look for her?" said William.

"I don't think we need to," said Art, through the tears. "Daphne told an effing TV production company all about it, so I suspect they'll be doing that for me, and opening up a whole festering can of worms. They called it 'my emotional backstory,' and it was the only reason they let M through the audition, so there was nothing I could do about it."

"Bloody hell," said William. "But maybe the old bird's done you a favor."

There was a small part of Art that agreed with this sentiment. He didn't have the courage to find Kerry himself, but now it was all rather out of his hands. Now he could just leave it to fate. He wasn't going to admit this, though, even to William. And certainly not to Daphne.

"Hardly. A favor would imply that she'd done it for the right reasons," said Art. "But it was purely selfish. That woman is evil. And where did she even come from? We know nothing about her, despite hours of playing Truth or Dare Jenga and Never Have I Ever. We've lived here our entire lives, and yet we'd never seen her before she turned up at the social club. Doesn't that strike you as a little odd?"

"Well, Hammersmith is a big place," said William. "But Daphne doesn't exactly blend in. We could hardly have missed her, could we?"

"That woman drives me mad. I really don't like her," said Art.

There was a long silence before William spoke again.

"You remember when we moved up to secondary school, and you told everyone how much you loathed football, just because you hadn't been picked to play on the A team?" he said, in an extraordinary change of subject. "But you were so intense and over the top about it that any fool could see how much you cared. Are you sure you're not feeling like this about Daphne because, deep down, you want to be on her team?"

"Are you mad?" said Art. "Besides, she's not the sort of woman who'd ever have a team. She's a lone wolf. A solo-flying, whiteboard-wielding witch. Luckily, it's Jeremy she has her sights trained on now, not us. I dread to think what she's planning for him."

Daphne

aphne was sitting at her desk, trying to write a letter of apology. It was rare that one came across a first at her age, but this was one, and it was much harder than she'd anticipated. Especially because the recipient of the apology was to be Art Andrews.

Daphne had been feeling *out of sorts* for the past few days. Ever since they'd got back from the auditions. She just couldn't shake the unaccustomed unease which, by process of elimination, she finally identified as *remorse*. She was, in actual fact, sorry. After all, she had more reason than most to understand the need for privacy, the value of secrets. Yet she had taken the secret Art had trusted her with and used it carelessly and selfishly.

Art had every right to be furious. And, to her immense surprise, Daphne realized she cared what he thought of her. Was that the definition of a friend? Someone whose opinion you actually cared about? Perhaps it was. And friends apologized to each other when they were in the wrong, didn't they?

So, Daphne found herself, fountain pen in hand, agonizing over a blank sheet of paper.

Dear Art, she wrote.

Dear? Wasn't that a little too *familiar?* She didn't loathe him as much as she once did, but that hardly made him a *dear.* She scrumpled the paper into a ball and threw it toward the wastepaper basket. Hole in one. Nice.

Hi! she wrote. Jaunty. Casual. Too casual, perhaps?

I feel I must say sorry for the way I've treated you, she wrote. She squinted at the words. While they were true, they looked so *weak.* So *apologetic.* She sighed, crushed the words into another ball, and potted another basket.

The wastepaper bin was almost full by the time she got as far as signing her name, two hours later, and even that wasn't straightforward.

Love, Daphne, she wrote with a flourish, then groaned. She certainly couldn't use the word "love"! He might get entirely the wrong idea. And even the name was a problem. Given that this was the most honest thing she'd written in years, she didn't want to end with a lie. With the name "Daphne."

Should she sign it with the nickname Art had called her? What was it? *Daffy?* No. Perhaps he wouldn't even remember having said it, and wouldn't it look a bit strange that she had?

Daphne rested her forehead on the cool leather top of her desk and tried to gather the strength to start again.

Ziggy

iggy lay on the sofa under the Buzz Lightyear duvet he'd had since he was five, wishing he could escape "to infinity and beyond." He scrolled through TikTok on his phone, while Kylie watched yet more TV. He was already an hour late dropping her off at nursery, but the more he anticipated Janine's disappointment-mixed-with-worry face, the less he wanted to go, and the longer he left it, the more disappointment and worry he could expect. It was a vicious circle.

The jarring sound of the doorbell made him jump. Was it Floyd? The police? Social Services? Someone from his school? The best strategy was obviously to pretend not to be there, since none of the options were good ones. He pulled the duvet over his head.

Kylie, however, had other ideas, and began to scream loudly.

He couldn't pretend not to be in when there was a baby yelling. They'd break the door down.

"You missed a golden opportunity there to remain silent," he said to his daughter, echoing the phrase his mother had said to him so many times.

Ziggy pulled the duvet around him, so he looked like a creature from *James and the Giant Peach*—a huge maggot with size-ten feet. He stood up and shuffled to the door, putting his eye up to the spyhole.

It was Daphne. For a minute, he felt relieved, before remembering that Daphne was quite possibly the most dangerous of all the potential variables. He leaned his back against the door. Perhaps she wouldn't know he was there.

"I KNOW YOU'RE THERE, ZIGGY!" Daphne shouted, mere inches away from his head, the force of her words making the door between them reverberate. He opened it, just a crack. Daphne thrust the end of her walking stick into the gap, narrowly missing jabbing him in the eye, and levered the door open wide enough to push her way past him.

"Right," she said. "We need to sort out this pickle you're in."

Ziggy sighed. "Don't even bother suggesting we go to the police," he said. "If I'm labeled a grass, my life, and Kylie's, really will be over."

"Believe me, I have no desire to go anywhere near the police, either," said Daphne, who had dragged the details of Ziggy's situation from him after she'd "rescued" him from the pub. "We're cutting out the middlemen and going straight to see the chap responsible for this irresponsible behavior of yours. What's his name?"

"Floyd," mumbled Ziggy.

"Speak up!" said Daphne.

"Floyd," mumbled Ziggy, a fraction louder.

"Go get dressed. I'll sit with Kylie," said Daphne.

When Ziggy returned, Daphne and Kylie were engrossed in something on Daphne's iPhone.

"What are you watching?" said Ziggy. Not because he cared, but because he was trying to delay the inevitable.

"Ask Iona," said Daphne. "This extraordinary young woman— Iona Iverson—helps people with their problems on YouTube. She tells it exactly like it is. She gets millions of views. It's hilarious, isn't it, Kylie?"

Kylie grinned back at Daphne, and clapped her tiny hands together. Ziggy didn't know if his daughter genuinely loved Daphne, or if she had Stockholm syndrome.

"Are you thinking she could help me?" said Ziggy, looking at the woman on screen and realizing that his definition of "young" and Daphne's were not the same.

"Good God, no," said Daphne. "Your little problem requires more . . . specialist knowledge. She's a lesbian, you know. I've always fancied having a go at being a lesbian."

Ziggy was so thrown by Daphne's lesbian ambitions that he forgot to ask the most crucial question: What specialist knowledge?

Floyd had a lookout stationed on the wall, as usual, swinging his legs and exhaling clouds of sickly sweet vape fumes.

"Are you sure this is a good idea, Daphne?" Ziggy whispered to her as they approached. "You really don't know what you're dealing with here."

"I can assure you, I do," said Daphne.

"It could end really badly," said Ziggy.

"For someone, maybe, but not for me," said Daphne. "And not for you or Kylie. Trust me."

Ziggy had to stop her. If Daphne ended up in the hospital—or worse—he'd never forgive himself.

"Daphne, let's just walk on by," he said, grabbing her by the sleeve and trying to drag her through the estate entrance. Daphne just dug in her heels and pulled out her arm, leaving him holding an empty jacket and looking like a cloakroom attendant.

"OI, YOU!" she shouted at the lookout. "I NEED TO SPEAK TO FLOYD."

The lookout peered down at her and laughed. "He's all out of dementia meds, grandma," he said.

Daphne gave him the sort of look that would have crumpled any-one not backed up by the sheer force of Floyd.

"OK. I'll speak to him," he said, rolling his eyes then turning away from them and talking into his phone. A few seconds later, he said, "Floyd says to come to his office. Ziggy knows the way."

Ziggy nodded, although the only other time he'd had an invite to the "office" was when Floyd had kicked the crap out of him for los-ing that package. It was the last place in the world he wanted to go back to. He wondered if there were still patches of his blood and vomit on the concrete floor.

Ziggy steered Kylie's pushchair toward the row of garages at the back of the estate, Daphne following close behind. When he reached the right one, he knocked.

"It's Ziggy," he said, forcing the reluctant words out of his mouth. Nothing happened. "Floyd's expecting me," he said, his head up against the metal door.

The garage door opened, just enough to let them through if they ducked a little, then closed with a metallic bang. The garage was lit by a single, bare, flickering light bulb hanging from the ceiling. Two or three flies buzzed around it, like electrons around a nucleus.

Floyd sat in a vast leather reclining chair, playing some game on a PlayStation that involved copious amounts of killing. He was probably limbering up for the real thing.

"You wanted to talk to me, grandma," he said, not taking his eyes off the screen.

"Yes. And look at me when you're speaking to me," said Daphne. Ziggy tensed, waiting for the inevitable explosion. Nobody talked to Floyd like that and got away with it. Nobody apart from Daphne, it appeared.

"Ha ha! You've got balls, I'll give you that," said Floyd, handing his controller to one of his minions to continue playing for him, and swiveling his chair to face Daphne. "So, what do you want?"

"I want you to leave Ziggy alone," she said. "He can't work for you. He has exams to do, and a child to look after."

"No can do, babushka," said Floyd. "He owes me."

"Don't you think it's a bit of a coincidence that someone just *happened* to steal his backpack at exactly the time he was carrying your package? And less than an hour after he'd told you he wanted to quit being your errand boy?" said Daphne. That thought had occurred to Ziggy, but he'd dismissed it. He was just incredibly unlucky. The chances of one of his sperm hitting the jackpot after just one unimpeded outing had been remote, too. And yet, here he was.

"You think it wasn't stolen at all?" said Floyd, narrowing his eyes. "You think he's been lying to me?" Oh God, she was just making things so much worse. *Shut UP, Daphne.*

"Look. I was in this game long before you were even born," said Daphne. "And I played it far better and harder than you. The people who worked for me could have chewed you and your minions up for breakfast, you pathetic little waste of space of a man." *Argh, stop, Daphne, STOP.*

"Careful how you speak to me, old woman," said Floyd, but he was watching her with amused interest rather than aggression.

"You're not even clever. It's the oldest trick in the book. You get one of your own people to steal your own stash from your courier, thereby ensuring that they're in hock to you for the foreseeable future," said Daphne. "That package wasn't stolen at all, was it? It was brought straight back to you. You beat Ziggy up for fun, and now you're ruining his life, just so you have a free dogsbody."

Ziggy waited for Floyd's angry denial, but he just leaned back in his chair and laughed. Was Daphne right? Had he been manipulated all this time?

"Look, I tell you what I'll do, grandma, since I like your style," said Floyd. "You give me that necklace, and we'll call it quits." He gestured at the diamanté choker around Daphne's neck.

There was a pause, while Daphne twisted the glittering stones at her throat.

"OK," she said, eventually. "But you're to leave Ziggy and his family alone. And tell all your friends to back off, too. *Capisce?*" She unclasped the necklace and passed it to Floyd.

"Sure. Whatever," said Floyd, tucking the necklace into his jeans pocket. It dangled from the top like a sparkling serpent, searching for air. "Now, bugger off. I'm busy." He took the controller back from the minion and turned to face the screen.

"I can't believe that just happened," said Ziggy as they walked back toward his flat. "How did you know all that stuff?"

"I watch a lot of television," said Daphne. "That was a mixture of *Happy Valley* and *The Sopranos*. Now, you need to get back to school and get your life back on track as quickly as possible, or I'll make you wish you were dealing with Floyd and his gang again. Understand?"

"Yes, ma'am," said Ziggy. "But, Daphne, I'm worried about that necklace. What's going to happen when Floyd realizes those stones aren't real?"

"Mmm. I'm worried about that necklace, too," said Daphne. "Time's running out, Ziggy."

"Time for what?" said Ziggy, but she just shook her head, leaving an awkward silence hanging in the air between them.

Then Ziggy had an idea. A way to show Daphne how incredibly grateful he was for what she'd done for him and Kylie. She'd be thrilled. He was a genius.

"Daphne," he said. "Would you consider being Kylie's god-mother? We'd love it if you would."

There was a pause. Daphne was obviously trying to work out how best to express her enthusiasm.

"Don't be bloody ridiculous, Ziggy," she said. "Of course I can't. What an incredibly stupid idea."

That was not the reaction he'd expected. But then, nothing about Daphne was what one would expect.

Lydia

Right, is everyone clear?" said Daphne, pointing at them somewhat aggressively with her piece of chalk. They'd borrowed the children's blackboard from the nursery next door, and Daphne had been outlining the plan, titled "LYDIA'S REVENGE," and the roles each of them were to play. She'd made them all repeat the instructions she'd given them until she was satisfied they'd remembered every detail.

Daphne was almost unnervingly impressive. So clear, logical, and persuasive. Anyone would have thought she'd been outlining complex strategies for years.

The problem was, Lydia couldn't even remember agreeing to the idea. Had she? It was her name in block capitals on the top of the blackboard, but she felt as if she'd just been swept up by the fast-flowing momentum of the whole thing, without a chance to think, let alone disagree.

"Are we really certain about this, Daphne?" she said. "Isn't it a little over the top? I'm sure the problems in our marriage were as much my fault as . . ."

She was interrupted, not for the first time, by a chorus of "IT'S NOT YOUR FAULT, LYDIA," from her seniors.

"He's not going to come to any actual physical harm, my dear," said Art. "His punishment is entirely in proportion to the crime. Now, I have a little something for everyone."

Art opened the bag that was sitting on his lap and produced six brand-new walkie-talkies, which he handed round. Lydia picked one up, turning it over in her hands and feeling like Kate Fleming in *Line of Duty*.

"You have to make sure you're tuned to channel three—then, so long as you're in range, we can all communicate with each other," Art said. "Also, don't forget to take photos, which you need to send to William. Surreptitiously, obviously."

"Uh, Art, don't take this the wrong way, but where did you get these walkie-talkies from?" said Lydia, who wasn't going to have her fingers burned twice.

"From a shop," said Art who, judging by his expression, had actually taken it the wrong way. "Don't worry. I paid for them."

"With my money," added Daphne.

"Why don't we just use a WhatsApp group?" said Lydia.

"A what group?" said Ruby, which rather answered her question.

"Have you seen how slowly Anna and William type?" said Art. "Anyhow, walkie-talkies are more fun, and you get to say 'Over and out,' 'Do you copy?' and 'Roger that.'"

"*Roger that*," said William, giggling. "Could be misleading. Ow!" He rubbed his forehead, where he'd just been hit by a piece of chalk, lobbed with impressive accuracy by Daphne.

"This is no time for your childish schoolboy puns," she said. "Right, let's synchronize watches. It's four p.m. That's T minus two hours. Everyone, get to your stations and we'll meet back here when it's all over."

Art

rt put his hand in his pocket and felt the stiff edges of an envelope. How strange. He was sure his pocket had been empty when he'd left home. Had he started stealing things subconsciously? That would not be a welcome development.

He pulled out the envelope and stared at it. *Art* was printed boldly in the center, in neat, cursive handwriting. How on earth had it got there without him having noticed?

Art opened the envelope, pulled out a single sheet of high-quality notepaper, and held it at arm's length, since he didn't have his reading glasses with him. The words gradually came into focus.

Art,

I'm sorry.

D.

Art smiled. That obviously hadn't taken Daphne long to write, but he genuinely appreciated it. Perhaps she wasn't such an evil old bat after all. Maybe they could even be friends. The woman had balls, and life was actually a lot more interesting with her around. Not always in a good way, admittedly.

For a minute, Art almost forgot why he was there, but pulled himself together, just in time.

"Subject is leaving the building. Do you copy? Over," he said, from his lookout point opposite the entrance to Jeremy's office, in the heart of the financial district.

"Loud and clear! Moving into position," said Anna.

"You have to say 'Over,'" said Art. "Over."

"Why?" said Anna.

"So everyone knows you've finished speaking. Over," said Art.

"You can tell I've stopped speaking when it goes quiet," said Anna.

"He's approaching the bicycle racks!" said Art. "There's a huge crowd already!"

"You didn't say 'Over,'" said Anna.

"I'm getting this all on film. Over," said William, who had positioned himself in a rooftop bar with a selection of extremely powerful lenses.

The channel went silent as they watched Jeremy push his way through the crush to find his scooter. The crowd parted easily around him. Art imagined he'd been elbowing his way to the front of the pack since he was a toddler.

Jeremy stared at the assembled bicycles and scooters, his brow furrowed, then took off his glasses and rubbed his eyes, as if that would make the extraordinary sight in front of him go away.

In the exact spot where he'd chained up his top-of-the-range scooter that morning was a giant, pale-pink knitted penis. Yarnsy, it turned out, had been secretly working on it ever since the accidental slideshow at the nativity, and had donated it to Daphne's plan.

The huge woolen shaft covered the entirety of Jeremy's scooter's front column and handlebars, and two massive knitted testicles covered the front wheel.

Jeremy grabbed the top of the neatly circumcised penis with both hands and tried to pull it off his scooter, but it had obviously been tied tight to the base. Beads of sweat were breaking out on his forehead.

"Is that your dick you're handling, mate?" asked a man with a hipster beard, his phone trained on Jeremy. A ripple of laughter spread in a wave through the crowd.

"Nothing to do with me," replied Jeremy, quickly releasing the phallus and blushing with what looked gratifyingly like deep humiliation.

Art crossed the road as Jeremy strode away from the knitted knob covering his scooter, powered by righteous indignation and fury. Right on cue, Anna, driving her pimped-up mobility scooter, blocked the pavement ahead of him. Jeremy pulled up short with a harrumph of annoyance, and Art, with fingers honed by years of pilfering, reached into his coat pocket and pulled out his mobile phone.

Art gave Anna a thumbs-up signal from behind Jeremy's back, and she moved her scooter out of his path.

"Quick," she said, as soon as Jeremy was out of earshot. "Try the PIN."

Art fumbled with the phone, inputting—as suggested by Lydia—Jeremy's birth date. The phone unlocked.

"The man's an idiot. If you use your birthday as your passcode, you deserve everything you get," said Art, before remembering it was exactly what he'd done. *Note to self: change PIN.*

Art scanned through Jeremy's text history until he found the information he was looking for.

"Daffy, do you copy? Over," he said into his walkie-talkie.

"Reading you loud and clear. Over," said Daphne.

"He's going to a restaurant called Le Pont de la Tour by Tower Bridge. Sounds fancy."

"Pon. It's pronounced Pon, not Pont. It's French. Over," said Daphne.

"Whateveur," said Art, in a cod fench accent.

"See if you can bag us a table and I'll meet you there once I've sent this text," said Art.

"Roger that," said Daphne.

Daphne

aphne sat at a table for two by the window, looking over at majestic Tower Bridge, which was glowing in the sunset. Across the river, she could see the aptly named Gherkin building, which had only just been built the last time she'd been in this neck of the woods, but now looked well settled in. She'd forgotten, holed up in Hammersmith for so many years, what a magnificent city she lived in. She was going to miss it.

She watched an impeccably dressed waiter lead Art over to her table. He was holding firmly on to Art's elbow, as if Art might collapse at any minute.

"We hope you have a wonderful dinner, sir," he said, pulling out the chair for Art, then shaking out the folded linen napkin and placing it on his knee. "We're honored that you chose our establishment for your bucket list."

"*Daphne*," hissed Art, as soon as the waiter had left. "What have you done now?"

"Well, they were fully booked," said Daphne. "For weeks, apparently. So I told them you were dying. Which is true, after all, just

not as imminently as I led them to believe. I said the final item on
your bucket list was dinner at this restaurant, and it couldn't wait a
minute longer. So please try not to look too healthy."

Art sighed and rolled his eyes but, if she weren't entirely mistaken, he also looked just a tiny bit impressed.

"I sent the text," said Art. "She's called Kitty, by the way. Silly
name for a grown woman."

"Well, it worked," said Daphne. "I saw her as I arrived. She was
about to head in, then she looked at her phone and did a U-turn,
looking like the Kitty that had got the cream. It was just in the nick
of time, as Jeremy turned up ten minutes later, looking as cross as
someone who'd recently found their scooter transformed into a
giant woolly penis. He's over there—look."

Jeremy was sitting at a table for two, which was draped in a linen
tablecloth and groaning with silverware and crystal. A champagne
bottle nestled in a large bucket of ice beside him. As they watched,
he acknowledged several of the diners at neighboring tables with a
half wave and a slight tilt of the head. These self-styled Masters of
the Universe communicated in a secret code, it seemed.

Jeremy raised his hand and gestured at a waiter, then pointed at
his menu and issued some instructions which they couldn't hear.

"I came here when Terence Conran first opened it in the early
nineties, with Jack," said Daphne.

"Who was Jack? Your husband?" said Art. And, much to her
surprise, Daphne found she wanted to talk about him. That was
what friends did, wasn't it? They told each other things about themselves that were true. Things that were important. And besides, it
could hardly make any difference now, could it? The countdown
had already started, and there was no stopping it.

So Daphne told Art about growing up as the Hopesburys' foster child, and her desperate desire to belong, pausing only to relay their food order to another obsequious waiter. She told Art how she'd been surrounded by luxury and riches, none of which were hers.

"And then," she said, "I met Jack. And in his smile, I saw everything I'd ever wanted. With Jack by my side, I had the respect, the belonging, and more money than even I had imagined possible. I was only eighteen when I met him."

"What did he do?" asked Art.

"Well, I thought he was just a businessman. A club owner, and import/export," said Daphne. "Needless to say, it was all a bit more complicated than that. I must have been terribly naive, or maybe just deliberately looking the wrong way. By the time I found out the extent of Jack's operations, we were married, and I was so firmly entangled that I couldn't see how I could get out."

Art looked as if he couldn't work out which of his many questions to ask first, which made Daphne realize how much she'd given away. Stupid woman. She needed to deflect the conversation back to Art. There was a question that had been niggling away at her ever since he'd taken her into Kerry's room.

"Art, I don't mean to pry," she said. Although she did. "But, Kerry's room. It looked like it was a room for two children?"

The expression on Art's face was one that Daphne was familiar with. It was how her own face had looked in the mirror, for years after she'd lost Jack. Unbearable grief and sadness, but also an undercurrent of guilt. Or perhaps she was just projecting.

She reached across the table and rested her hand on Art's arm. Then took it away again and shoved it into her lap.

"Kerry was a twin," said Art, so quietly that Daphne had to strain to hear. "Katie, her sister, died, incredibly suddenly, of meningitis. She was just fifteen. Then, just days later, Kerry and her mum left me. They say time heals, but I've never got over it. I think about her, about all of them, every single day."

"I'm so, so sorry," said Daphne who, now she'd got into the habit of apologizing, seemed unable to stop. But there was nothing else she could say. She couldn't imagine what it must be like to have a child, let alone to lose one so very young. Poor, poor Art.

"Is that concern, Daphne? Empathy?" said Art, with a shaky smile.

"No. Indigestion," said Daphne. "I shouldn't have ordered the beef carpaccio. Although it was delicious."

"Why am I not at all surprised that you like eating raw meat?" said Art, shoving the painful memories aside in the practiced manner of someone who'd been doing exactly that for more than thirty years.

"Look," she said, nodding over toward Jeremy. "Idiot man ordered for Kitty, too. Of course he did. I bet she doesn't even like steak. She looks more like a tofu kind of girl."

"What does a tofu kind of girl look like?" asked Art.

"Skinny. Pale. And weak," said Daphne.

"For someone who rails against the stereotypes of aging, you really do make some heinous generalizations," said Art.

They watched as a waiter placed a large rib eye steak in front of Jeremy, and another in the empty place opposite him at the table. Jeremy, who was looking increasingly angry, kept checking his watch and reaching for a phone which wasn't there. According to the plan, Art should have passed it to William, who would have taken it back to Lydia in Hammersmith.

Half an hour later, Daphne had eaten most of her Dover sole, along with half of Art's oysters.

"You can't eat too much," she'd told him as she'd stolen the food from his plate. "You're dying, remember. Your digestion simply isn't up to it."

Jeremy, meanwhile, had finished his steak, and Kitty's was still sitting on the table. Forty pounds' worth of untouched prime organic grass-fed beef. The blood that had seeped from the rare meat was congealing around the edges of the plate. The acquaintances Jeremy had greeted so proudly as he'd arrived were looking over at him, whispering behind their hands.

Jeremy stood up, throwing his napkin onto his chair, and stalked over to the maître d', asking, presumably, for the bill. The fact that the first two cards Jeremy tried to pay with were rejected only accentuated his public humiliation and made it clear that Lydia had executed the financial phase of Daphne's plan. Good girl.

Lydia was out of range, so Daphne pulled out her phone and sent her a text.

All going to plan. He's on his way home now. She resisted the urge to add her name, since Ziggy had informed her that signing your texts was ageing.

"So, now we've played our part, what do we do next?" said Art.

"We order some more wine and ask for the pudding menu," said Daphne. "And for God's sake, try to look at least a little bit sick."

"Spending time with you makes that rather easy, actually," said Art. But he winked at her, turning his words into a joke between friends, rather than an insult.

Daphne smiled and leaned back in her chair. She'd missed having a sparring partner. She hadn't enjoyed herself this much in years.

Lydia

ydia watched Jeremy climbing out of the black cab which had drawn up outside their house. Her hand, pulling back the edge of her bedroom curtain just an inch or two, was trembling, making the fabric twitch. Fear, or just adrenaline? It was hard to tell the difference.

Joe Brent, from two doors down, rushed up to Jeremy, clutching a bottle of what Lydia knew was one of Jeremy's prized Chablis Grand Crus. Lydia was certain Jeremy couldn't remember Joe's name. She did all that stuff. Buying presents, writing thank-you letters, posting Christmas cards, and remembering names. Jeremy just brought in the money, took out the rubbish from time to time after much nagging, and shagged other women.

Lydia couldn't hear what Joe was saying, but imagined it was fulsome gratitude for the generous gift that had been left on his doorstep. Jeremy's posture, and the way he ruffled his hair, conveyed his utter confusion.

Joe waved a piece of paper at him—the one that had been wrapped around the bottle. Lydia knew what it said, as she'd typed and printed it herself.

Please accept this wine with thanks for being such a great neighbor! Do text me a pic of you enjoying it! Love, Jeremy at 34 Hollyoak Road.

Jeremy's mobile number was printed on the bottom along with the words: PS. Save Mandel Community Center for the community!

Lydia had already seen several photos sent to Jeremy's phone of their neighbors enjoying the wine that she and Ruby had spent the past two hours delivering. They'd completely emptied Jeremy's cellar, and it was lovely seeing the joy they'd spread around the neighborhood, even if the drinkers weren't quite the connoisseurs that Jeremy was, and had no idea that the wine they'd been given was worth, in some cases, thousands of pounds.

Number 16 had sent a pic of them all drinking a Pouilly-Fumé Grand Cru with a Nando's takeaway. The teenage kids of Number 27 appeared to be glugging a rare Châteauneuf-du-Pape from tumblers. Number 80 had mixed one of Jeremy's prized Gavi di Gavis with lemonade and ice and were drinking it through a straw. Jeremy was going to be utterly livid.

Lydia held her breath as Jeremy tried to put his key in the lock. She still couldn't believe she'd had the nerve to do all this. Daphne had spent so long drilling her on her parts of the plan that she hadn't really stopped to think. She'd just carefully executed them, one by one. Including calling the emergency locksmith.

"LYDIA!" yelled Jeremy, shouting up at the window she was now crouching under, heart pounding. "LET ME IN! MY KEY DOESN'T WORK!"

Lydia heard Jeremy cursing the door, the key, the world, and, of course, her as he tried over and over again to open a lock made for an entirely different key. He started banging hard on the door with both fists. That must hurt. Poor Jeremy. Perhaps she should just rip up the rest of Daphne's instructions and let him in? After all, she wasn't entirely blameless herself.

"LYDIA, YOU FAT, LAZY, DUPLICITOUS BITCH! OPEN THE FUCKING DOOR!" yelled Jeremy, just a few feet below her.

Forget that. Jeremy deserved everything that was coming for him.

She fumbled for her phone and called Jeremy's number, as per the next item on her list of instructions. Even from up here she could hear the faint ringtone of the phone that Art had liberated from Jeremy's pocket and William had delivered back to Lydia.

The banging on the door stopped, and Lydia risked tweaking the curtain slightly so she could watch Jeremy looking around for the source of the ringing. Within seconds, he'd opened the door to the bin cupboard, and Lydia could see the screen of his phone shining in the dark. She hung up.

Lydia watched as Jeremy read through his recent messages, glaring at the pictures of their neighbors tucking into his wine, while pacing up and down under her window. She wondered if he'd found the most important text yet. The one Art had sent to Kitty from his phone.

I've canceled the table for dinner! I'm coming to stay with you for a few weeks! See you soon!

Within seconds of Art sending that text, Kitty had replied with a flurry of excited messages, liberally scattered with heart emojis of varying colors and, most recently, a pic of Kitty herself, dressed in the sheerest of negligees, draped across a double bed. When she'd seen that one ping onto Jeremy's phone screen, Lydia had rushed to the bathroom and dry-heaved over the lavatory.

Lydia watched as Jeremy picked up the keys to his Mercedes and the small bag of clothes and toiletries, which she'd left with the phone. The bag hadn't been part of Daphne's plan, but it didn't seem fair to leave Jeremy without clean pajamas or a toothbrush.

After a few more expletives yelled at her window, Jeremy walked over to the car.

And left her.

Ziggy

The three weeks of school that Ziggy had missed had felt like months. Ziggy had never imagined he could be so excited about a day of lessons. He was walking around with a stupid grin on his face. Just the unique corridor smell of dust, disinfectant, and the sharp tang of body odor, mixed with illegal vape fumes and wafts of school dinner coming from the kitchens, was making him high. High on the *ordinariness* of it all.

Having seen the alternative, no number of arbitrary rules, pieces of homework, or detentions could dent his mood. There was, however, one encounter he wasn't looking forward to.

Ziggy knocked on the door to Mr. Wingate's classroom.

"Come in!" said Mr. Wingate.

Ziggy pushed open the door and watched the curious, welcoming expression on Mr. Wingate's face harden into one of annoyance.

"So, you've decided to grace us with your presence again, have you, Ziggy?" Mr. Wingate didn't even look up from the pile of papers he was marking. "Are you planning to stick around this time?" he said, as he wrote the words C+ Could try harder in red pen on the top page. Ziggy hoped it wasn't his fault the paper was being marked harshly.

"I'm really sorry, sir," said Ziggy. Words which he knew were wholly inadequate for the task, but he couldn't find the right ones. Numbers were his thing, not words. Numbers always did what you expected, whereas words could so easily be mixed up or misinterpreted. "I got caught up in something rather . . . bad. But it's all sorted now."

"I trusted you, Ziggy. I *believed* in you. I gave up my free time for you," said Mr. Wingate, not sounding angry, but sad. Which was worse. Ziggy knew what was coming next. He'd let Mr. Wingate down, and himself, and Kylie.

"You let me down," said Mr. Wingate. "But, worse than that, you let yourself down. And your daughter."

"I know," said Ziggy, looking down at his feet. "But, please believe me, everything I've been through over the last few weeks has just made me more determined. I have to get out, Mr. Wingate. I have to get Kylie out. I need to make us a better life. And I will do. I know you don't owe me anything, but please will you help me?"

There was a long pause. Mr. Wingate sighed deeply, and drummed his fingers on the desk in front of him. Then, finally, he swung his chair around to face Ziggy, who tried to meet the gaze of the man who held his future in his hands without flinching.

"OK. I'll give you one last chance, Ziggy, since I don't expect you've had many chances in life. But you're going to have to work your arse off to catch up, and your UCAS form is due in by Friday. Don't you dare let me down again," he said.

"I won't, sir. You won't regret it. Thank you, thank you," said Ziggy as he virtually skipped out of the classroom. And bang into Alicia. Shit.

Ziggy took a few paces back, and waited for Alicia to blank him, or shout at him, or march him straight back to the headmaster, with whom Ziggy had just spent the last half hour persuading him to let Ziggy back into school.

"Welcome back, Ziggy," she said, with an actual smile. God, she had a wonderful smile. If you could bottle the effect of that smile, Floyd could sell it on the estate for a fortune. "It's so good to see you!"

"Really?" he said. Had he fallen through a gap in the space-time continuum? That seemed more likely than this reaction. "I thought you'd never want to see me again, let alone talk to me. I'd completely understand if you didn't."

"I had no intention of ever seeing you again, obviously," said Alicia. "I was actually planning to report you to Social Services. But then, I was in orchestra practice, and this extraordinary woman stormed in. Miss Garson stopped the rehearsal and said, 'Can I help you?' and the woman said, 'I urgently need to speak to Alicia. I'm her grandmother.'"

"I take it she wasn't your grandmother?" said Ziggy.

"Absolutely not," said Alicia. "My granny's nowhere near that cool. She could never have blagged her way past the school receptionist, let alone into rehearsal. Anyhow, Miss Garson said she'd have to wait until the end of the session, and she said, 'Surely you have back-up oboists?' When Miss Garson told her I was the only one, she just said, 'Well, that's terribly bad planning, isn't it? But hardly my fault, or my granddaughter's.' And by this point Miss Garson had lost the will to live . . ."

"I know that feeling," said Ziggy. "And that fake grandmother."

"So, I got let off early. And we went for tea in the café, and had a chat," said Alicia.

"I take it her name was Daphne?" said Ziggy.

"It was, actually. She told me all about the gang, Ziggy, and how you'd faced them down and outsmarted them. You were *so brave*," said Alicia, staring at him with an expression he really wished he deserved, but didn't. Not in the slightest.

Ziggy was about to stop her, to explain that it was Daphne who'd pulled him off the sofa he'd been wallowing on and sorted everything, but maybe it wouldn't do any harm to just keep quiet at this point? He could hear his mum saying, *You missed a golden opportunity to stay silent, Ziggy.* Perhaps it was time to start taking her advice.

"Daphne said it's all behind you now, and you're going to completely turn your life around. That's so impressive. She reckons in ten years' time you'll be the most successful man I know," said Alicia. "And you know what?"

"What?" said Ziggy.

"I believe her," said Alicia.

They walked together down the corridor, matching each other's strides. Ziggy reached for Alicia's hand, but she batted his away. Kindly, but firmly.

"I'm not going to call Social Services, Ziggy. And I'd like to be your friend, but don't push it, OK?"

"OK," he replied. Strangely, and just for a moment, Alicia reminded him slightly of Daphne. Perhaps Daphne was a little bit catching. Like a virus, but a good one. On balance.

Alicia chattered away about ordinary stuff, like the auditions for the school play, who was dating who and what was for lunch.

Ziggy didn't think he'd ever felt so happy.

Lydia

All of Lydia's worst nightmares had come true.

She was totally alone. Abandoned. The girls had gone back to university, and Jeremy had moved in with another woman, one at least twenty years younger, and several sizes slimmer, than Lydia. Apart from her very meager salary, and the fighting fund she'd been able to squirrel away from Jeremy's current accounts while she'd had access to his mobile phone, she had no ongoing means of support. There was no way she could afford their mortgage repayments, let alone anything else.

Yet Lydia hadn't felt this free, this full of optimism, this young since she was first married. She was invincible. Well, maybe not invincible, but certainly relatively proficient. She'd even bagged up her entire collection of self-help books and taken them to the charity shop. Except for Michelle Obama, obviously. She didn't need all the self-help anymore, since she'd realized she was entirely capable of helping herself.

Lydia walked toward the community center carrying a lemon drizzle cake and wearing a pair of Daphne's tight leather trousers and platform shoes. The trousers were squeaking a little unnervingly, and her journey took her much longer than usual, on account of the shoes, and because she kept being stopped by neighbors telling her how much they'd enjoyed Jeremy's wine. She'd never felt so popular! Revenge, it appeared, had never tasted so sweet. Or fruity, or oaky, or with delicate undertones of black currant.

Today, she was finally going to get to use the macramé plantholder kits she'd had lined up for weeks. It would be such fun, and an entirely age-appropriate activity, thank goodness.

"Come in, Lydia!" said Art as she arrived. "We have a surprise lined up for you."

Lydia sighed. She wished that, just once, she'd be allowed to set the agenda and be in control. Her so-called charges seemed to be constantly taking charge. If it hadn't been for the homemade cakes she always brought with her, she'd have been utterly redundant.

"Popcorn, madam?" asked Anna, gesturing at a collection of buckets of popcorn in the basket of her mobility scooter. Great. It appeared they didn't even need her cake.

Wordlessly, Lydia put down the cake, took some popcorn, and followed Art into the darkened room. All the blinds were down, and the chairs were arranged in rows, pointing toward a projector screen.

Lydia had a terrible sense of déjà vu. Last time she'd watched a slideshow in this hall, it had not ended well.

"Sit! Sit!" said William. "Now the guest of honor is here, we're all ready to go!"

Lydia sat down, next to Ruby, who patted her knee. Ruby's own knee was covered, as always, in knitting.

Some music started playing. "The female of the species is more deadly than the male," sang the artist of a song she remembered from the 1990s, when she and Jeremy had been newlyweds. She remembered Jeremy scoffing at the lyrics.

"I chose the music!" said Daphne, from right behind her. Daphne had a habit of just appearing from nowhere, exactly where the action was taking place, as if the usual rules of entrances and exits didn't apply to her.

"That figures. Ow!" said Art, as Daphne poked him in the back with her walking stick.

A title came up on the screen: THE MANDEL COMMUNITY CENTER SOCIAL CLUB PRESENTS . . . The words faded out, to be replaced with JEREMY HAS A BAD DAY. Followed by: OR LYDIA'S REVENGE.

Everyone cheered and clapped. There were even a few whoops.

Lydia took a large handful of popcorn and leaned back in her chair. This might be more fun than the macramé plant-holder kits, after all.

William had, it appeared, edited together all the photos they'd taken on the night of Daphne's grand plan, so they could each enjoy the parts of the action they'd missed. The first pictures on the screen were of Jeremy trying to remove the giant wool penis from his scooter.

"Look! It's a huge prick! Holding another huge prick!" said Art. "Oh, I'm sorry, Lydia. You must have loved him once."

She had loved him once, more even than she'd loved herself. And perhaps that was the problem.

"I think that's some of Yarnsy's best work yet," said Anna. They all seemed to have an unspoken agreement to play along with Ruby's incognito act.

"You think so?" said Ruby. "Yes, I like the attention to detail.

Did you notice the pronounced vein running down the shaft? And the little nest of pubic hairs at the base?"

"I did, Ruby, I did," said Anna. "She's a genius."

"Or he. Or they. Nobody knows," said Ruby.

"Right," said Anna, rolling her eyes. "Nobody knows." Anna leaned in toward Daphne and whispered, "How long do we have to carry on with this charade?"

"What charade?" said Daphne.

The next picture, caught by a telephoto lens, was Art's hand removing a phone from Jeremy's pocket, then the camera pulled back to reveal Anna blocking the pavement with her mobility scooter.

"I think I was a highwayman in a former life," said Anna. "Stand and deliver!"

"God help us," said William.

The next series of photos were taken in a fancy restaurant. Jeremy sitting alone with two giant steaks, looking increasingly cross. Then there was a selfie of Art and Daphne, champagne glasses raised, smiling broadly. Lydia suspected it was the first selfie they'd ever taken, since it was crooked, a little blurry, with the edge of a thumb added and half of Art's head missing.

"What's that photo doing in there?" said Daphne. "It's not part of the plan."

"I had to include it," said William. "Because you two look like you actually like each other."

"Humph," said Daphne and Art simultaneously.

Next came shots of Jeremy being accosted by the grateful neighbor with the wine, followed by video footage of him shouting up at Lydia's window, his angry face resembling a stewed plum.

Lydia almost felt sorry for him. But not quite.

The final photos were a complete surprise. Jeremy with the door of his Mercedes open, vomiting into a gutter.

"What's going on there?" asked Lydia.

"Well, I know this bit wasn't in Daphne's outline, but Art and I did a teeny bit of improvisation," said William. "You know we asked you what Jeremy loved most in the world, after his daughters? And you said his wine cellar and his Mercedes?"

Lydia nodded.

"Well, you and Ruby handled the wine cellar, and Art and I dealt with the Mercedes," said William.

"What did you do to it?" asked Lydia.

"We put a rotting kipper under the bonnet," said Art, giggling. "When the engine warms up, the smell goes through the heating system."

"You're such children," said Daphne. "And that's hardly original— such a cliché."

"I prefer to think of it as an *old classic*, rather than a cliché. A bit like us, Daffy," said Art, and he grinned at Daphne. *Daffy?!?* Daphne was *not* going to like that. It was hardly respectful. Lydia waited for the inevitable explosion, but Daphne smiled back at Art, looking almost . . . pleased.

"Play it again!" said Ruby, but before William could restart the show, the door opened, letting a shaft of light in from the hall.

"Err, hello?" said a man. "Is this the Senior Citizens' Social Club?"

"Yes, it is," said Lydia, jumping to her feet and rushing over to turn on the lights. "I'm Lydia. I'm in charge." *In theory*, she nearly added.

"Where are all the others?" said the man, looking around as if there might be twenty more OAPs hiding behind the furniture. Lydia hadn't actually told anyone at the council that she only had six club members, and one of them was technically dead.

"Oh, they're doing the alternative outing today," lied Art, before Lydia had a chance to tell the truth.

"What outing?" said the man.

"Uh, a tour of the local cemeteries," said Daphne, picking up the baton.

"Oh, right. I can see how that might be useful," said the man. "I could arrange a trip to our local hospice, too, if you like. Forward planning is essential! Anyhow, I wanted to do you the courtesy of coming down in person to let you know that the council had a vote last night on the future of the community center." He paused, as if waiting to be thanked for his consideration. They stared at him, silently.

"We've had a great offer from a developer," he continued. "And the money they're offering will benefit the whole community. So, unless anyone can find the hundred thousand pounds we'd need for repairs and maintenance by two weeks today, we're going to cut our losses, board the place up, and hand over the keys. I'm sorry."

He didn't look sorry.

"Wait. I thought it was eighty thousand we needed," said Daphne, as if it made any difference which unfeasibly large amount was required.

"That's just for the initial repairs. Then another twenty for ongoing maintenance and contingency," said the man.

"And is anyone close to raising that money?" said Art.

"Not as far as I'm aware," said the man.

"We have three hundred and sixty-five pounds and forty-nine pence in the appeal fund so far," said Lydia.

The man chuckled and left, sucking all the air out of the room before closing the door behind him.

"We're doomed," said Lydia, sitting down heavily. She'd already lost her husband, her daughters (most of the time), and her primary means of support. She couldn't lose her job, too, or the club members, who she counted as friends. Which may be why she lacked any form of authority.

"Two weeks today," said Daphne. "That's the day of the talent show. We still have time."

"What talent show?" asked Lydia.

"Maggie and Art have won a place in a TV talent show. The prize money is a hundred grand," said Daphne.

"Blimey! Do they have any chance of winning?" said Lydia, trying not to sound skeptical.

"Totally!" said Daphne, who either had huge faith in their dog or was a very good liar. Lydia suspected the latter.

"We only have fourteen days to get a really slick act together," said Art. "It's a tall order."

"You know what we should do?" said William. "Art and Maggie might get a sympathy vote, but they're not going to get the 'aah' factor."

"Thanks, mate," said Art. "But I take your point."

"We need to add some cute into the mix. Remember the nativity? It was genius, until it all went tits up. We should rope in some of the kids," said William.

"Brilliant idea," said Art. "I'll talk to Janine."

"In the meantime, does anyone fancy doing some macramé?" said Lydia.

Daphne

Daphne stared at her whiteboard from her bed.

She'd managed to cross off Deal with Ziggy's gang, and had thrown in Sort things with his love interest as an extra bonus item. She'd also engineered Revenge on Jeremy rather spectacularly, due to all her friends pitching in to help.

All her friends. Daphne rolled those words around in her head, loving the way they sounded, the way they made her feel. God, she was going soft in her old age. She'd always prided herself on being self-sufficient. She was a lone wolf. Even during all those years she'd been with Jack, she'd not had any friends to speak of, besides him. She'd not needed any; people were wary of her and she could never trust their motives, which made genuine friendships impossible.

Daphne wasn't entirely sure that her new friends actually liked her, but she liked them, on the whole, so that was a good start, wasn't it? Unfortunately, it was also an end. The ticking of the clock had become louder and louder until it was about the only thing she could hear. It was keeping her awake at night. She was tired. Tired of it all.

She still had three items on the list (having dealt with the lack of loo roll some time ago). Find Art's daughter she'd managed to delegate to some professionals. She had no doubt that a top TV production company, who'd had a perfect feel-good story dangled in front of them, would be able to locate Kerry in no time.

The next item—Save the community center—was the real problem. The talent show appeared to be their only chance, and she really wanted to be there to make sure it all went to plan. Art was enthusiastic, and dangerously softhearted but couldn't really be trusted not to make a huge mess of it all. Just look what had happened at the nativity.

So, she had to stick around for nine more days. Nine more days of looking over her shoulder and having palpitations whenever she heard someone call her name. Nine more days of ducking her head and rushing off whenever anyone on the street caught her eye for a minute too long.

And she didn't want to leave. Last time it had been an escape. A relief. It had felt like amputating a gangrenous limb. Incredibly hard and life-altering, but the only way to survive.

This time was different. She'd started to make a life for herself, a life of her own, and she really didn't want to abandon it. She wasn't sure she'd have the strength to start over, and even if she did, she'd only end up in this position again, eventually. Building a life meant making connections, and that meant being visible, which made you vulnerable.

All this ruminating led her right back to Sidney. Could she tell him she was leaving? Could she maybe even persuade him to come with her? She'd love to have a wingman. It would make this next step feel like an adventure instead of a punishment. They could be like Bonnie and Clyde, without being shot to death, obviously.

She stared at the final remaining item on her list: Ask Sidney to come with me? Then picked up her phone, found Sidney's number and typed out a text.

Daphne pushed open the door to the café and paused for a minute while she surveyed the room. Sidney was, as ever, early. Waiting for her. As she approached the table, he pushed back his chair and stood up, leaning forward to kiss her, as he always did. Such a gentleman, which was a rare thing these days.

But something was different. Sidney, usually so relaxed and confident, was on edge. Daphne was an expert on *edge*; she could spot it a mile off. She was, after all, often the reason for it.

"I ordered your double espresso," he said.

"With two sugars?" said Daphne.

"Of course," said Sidney. How nice it was to have someone who knew exactly how you liked your caffeine.

"And I took the liberty of choosing a couple of slices of cake. I thought you'd like carrot cake."

"Fabulous. One of your five a day. Two, if it has lemon frosting," said Daphne, shrugging off her coat, which she hung over the back of her chair.

"I have something I need to talk to you about," he said. "Something important."

"OK," she replied. "I have something important to talk to you about, too, but you go first."

"It's Sonny," said Sidney, with a heavy sigh. "He's been injured. Just outside Kyiv. I thought he was staying at the border. I had no idea he was venturing so far into Ukraine, to help people escape. Stupid, stupid boy. I warned him not to be a hero."

Daphne took his hand in both of hers. "I'm so sorry," she said. "How bad is it? Is he going to be OK?" She couldn't bear the idea of this young, vital man, so brave and kind, having his life cut short, or forever altered.

"I don't know," said Sidney, resting his head on their clasped hands. She could feel his ragged, shallow breath, hot against her skin. "I need to get him airlifted back home. But it's going to cost ten thousand pounds."

"Do you have the money?" said Daphne.

"Yes," he replied. "But I can't access it quickly enough. It'll take a month to liquidate the capital, and I need to get Sonny back here now. Daphne, I hate to ask this of you, but I feel so close to you. You're the only woman since my darling wife died who I've been able to love."

"*Whom* I've been able to love," said Daphne, which, judging by Sidney's expression, wasn't the reaction he'd been expecting to his declaration.

"So, I wonder if you might be able to help me? Help Sonny. I'll pay you back, of course. With interest," he continued, looking up at her, unblinking, waiting for her response.

"Sure," she said. "Of course, I'll help you."

Sidney beamed and passed her a piece of paper with some numbers scrawled in Biro.

"Honestly, I can't thank you enough. Here are the bank details. You need to transfer the money by this time tomorrow," he said.

Daphne picked up the paper and put it in her pocket. "What are friends for?" she said.

"What did you want to talk to me about?" said Sidney, all remnants of his earlier distress having vanished now a solution had presented itself.

"You know, I can't even remember," said Daphne.

Daphne stood in front of her whiteboard, pen in hand. Underneath Save the community center she wrote Buy butter. Then she crossed out Ask Sidney to come with me? and replaced it with Make Sidney pay.

What kind of stupid fool did he take her for? The injured child in a war zone? That was the second-oldest trick in the book. She remembered the words she'd written with such hope and determination on her whiteboard, two months ago: Be more trusting. And look where that had got her. She was just as stupid as Sidney.

She sat down heavily on her bed, took the piece of paper Sidney had given her from her pocket, ripped it into tiny pieces, then put them into the heavy cut-glass ashtray on her bedside table and set them alight with her Zippo.

For the first time since she could remember, Daphne cried. She'd thought she was gradually learning to love again. She'd thought she'd found someone who could genuinely love her back. She'd thought she could see a future where she wasn't alone.

But it had all been an illusion. Her wingman had just shot her in the back of the head. She'd been betrayed by someone close to her.

Karma, it appeared, was a bitch.

Art

They had just four days left before the talent show, which was being broadcast live on national TV. A film crew had already been to the hall, to interview Art and Maggie, and to find out more about Art's "emotional backstory." Lydia had filled them in on the plight of the community center, and they'd filmed some really cute footage of the kids from the nursery, playing with Maggie and fluffing their lines.

The act was shaping up nicely. They might actually do this. They just needed to focus. Nursery pickup was in half an hour.

"Lucky," said Art, "come and sit here." He gestured at the chair next to him and Lucky sat down. The boy who, just a couple of months ago, had seemed to exist in a different dimension from everybody else. Present, but not connected, like a TV in standby mode.

"I just wanted to say how proud I am of you. You're a fine actor," said Art. "And it doesn't matter a jot if you don't want to speak. Charlie Chaplin never did, and he was one of the most iconic actors of all time. I've not had many speaking parts myself, to be honest."

Lucky said nothing, and just stared at his feet, but Art was sure he could see the corners of his mouth twitch in a vague semblance of a smile.

A head poked round the door. Ziggy, with Kylie.

"Uh, are we in time for our starring role?" he said. "I left school as early as I could."

"Yup. We're just starting another run-through," said Art from his director's chair. "Cue music!"

The soundtrack to *Mission: Impossible* filled the room, and Maggie, dressed in a red polka-dot neck scarf and black eye mask, made her way through a complex obstacle course of tunnels, ladders, and planks, coaxed by Art with pieces of sausage, toward a small fridge with *SAFE* written on it.

"OK, Zack, you're on!" said Art. Zack appeared, dressed as a policeman, holding a plastic gun.

"Thief!" he said, pointing at Maggie. "She's trying to steal the crown jewels!"

"Stop right there!" said Tallulah, also in uniform, brandishing a truncheon.

Maggie, knowing there were treats inside the safe, pulled the door open by grabbing a short rope attached to the handle with her teeth.

Art held his breath. They'd been trying to teach her to pick up the bag filled with plastic jewelry for the past three days, but she'd not managed it yet.

Maggie, smelling the sausage nestled among the jewels, grabbed the bag in her mouth and ran across the stage, chased by the children.

Lucky, the final policeman—with no lines, obviously—tried to block her path, but she, as practiced, ducked straight between his legs. Then, as Ziggy wheeled Kylie across the stage in her pushchair, Maggie dropped the jewels in Kylie's lap, jumped into the chair, and burrowed under the blanket, where Art had hidden more sausage.

The three miniature policemen looked around for the jewel thief, puzzled, while Ziggy slowly pushed Kylie and Maggie offstage.

The audience rose to their feet, which, in most cases, took a few seconds, some false starts, and several wobbles. It gave a whole new meaning to "stand-up comedy." They cheered wildly.

"YOU DID IT, ART!" shouted William. Always his greatest cheerleader.

"Maggie did it," said Art, slightly misty-eyed, as the children crowded around the dog, patting and stroking her. "And the kids, of course."

Art looked at his friends, thinking what a wonderful thing an appreciative audience was.

A group of men, wearing hard hats and high-viz jackets, as if they were in imminent danger, barged into the room without even knocking.

"Don't mind us," they said. "We'll work around you."

"What are they doing?" hissed Daphne in Art's ear.

"Sshhh!" he said as they all strained to listen.

"These are just stud walls, not load-bearing, so they'll come out easily. We'll take them down first," said one of the men, rapping on the internal wall with his knuckles.

"It's not going to take much to bring down that ceiling," said another, gesturing up at the gaping hole at the cordoned-off end of the room. "Thank goodness there's no asbestos."

"They're planning our sodding demolition! Before we've even left the building," said William.

The group bustled out of the room, into the nursery next door, leaving a pile of coats, an umbrella, and a stack of A4 paper on the table. They'd barely closed the door before Daphne was leafing through the documents.

"Finances, schedules, measurements, contact lists," she said.

"I think we need a quick break from rehearsals," said Lydia. "Anyone fancy a crafting session?"

What was the woman *thinking*? They had a community center to save, and the demolition team were, quite literally, on their doorstep. This was no time for *crafting*.

"I was thinking a little *origami*," said Lydia. And the penny dropped.

"Is that a pair of scissors you have in your bun, Daphne?" said Lydia.

Daphne reached round to the back of her head, then stared at the crafting scissors in her hand, and smiled.

By the time the hard-hat brigade returned, everyone was busily at work, trying to appear nonchalant as the men looked around in confusion for their documents.

"Uh, have you seen the stack of papers I left here?" said one. "They're rather important."

"Oh, gosh. I am sorry," replied Lydia. "I thought that was our waste paper for crafting. We always try to recycle, you see."

"So, where are they?" asked the man.

Art gestured to the table in front of the assembled group of seniors and toddlers, which was covered in a pile of origami swans.

Daphne

It was the day before the talent show.

Daphne made her way through the estate toward Ziggy's flat. She was almost disappointed to see no sign of Floyd, or his minions. She'd rather enjoyed their little chat. Her phone pinged with another message from Sidney.

Is the money on the way? Why is it taking so long? Sonny is deteriorating. Every hour counts.

She resisted the urge to throw her phone to the ground and stamp it into smithereens. If it hadn't been an iPhone 14 Plus, with a dual-camera system, face ID, and 512 gigabytes of storage, she would have done.

Could she possibly be wrong about him? Perhaps Sonny really did exist, and Sidney did genuinely love her. Perhaps he really did need the money and was intending to pay her back.

Maybe she just saw evil where it didn't exist. Maybe the evil was only inside her, and her reticence and distrust were going to kill an innocent boy. A dying hero.

Or maybe not.

She rang the bell and, within seconds, the door was opened by Ziggy.

"Thanks for doing this so quickly, Ziggy," she said. "I'm not getting you into trouble at school, am I?"

"No, no," he replied. "I have two free periods this afternoon. I've been working my arse off, actually. I've had an offer from Bath uni. One of the best for computer science. They've given me a lower offer than usual on account of my *extenuating circumstances.*" He made air quotes around the words "extenuating circumstances." "But I still have to get two As and a B."

"That's amazing, Ziggy," said Daphne, giving him a pat on the back. Because she was the kind of person who did physical displays of affection now, it seemed. Who would have thought? "It would be so good for you and Kylie to get away from here. From Floyd and all that baggage."

"I know. But I'm worried about leaving my mum here on her own. She won't come with me. She says she's never lived anywhere other than Hammersmith and she's not starting now. All her friends are here," said Ziggy. "By the way, Floyd was arrested yesterday. Nobody seems to know why."

"Mmm. The possibilities are endless," said Daphne. "It was always going to happen eventually. He's not clever enough to avoid retribution. Anyhow, did you look into those photos I sent you?"

"Yup, I did a reverse image search," said Ziggy, in the reluctant tone of someone with bad news to impart. Or perhaps she was being paranoid?

Ziggy led Daphne over to his computer. She held her breath, grasping at a vanishingly faint hope.

"The pic Sidney used on that dating site—it's on several other sites, too, under different names," said Ziggy, flipping between various windows of dating sites, all showing the same picture that had originally attracted Daphne: a grinning "Sidney," barefoot and laughing on a windswept beach, jeans rolled up to his knees, catching a ball thrown by someone off camera. "I Googled some of those names, and there are several posts online from women who've been conned by him. Women who thought he loved them, and gave him money under what turned out to be false pretenses. They never saw the money again. Or him. I'm so sorry, Daphne." The vanishingly faint hope vanished.

Daphne sighed. "Don't worry, Ziggy. It's what I expected," she said. "And Sonny?"

"He's a genuine hero, in an actual war zone. But he's not called Sonny, and he's not related to Sidney, or whoever Sidney really is," said Ziggy. "As of yesterday, he was alive and well and posting on Instagram from Lviv. What are you going to do now?"

Before Ziggy could reply, the doorbell rang, echoing around the tiny flat.

"Are you expecting anyone?" said Daphne.

"No," said Ziggy, walking over to the door and pressing his eye against the spyhole. "Fuck me. It's the cops."

The bell rang again, longer and more insistent. Ziggy opened the door. There were two police officers standing on the threshold.

"Is your name Ziggy?" said one.

Ziggy nodded. Daphne had never seen someone look so needlessly guilty. She really hoped he got that the university place, because he was never going to be able to pursue a career as a criminal.

"We need to talk to you about a necklace," said the first policeman.

"We arrested a man called Floyd Daniels yesterday, on suspicion of handling stolen goods. But he claims the diamond necklace in question was given to him. By your grandma, apparently. Seems unlikely, but we thought we should check it out. Due diligence."

Daphne stepped forward. She remembered the words on her whiteboard. Make Sidney pay. It seemed an opportunity had presented itself to strangle two birds with one necklace, so to speak.

"It wasn't Ziggy's grandma, officers," she said. "It was me. I gave Floyd the necklace. He didn't steal it at all."

"Well, there's a surprise," said the other officer. "And you are?"

"Daphne Smith," lied Daphne.

"But that rather begs the question, Ms. Smith: where did you get it from? You see, when Floyd tried to pawn it, it triggered an Interpol alert. It was one of a number of items stolen in an infamous heist in 2008. The Jones Gang. You might have heard of them? The culprits are all inside, or dead, but the jewelry was never found."

Ziggy was staring at her, eyes bulging.

"I was given it as a gift," she said. "For Christmas. From my boyfriend. Although sixty-five is probably too old to be described as a boyfriend, don't you think? He said he'd had it for fifteen years, just waiting for the right woman to give it to. But it turned out he wasn't the man I thought he was." She added a theatrical sob.

The policemen tried and failed to hide their mounting excitement.

"What's his name, Ms. Smith?" said the first officer, his pencil hovering expectantly over his notebook.

"Do call me Daphne," she said, with her most winning smile, which wasn't quite as effective as it had been in the old days. "I'm afraid I don't know his name. I thought it was Sidney Wilson, but I've just discovered that he operates under a number of different aliases. He was trying to con me out of rather a lot of money, you see. Ziggy here will show you all the proof. You might want to ask Sidney about that, too, while you're at it."

"Do you have an address for him?" they asked.

"No, he never invited me to his home. Of course, now I know why. But I know where you'll be able to find him in an hour from now," Daphne said.

She took out her phone and typed, **Sorry for the delay. Having problems with the bank transfer. I'm such a Luddite. Can you help? Meet you at our regular café at three p.m.**

The reply came as swiftly as she'd expected.

No problem.

For the second time in her life, Daphne watched as someone who professed to love her was arrested. This time, it hurt a lot less. The first time had felt like watching the gangrenous limb being amputated without the aid of anesthetic. And it had been all the more painful because she'd known that it was entirely her fault.

Daphne sat at the bus stop, across the road from the café, as Sidney emerged in *actual handcuffs*, flanked by her two favorite police officers. They even did the thing she'd seen on TV cop dramas, putting a hand on the top of Sidney's head and ducking him down into the back seat. She waited for the rush of triumph and satisfaction, but she just felt empty. She wondered how long it would take Sidney to convince them he'd never seen her diamond necklace before, and had nothing to do with the Jones Gang. Eventually, she imagined, they'd come back to her and start asking more questions. She'd only bought herself a little more time.

By the time she arrived at the community center, the final dress rehearsal was in full swing, and the excitement was palpable. Lydia spotted her and rushed over.

"Daphne, I need to talk to you," she said, looking worried. But then, Lydia usually looked at least a little worried. "Someone just came looking for you, or for someone who looks like you. He said he knew you from the old days and wanted to catch up. He showed me that video of you—you know, the meme? Edward effing Scissorhands?"

Daphne nodded, her face stonily impassive as fear twisted in her guts.

"Did you tell him where to find me?" she said, her voice a strangled croak.

"Well, no. Because he didn't know your name, you see. He said you were called . . . What was it? I wrote it down on my phone so I wouldn't forget. Here it is! Delilah Jones," Lydia said, triumphantly, waving her phone at Daphne. "So I said I had no idea whatsoever where you were. Was that the right thing to do?" Lydia looked at her, nervously.

"Yes. Thank you, Lydia," she said. "I'd better go now." Which Lydia must have thought odd, given that she'd only just arrived.

She hoped that Lydia didn't Google Delilah Jones. It felt so strange to hear that name again, after so long. So familiar, and yet also the name of a stranger. A very different woman from Daphne.

The countdown clock was rapidly ticking toward zero. Daphne couldn't go home. Not now, or ever. Someone would point them in the right direction. It wasn't safe any longer. She felt a huge pang of sadness for all her lovely things, which she'd probably never see again.

Where could she go?

Daphne, the master strategist, who always had the next moves planned, along with numerous contingency options, was at a loss.

She stood in the entrance hall of the community center, utterly frozen. There were four doors off the hall. The one she'd just walked through, the door to the nursery, the door to the outside, and one remaining.

Daphne opened the final door and found herself in a storage room, filled with spare chairs and tables, some cleaning materials, and a stack of macramé plant-holder kits. There was a tiny window, letting in a little light from the darkening winter sky outside. Daphne dusted off a chair in the corner, sat down in the safety of the gloom, and waited for inspiration to strike.

Lydia

ydia waited until everyone was occupied with the rehearsal, then hid herself away in the little kitchenette. She picked up a knife and shaved off some of the coffee-and-walnut cake she'd baked that morning. It didn't count as an actual slice, more just tidying up the edges. She squinted at the cake. It still wasn't quite even, so she shaved off a little more. Which made it even more lopsided. What a shame.

Lydia ate all the tidied-up pieces of the cake, which was now significantly smaller, and sat down, feeling a little sick. She wiped the icing off her fingers, picked up her phone and Googled Delilah Jones.

The results showed page after page of entries, mainly from the nineties and early noughties. None at all after 2008.

Delilah Jones, it turned out, was a younger, terribly glamorous version of Daphne. There were photos of her at Ascot, Henley, and Wimbledon, at parties and clubs, wearing fabulous jewelry and lush furs, smoking cigarettes in a long cigarette-holder and drinking cocktails. Pictures of Delilah's houses—a country estate in Essex and a grand Georgian town house on Blackheath. One image made

Lydia gasp out loud: Delilah wearing the exact Dior jacket that Daphne had given to Lydia.

And always, right next to Delilah, his hand draped proprietorially around her waist or her shoulders, or clutching her at the elbow: Jack Jones. Her husband. Jack Jones, the notorious East End gangster and thief, who'd evaded the police for decades before they'd finally arrested him and his accomplices for emptying the safe of a famous jeweler in Belgravia. The gang had all gone to prison, but most of the jewelry had never been found.

And Delilah Jones, it seemed, had just disappeared.

Art

rt said goodbye to Lydia, who was going to take Maggie home for a well-deserved rest before her big day tomorrow. He suddenly felt unbearably, unimaginably tired. Was all this effort a terrible waste of time?

He picked up the bags containing the costumes and props, and carried them to the storage cupboard in the hall. The hall was filled with parents and carers, collecting the children from the nursery. He felt an overwhelming urge to be alone, just for a moment. He quietly pushed the door to the cupboard open, slipping into the gloom behind it and placing his bags down in the corner. The room was filled with spare chairs and tables, so he groped for the nearest chair and sat down heavily, burying his head in his hands.

He needed a few minutes alone to breathe and pull himself together.

"Hello," said a familiar voice from the corner.

Art started so violently that he nearly tipped his chair over.

"Daphne!" he said. "What the hell are you doing in here?"

"I could ask you the same," she replied.

"I was putting the costumes away," said Art. "And I just needed to escape for a few minutes."

"Ah. Well, I also need to escape," said Daphne. "But rather more permanently."

Art wasn't at all sure where to start with this extraordinary statement.

"Why?" he said.

"I've been hiding for so long, Art," she said. "I don't mean here, in this cupboard; I mean for the past fifteen years. I've done some terrible things, and now it's all catching up with me."

"Hey," said Art, reaching through the dark to hold her hand. It felt softer than he'd imagined. Fragile. And he had a strange urge—which he resisted, of course—to stroke it. "I've done some awful things, too, as you know. You don't get to our age with a completely unblemished record. Not unless you've not lived. The trick is just to try to ensure the balance falls on the side of the good."

"That's kind of you, old man," said Daphne. "But you really don't know me. You don't even know my name. And your part-time shoplifting hobby is nothing like what I've done. Not that it's a competition."

"What is your name, then?" said Art.

"Delilah," said Daphne. "Delilah Jones."

The hallway outside had gone quiet. They heard a voice say, "Come along, Maggie, let's get you home," and the sound of the heavy outer door closing. And a key turning in the lock.

"Oh, bollocks," said Art as the implications hit him. "She's locked us in. How on earth are we going to get out? We could be here all night!"

Daphne just shrugged, as if that were the very least of her problems.

"Do you want to tell me about it, Daffy," said Art, "as it looks like we're both stuck here together for a while?"

"I guess there's no harm in telling the story now," said Daphne. "Since in a day or two I'll either be arrested or dead, or, if I'm lucky, I'll be somewhere else, pretending to be someone else."

"This sounds like a story that needs to be accompanied by tea and cake. Why don't you stay there, and I'll see what Lydia's left in the fridge?" said Art.

By the time Art returned with two steaming mugs of tea and generous slabs of cake, Daphne had uncovered a portable electric heater and found a couple of abandoned coats, one of which she'd spread over her knees.

"I found some of Jeremy's wine, too," said Art, pulling a bottle out of his coat pocket. "Right, talk. I guess this all has to do with your husband? Jack, wasn't it? You told me that he wasn't what he seemed."

"Yes. It turned out he was a thief, too. But on a much more impressive scale than you. No offense."

"None taken," said Art.

"It was impossible to be married to Jack and not get involved. I convinced myself that our crimes were victimless. The only people who suffered from our scams and robberies were the insurance companies and the very rich, who should have been spreading their wealth around more fairly, in any case. They'd inherited their money and their jewels, in most instances. We, on the other hand, had worked for them."

Daphne, who wasn't Daphne, paused to sip her tea. Art, who was completely au fait with this type of self-justification, nodded, but stayed silent, not wanting to break the spell.

"And I was good at it, too," said Daphne. "I was better than Jack, or any of his men, at the strategizing, the delegating, the contingency planning. And I made sure everyone stuck to a strict moral code: no killing, play fair, look after each other."

This, Art realized, would explain Daphne's seamless planning and execution of Lydia's Revenge.

"But I didn't realize that there was a whole other side to Jack's business that he kept from me. Drugs, mainly. And that game wasn't being played fairly. People were being killed—both directly and indirectly. But by the time I found out, I couldn't leave. I was too deeply embedded. Jack would never have let me go. His pride wouldn't have allowed it and, besides, I knew all the secrets."

Art wasn't sure if he was expected to say anything. And he didn't know what to say, in any case. So he settled for, "Are you going to eat that cake?" Daphne shook her head and gestured for him to take it.

"So, as soon as our last job was finished—a huge jewelry heist—I gave the police an anonymous tip-off. Where to find them all, along with enough evidence to put them inside for years, to stop them ruining more lives. And I ran away. And became Daphne," said Daphne, looking as wrung-out as he felt.

"OK. You win," said Art, after a long silence. "Definitely more impressive than my shoplifting hobby."

Daphne smiled. "I thought I told you it wasn't a competition," she said. "I always win competitions."

"This needs wine," said Art. "But we don't have a bottle opener."

"That's what you think," said Daphne as she pulled a slim cork-screw from her bun. How did she always manage to produce exactly what was needed? The woman really was a witch. Although an impressively useful one.

"Why didn't you ask for police protection in exchange for information?" said Art as he poured the wine into the two empty mugs.

"Because Jack had friends *everywhere*," said Daphne. "Including in the police. I'd never have been safe. At least this way, I thought, maybe they'd not know for sure it was me who'd given the tip-off. And the police weren't looking for me. I told you about making the stereotypes work to your advantage?"

Art nodded.

"Well, they didn't believe that a *woman* could have planned all of that. A fifty-five-year-old woman. They thought they had their men all bang to rights. And the gang wouldn't have given me up. Even if they'd suspected I was a grass, they'd have dealt with me themselves, not let the police do it. Honor among thieves, and all that," said Daphne.

"So what's changed?" said Art.

"Well, I came across a small article in a newspaper, a few months ago. It said Jack had died, in the prison infirmary. Lung cancer. So, when my seventieth birthday came around, I thought, *Why not try living again?* You see, I'd created my own prison, which was what I thought I deserved. I'd hardly left my apartment for fifteen years. I thought maybe now I'd done my time, paid my dues. I thought perhaps I'd finally be safe, that the ravages of age could provide the best disguise," said Daphne.

"But I'd stupidly kept hold of the jewelry. And now the police have one of the necklaces. It won't be long before they put two and two together. Also, that awful meme of me must have been noticed by one of the men I'd put away, because someone's been round here, asking after Delilah Jones. I don't expect they're looking for a chat and a cup of tea."

"What are you going to do?" said Art.

"I have a bag packed ready in a locker at St. Pancras, the Eurostar terminal," said Daphne. "I was just waiting for the talent show. And I need another new name, and a passport. But I no longer have the contacts for that kind of thing."

Art put his arm around Daphne, or Delilah, and she leaned her head against his shoulder. They sat in silence, her head growing heavier and heavier, and her breathing deeper, until eventually she fell asleep.

Art's arm started going numb, but he didn't dare move it. Daphne looked like she badly needed a few hours of oblivion.

Art had realized some time ago that it would be easy for them to get out of the hall. All they had to do was phone Lydia and ask her to come back and unlock the door. But Daphne, for all her clever strategizing, obviously hadn't thought of that.

Or perhaps she, like him, preferred to be right here, right now, than anywhere else.

Ziggy

This was shaping up to be the most exciting day of Ziggy's life so far. Even surpassing the birth of his daughter, which, to be honest, hadn't actually been exciting at all, just utterly, incomprehensibly terrifying. He still had vivid flashbacks of the delivery room. Jenna, spread-eagled and sweaty, on the bed, calling Ziggy every name under the sun. Then some that hadn't even been invented yet. Jenna's mum and his mum fighting about whose child was most to blame. The midwife trying, and failing, to keep the peace, to get them all to focus on the miracle of birth. Then all the blood and gore and . . . Ziggy shook his head to dislodge the memory, and to focus on *today*.

They were meeting at the community center at eight a.m., and taking a minibus to the film studios in Bristol, where they'd spend all day rehearsing before the live show that evening. Ziggy had been given the day off lessons, and the headmaster had told the whole school at yesterday's assembly about the talent show, so they'd all be watching him and Kylie on actual TV.

The side effect of all this was that his previous popularity had been, at least partially, restored. It turned out that the kudos of starring on live TV almost, but not quite, erased the negative credits of being an eighteen-year-old single father.

Ziggy was so keen not to be late that he and Kylie were there ten minutes early, before Lydia had even unlocked the door.

"Morning, Lydia!" he said. "Morning, Maggie! Does this belong to you?" He gestured at the bulging plastic bag sitting on the front steps.

"I wasn't expecting anything," said Lydia, leaning over to open the bag. Sitting on the top was a note: To the heroes of Mandel Community Center, from Yarnsy.

"Oh my God! Look at these!" said Lydia, pulling out three gorgeous wool replicas of Maggie, wearing little sweaters saying VOTE MAGGIE. The woolen Maggies were on sticks, so they could be held above the heads of the audience during the show.

"Oh, so cute!" said Ziggy, accidentally letting his practiced teenage cool slip for a moment and waving a woolen Maggie in each hand.

Lydia pulled out a giant bunch of keys from her pocket and unlocked the front door.

As Lydia, Maggie, Ziggy, and Kylie pushed their way into the entrance hall, a door opposite them, which Ziggy had never really noticed before, opened. Out walked Art and Daphne, looking rather sheepish and disheveled. *What on earth were they doing in there? Had they been there all night?* If they hadn't both been completely ancient, Ziggy would have assumed they'd been . . . Ziggy knew only too well what could happen if you spent too long in a cupboard with a member of the opposite sex. Oh God, another image he didn't want to have to see. Not so soon after breakfast.

"Morning! Sorry, can't stop to chat," said Art, pushing past them, pulling Daphne by the hand. "We're going to my place to shower. See you back here in a jiffy."

"But . . . What . . . ? How . . . ?" said Lydia, which perfectly encapsulated Ziggy's feelings on the matter.

Daphne looked back over her shoulder at them, and *winked.*

"When they said they were going to shower, do you think they meant . . . ?" Lydia tailed off.

"Separately. I'm sure they meant separately. One at a time," said Ziggy, firmly.

Within a few minutes a crowd of people had shown up, including several extremely pregnant ladies, and a whole group of people of various ages in karate kit.

"Are these people all coming with us, Lydia?" asked Ziggy. "We're going to need a much bigger bus."

"Ha! No. The antenatal class, karate club, and AA group have volunteered to hold a sit-in all day, to stop the council boarding up the hall until Maggie wins the show and saves the day," said Lydia, who was obviously feeling more optimistic about their chances than Ziggy was.

"Thanks for coming, everyone!" she said, addressing the crowd with aplomb. "Help yourselves to tea and coffee. I've brought cakes, and there are some macramé plant-holder kits in the cupboard to stop you all from getting bored. Ziggy, can you make sure the social club and all the performers with their responsible adults get on the bus? Here's a list, so you can tick them off." Lydia fished around in her bag and thrust a piece of paper at Ziggy. Ziggy wondered why adults were so often referred to as "responsible," when the past few months had proved they were often anything but.

Ziggy stood in front of the minibus, next to Kylie in her pushchair, crossing names off Lydia's list as everyone arrived. Anna. Ruby. William. Janine. Lucky. Zack. Tallulah. Zack's and Tallulah's mothers.

"Is everyone here, Ziggy?" said Lydia, jogging toward him looking flustered and sweaty.

"Just Daphne and Art missing," said Ziggy.

As if he'd manifested them with the power of thought, Daphne and Art walked up the path, looking cleaner than they had earlier, if a little damp. Whenever Ziggy had seen the two of them in the past, it had seemed as if there were static electricity between them, pushing them apart. Whereas now, if he weren't mistaken, they looked very much *together*. How on earth had *that* happened? And was it really a good idea?

"Thank God you're here," said Lydia. "Right, get on, get on. We should have left ten minutes ago."

"I've never driven one of these before," she said, climbing into the driver's seat. "But how hard can it be?"

She shouted at them all to make sure they had their seat belts on and, after some crunching of the gears, they were, finally, off.

Art

As Art climbed onto the minibus, Lucky waved at him, gesturing for Art to sit in the empty seat beside him. Lucky—still silent, but so different from the boy who'd refused even to look at him three months ago.

Art sat down and stared at Daphne, sitting a few rows ahead of him, just behind Lydia. How had he got her so wrong? He'd thought her so cold and aloof, so irritatingly perfect and patronizing. Yet now he knew she was just as flawed and vulnerable as he was. More so, even. But she was also *magnificent*. None of them would be here now if it weren't for her. They were changed, as if her energy had somehow leeched into them all, without them noticing.

"What on earth have you got in your bag, Anna? We're only going away for a day," Art said, gesturing at the huge, battered leather bag Anna had on the seat next to her, across the aisle from him.

"It's my travel bag, from my days on the road. We learned always to pack for every eventuality: spare undies, toiletries, torch, first aid kit, Kendal Mint Cake, Mace, Lucozade, and passport," said Anna.

"You don't need a passport to get to Bristol," said Ziggy.

"I know that, obviously," said Anna, who was wearing a T-shirt emblazoned with the words KEEP ON TRUCKING. "But old habits die hard. I never knew when my route might change, and I'd end up taking a load to Düsseldorf. Better safe than sorry."

The mood on the bus was jubilant, only dented slightly by the need to stop for Ruby to go to the loo. And just thirty minutes later, she announced she needed to go again. The bus had also started to smell a little pungent, on account of baby Kylie.

"OK, OK, I'll stop at the next services!" said Lydia.

"Nee-nah. Nee-nah," said Kylie, peering out of the rear window.

"Bloody hell, it's a police car," said Ziggy. "I think they want us to stop right now, Lydia."

The minibus fell eerily silent, except for the ticking sound of the indicator and the police siren, as Lydia maneuvered it onto the hard shoulder. She turned off the engine and pressed the button to open the bus doors. They all stared as a young, slightly weary-looking, female police officer climbed on board.

"Why did it take you so long to pull over?" she said, clearly not at all happy.

"So sorry, officer. I was looking for a service station for another urgent toilet break. You have *no idea* how many of those we need with this lot," said Lydia. "It's a miracle we get anywhere, to be honest. So initially when you started flashing all those lights and the traffic began moving out of our way, I thought maybe you were giving us a helpful escort. But then I realized that you couldn't have known about the state of Kylie's nappy, or Ruby's weak bladder, and you were being rather insistent, so I thought it best to stop."

"I don't think you're allowed to disclose sensitive and personal medical information like that without permission, Lydia. Or a warrant. Does she have a warrant?" said Ruby.

"I wasn't speeding, was I?" said Lydia.

"No. In fact, if anything, you were driving dangerously slowly. But we've been asked to apprehend this vehicle. I believe someone in this minibus is wanted by the Met for questioning," said the police officer.

Art looked over toward Daphne. He could see the back of her elegant neck, tense and unmoving, a deer caught in the crosshairs. He could feel the adrenaline emanating from her skin, as if the intense night they'd spent in that cupboard had connected them somehow, in a way he sensed was irreversible. In a way he *wanted* to be irreversible.

"Oh gosh," said Lydia. "Is he pressing charges? I'd thought he might. I just snapped, you see. After twenty years of dismissive comments, criticisms, or—even worse—being completely overlooked and ignored, I'd just had enough. Although I admit it was partly my own fault."

"It was not your fault, Lydia," chanted Art, William, Ruby, and Anna for the hundredth time.

"That photo montage was the final straw," continued Lydia. "The one that broke the camel's back, I guess you could say. Are you going to arrest me? What on earth are the girls going to think? Their own mother, a common criminal . . ."

Art reached his hand across the aisle. The upside of ten years of shoplifting was fingers which, despite resembling gnarled knobs of ginger, were incredibly deft. Checking that everyone was distracted by the drama at the front of the bus, he slowly pulled open the zip on Anna's bag. Luck was on his side, as his fingers closed around the thing he was searching for, right at the top. He tucked it into the seat pocket in front of him. He just had to get the police officer away from Daphne, farther down the bus.

"Lydia, my dear," he said, "I don't think they're looking for you. It's me they're after. You know, it's almost a relief after all these years. It had become an addiction, I think. But the stakes had to get higher and higher to create the same rush. I should have stuck to bingo, like an ordinary pensioner. I think the only way I was ever going to be able to stop was to get taken down. And now, it seems, that time has come. Bang to rights."

He held his hands out in front of him, clenched into fists, just like he'd done in every police show in which he'd played an insignificant criminal with no lines and no major role in the plot development. To his relief, the policewoman walked down the aisle toward him, and he could see Daphne edging over, toward the open door of the bus.

"HIDE EVERYTHING! IT'S A FUCKING RAID!" shouted Lucky, right next to him. The police officer took a few paces back in shock. But she wasn't as shocked as the rest of them were to hear Lucky speak. Not just a word, but two whole glorious sentences! With an adjective, even! The whole bus erupted into applause. Except Maggie, who started barking in alarm.

"Shut UP, Maggie Thatcher!" said Anna.

"Bravo, Lucky! We knew you could do it!" Art said to the little boy next to him, who looked even more surprised at himself than Art was. "Sorry," he said to the stunned policewoman. "It's just those are the first words we've ever heard him say, and he's nearly five. Not an ideal choice of vocabulary, obviously. Better if he'd started with a 'hello,' or a 'thank you,' but hey-ho. You work with what you're given."

"What did he mean—*hide everything?*" she said, rubbing her forehead and looking completely overwhelmed.

"Who knows, dear girl. Lucky's past is a bit of a black box. He's the most inappropriately named child you can imagine," he said. "Anyhow, he wasn't referring to me. None of my ill-gotten gains are aboard the vehicle. Well, not many, at least."

"Look," said the officer, with a sigh. "I have no idea what you've been up to, and I'm quite honestly not sure that I want to know, but it's not you I'm after. Or her," she said, nodding at Lydia.

Art saw Daphne, who'd moved over to the seat nearest the open door, freeze as the police officer looked in her direction, like a playground game of Grandmother's Footsteps. Then, as she turned away again, Daphne stood and started climbing slowly down the steps.

"Did Social Services send you?" said Ziggy, from the back of the bus. The police officer began walking down the aisle toward him, and away from Art. "I honestly had no choice, and I swear I'll never, ever do it again."

Art stared out of the window at Daphne, standing on the hard shoulder. She looked up at him and gave him a jaunty salute. He took Anna's passport from the seat pocket in front of him, slid open the little ventilation window above Lucky's head, and tossed the passport out toward Daphne.

Anna didn't look much like Daphne, but he remembered what Daphne had said about using the stereotypes to your advantage. To most people, especially the young, one geriatric looked much the same as another. If Daphne dyed her hair the same lurid scarlet as Anna's hair in her passport photo, that would be all most observers would see.

Good luck, he mouthed at her.

"If you're here on behalf of the council, then tell them it's not criminal damage, it's art. They're just a bunch of philistines who can't tell the difference," said Ruby to the policewoman.

"Well, I'm not going in for questioning again. How many times do I have to tell you lot, they all died of natural causes? I'm just extraordinarily unlucky with husbands." said Anna. She was, Art thought, in danger of protesting too much.

"Not as unlucky as them," he muttered.

"WILL YOU ALL PLEASE STOP CONFESSING!" shouted the police officer, who was holding a photocopied picture in her hand. A picture that was, unmistakably, of Daphne. She waved it at them all rather aggressively. "THIS is who I'm looking for."

Everyone went silent. Almost as one, they turned and stared at the seat immediately behind Lydia. The empty seat. Then, they all swiveled to look toward the open bus door, and the motorway beside them, where they could clearly see Daphne, walking stick tucked under her arm, vaulting the central reservation.

Art didn't think he'd ever met such an extraordinary, vital, and beautiful woman.

If only he'd realized that before she'd gone.

Lydia

Lydia was sitting with her seniors and carers in the audience, clutching their Maggie mascots. They became increasingly less buoyant and animated as brilliant act followed brilliant act. How could they possibly compete? When a little blind girl came onstage with her guide dog, Lydia told herself it was all over. How could you not vote for the blind girl?

The seat next to Lydia's, which should have been Daphne's, was empty. Just when Lydia needed her confidence and energy more than ever. Where had she gone? Would Lydia ever see her again?

"And now, our final act!" said Ant, or Dec. Lydia was never sure which one was which. "It's Maggie with the kids and seniors from Mandel Community Center!"

There was a roar of applause, and they all sat forward on their seats and waved their woolen Maggies on their sticks. Lydia felt sick. Then even more sick when the giant screen behind the stage came to life and a huge image of Lydia's face was beamed into the studio, along with millions of homes across the land.

Lydia peered at the screen in horror, through splayed fingers.

You could see every line. Every blemish, every enlarged pore. But, actually, she looked OK. Her cheeks were flushed with passion and determination as she explained, remarkably fluently, the plight of the community center and its occupants.

Thankfully, the screen cut to footage of their rehearsals. Of Art patiently helping Lucky with his stage directions. Of Maggie stealing some cake from a table. Of everyone laughing as Tallulah fluffed her lines.

"So you see," giant on-screen Lydia told the interviewer, "we really need Maggie to win, so we can rescue the community center for the community. My seniors are counting on her. The kids are counting on her. The pregnant ladies, karate club, and AA members are counting on her."

The action on screen cut to a wide shot of the rapt live audience in the studio, then homed in on Lydia and her friends, who all waved their woolly talismans furiously as everyone cheered, and the people behind them patted them on their backs and grinned at the cameras, mouthing, *Hello, Mum!*

It didn't matter one bit if they won or not, thought Lydia, wiping a tear from her eye. This was enough.

The screen went blank, and the studio fell silent as Art, Maggie, Ziggy, and Kylie took their places in a spotlight on the stage, along with the three children dressed as miniature policemen.

"How are you feeling, Art?" asked Ant or Dec.

"Excited!" said Art. "I just want us to do our very best, and to save Mandel Community Center for the community." The presenter was about to turn away, but Art grabbed on to the microphone.

"We have a GoFundMe page, if anyone wants to help," he said, gesturing over at where Lydia was sitting. The camera followed his gaze and panned to their group, where Anna and Ruby were holding a banner with the web address of a fundraising site set up by Ziggy.

"We sent our roving cameraman to your community center to film the sit-in that's taking place right now. Can you hear me, Ted?" said the presenter, holding up a finger to his earpiece.

The footage on the giant screen changed to a cameraman wearing headphones and clutching a large microphone.

"Yes, I can, Dec," he replied. "I'm here, live at Mandel Community Center, with the brave protesters." The camera panned around the room, which was filled with pregnant ladies, and kids in karate kit, along with a host of others who all started waving. In among them were a number of men in high-viz jackets. The cameraman held the microphone up to one of them.

"I believe you're here on behalf of the council, to board up the hall," he said. The studio audience booed and hissed, as if they were watching a pantomime.

"Well, yes, but we can't start work on account of this lot." The man gestured at the crowd around him. "So we thought, if you can't beat 'em, you might as well join 'em."

"So what have you been doing instead?" asked the cameraman.

"Actually, we've been making macramé plant holders and eating cake," he replied. "And now we're watching the show, obviously. Go Maggie!" He pumped a fist into the air.

"Art," said the presenter in the studio. "I believe you have a personal mission, too? Some deep, tragic heartache?" He furrowed his brow in exaggerated concern, and the audience all leaned forward on their seats, anticipating an emotional backstory.

"Uh, I guess so," said Art, looking nervous for the first time since he'd appeared onstage.

"Yes, Art here hasn't seen his daughter, Kerry, for over thirty years," said the presenter to camera. "He's never met his grandchildren." The screen behind him filled with pictures of a young girl, then a teenager, dressed in the fashions of the 1980s. "Maybe Kerry Andrews is out there, somewhere, watching you," he said.

The camera cut to members of the audience, probably planted by the producers, looking sentimental and dabbing at their eyes with tissues.

"So, Art. Let's see what you, Maggie, and the kids can do!" said the presenter, with a flourish.

The theme tune to *Mission: Impossible* filled the studio, and Lydia stopped breathing as Maggie traversed an obstacle course and effected a daring jewelry heist, chased by three pint-sized policemen whose slightly too big helmets kept falling over their eyes, before eventually escaping offstage in Kylie's pushchair.

The audience rose to their feet as one, and Lydia found herself jumping up and down, shouting, "BRAVO!" with tears running down her face.

"Well, what a fabulous performance to end on!" said the presenter, his arm around Art's shoulders. "But before we announce the winner of *Me and My Dog*, we have a surprise for you, Art. A very special guest . . ."

A spotlight panned to the wings, and on walked a woman, not much younger than Lydia, her eyes flicking nervously between the people on the stage and the cameras, which were trained on her from all directions.

"Art. We found her. It's Kerry," said the presenter. The audience was so quiet that they could hear Kerry's footsteps reverberating on the wooden stage.

"Kerry," said Art in a croak, his arms open toward her.

"Dad," she said in a tense, tight voice, then pulled back her arm and slapped him hard, leaving a speckled red imprint of her palm on his papery cheek.

There was a mass gasp from the audience, along with a few nervous titters.

"And that is the joy of live TV!" said the presenter, who was obviously a pro. "We're going to a commercial break now, but we'll see you on the other side for the moment of truth."

"Bloody hell," said Lydia.

Art

The safety curtain came down, and Ant and Dec disappeared offstage, leaving Art and Kerry feeling entirely alone, despite being in a room filled with thousands of people. Kerry. The woman he hadn't seen since she was seventeen years old. He could still make out the girl she'd been, but every change, every wrinkle, every gray hair was a rebuke. A reminder of how much time had been lost.

"Kerry," Art croaked again. "I can't believe it's really you."

Art reached for her hand.

"You can't manipulate me into meeting you like this and expect a fairy-tale happy ending," said Kerry, snatching her hand away. "I've hated you for so long."

"Not as much as I've hated myself," said Art. "Ever since you left, there's been a hole inside me. I've tried and tried to fill it, but it's impossible. I can't tell you how much I've missed you. I've replayed that day thousands of times in my head, wishing I could go back and make it different."

"Katie died asking where you were, Dad," said Kerry. "The last words she heard Mum say were a lie. She said you were on the way to the hospital. She didn't tell Katie the truth: that she'd tried and tried to find you, calling you on the set where you'd told her you were working, not knowing you'd been shacked up with another one of the extras in a Travelodge for two days."

"I know. It haunts me every day. It replays every night in my dreams," said Art. "I lost a daughter and didn't even get to say goodbye."

"I lost a *twin*. A part of myself. I know now that it wasn't your fault. It was meningitis that killed her, not your lies or betrayal, but for so long my anger and grief were all mixed up, and I couldn't separate them out."

"I know," said Art again, because there was nothing else he could say.

"Why didn't you come and find me?" she said.

"I did. I tried and tried. Your mother wanted nothing to do with me," he said.

"You made some effort, for a year or two. But then you just gave up," said Kerry, her voice hard and cold.

"You moved. You changed your numbers. I could have tracked you down, of course, but it was too difficult," said Art. "It hurt too much. Anyhow, you knew where I was. I'm still in the same house. Your house. I couldn't move. I kept your bedroom for you. It's still there."

"It's too late now, Dad," said Kerry, with the same determined, stubborn look he remembered from her teenage years. "There's too much damage done."

"We're live in one minute!" shouted a voice from offstage. "Clear the set! Places, please!"

A runner approached both cautiously and urgently, as if he'd been sent in to defuse a ticking bomb. "Sorry, but you need to move," he said.

And then Kerry was gone, and Art was in a large, crowded room backstage with Maggie, alongside all the other human and canine contestants, but feeling more alone than ever. There was a huge screen on the wall, transmitting the live show.

"Welcome back to *Me and My Dog!*" said the presenter, standing alone in the spotlight. "It's time to announce our three finalists, in no particular order." Art could never have imagined that around thirty people and forty dogs could be so silent.

"Tony and the Tiny Tots!" the presenter announced, and backstage the man with the three slutty Chihuahuas yelped, and was ushered toward the wings by two men in black wearing headsets. "Mary and Mungo!" said the presenter. Art held his breath. "And Art and Maggie!"

Art and Maggie were escorted through the crowd by the men in black, emerging, blinking, back into the blinding lights on the stage.

The three final acts stood around the presenter. Art was unable to follow what he was saying. He could hear the highlights of the three acts playing on the screen behind him.

"And in third place . . ." said the presenter. An unnatural, cruelly long silence followed, before he said, "TONY AND THE TINY TOTS!" The audience cheered, and Tony beamed and wept simultaneously, smothering his tiny Chihuahuas in kisses.

"And in second place . . . ART AND MAGGIE!"

Mary leaped into the air as her first place was announced, and Art used every ounce of his acting skill to look thrilled. He smiled broadly, and leaned down to pat Mungo, a stupid little sausage dog in a tutu, with a ridiculously long back and legs far too short to be useful. A dog designed so badly that it couldn't even climb a flight of stairs.

Mary gave him a hug as she sobbed and jabbered incoherently, thanking everyone from her parents to Mungo's vet. Art told her how incredibly delighted he was for her, how much she deserved the prize, and he tried not to imagine himself plunging a knife into her back. He should have been deliriously happy. Second place was amazing. But it just wasn't amazing enough.

A microphone was shoved into Art's face and he gushed to the presenter about how thrilled he was, and how he'd never, in a million years, expected to get this far.

It was, Art thought, his best ever performance.

The mood on the bus ride home was both jubilant and subdued, as they replayed every single minute of their day and the triumph that it had so nearly been. Apart from Art's reunion with Kerry, which no one was mentioning.

They were all desperate to know what Daphne had done to make her flee so spectacularly. Except for Lydia, who was keeping remarkably tight lipped, making Art suspect that she, like him, knew Daphne's secrets, and was keeping them to herself. It was safer that way and, besides, he didn't like the idea of everyone knowing Daphne, or Delilah, as well as he did.

Art kept looking across at the empty seat. The seat that Daphne had occupied that morning. He wondered where she was now. Did she know about their success, and their failure? He wished he could tell her about Kerry. How he'd found her and then, just a few minutes later, lost her again. He wished he could give her the piece of the jigsaw puzzle he'd deliberately withheld: the reason he'd not been there the day Kerry's twin sister had died so suddenly of meningitis. Then tell her how Kerry would never forgive him. How the hole she had left felt more gaping and irreparable than ever.

"That's strange," said Anna, across the aisle from Art.

"What?" he said.

"I'm sure I had my passport in this bag, but it's gone," she said, rummaging through the bag's contents.

"Anna," said Art, quietly, "do you think you'll ever need that passport again?"

"Hell no," she replied. "I've done enough traveling to last a lifetime. And I'm not exactly mobile anymore, am I?"

"Well, might you be able to stay quiet about it going astray? At least for a while?" said Art, and he nodded over toward Daphne's empty seat.

He watched Anna's expression slowly morph from confusion to understanding.

"What passport?" she said, finally, zipping up her bag and putting it back on the seat beside her.

"OMG!" said Ziggy from the back of the bus, waking up Kylie, who began yelling indignantly. "You know that GoFundMe page I set up? It's gone crazy! We've raised over seventy-nine thousand pounds, and it's climbing every second. We're going to do it! We're going to save the community center!"

THREE
MONTHS
LATER

Art

Art had fallen to pieces for a while after the show. He'd felt the loss of Kerry, her twin sister, Katie, and his wife as if they were fresh wounds. But this time, instead of hiding from the pain and the shame, he'd faced them head-on.

William had sat with him while he wrote and rewrote a long, tortured email to Kerry, which a sympathetic assistant at the production company had promised to forward on to her. And then, a few weeks later, she had called him. She still wasn't ready to meet, she said, and wasn't sure she ever would be. But that phone call was, at least, a start. The smallest of leaves on the tiniest of olive branches.

Art's agent, Jaspar, had been in touch, too, eating significantly large slices of humble pie. His phone had, apparently, been ringing off the hook with requests for appearances from Art and Maggie.

So, Art was busier than he'd ever been. But, strangely, he missed Daphne. Really missed her. For someone who'd been in his life so briefly, she'd made an incredibly large impression. He often wondered where she was, and if she was safe. He'd wake up in the morning realizing he'd been dreaming about her. Replaying in his sleep their dinner at Le Pont de la Tour, her rescuing him from the store detectives, and, of course, the night they had spent in that store cupboard.

Art picked an envelope off his doormat. It had a foreign stamp and postmark. He turned it over and ran his thumb under the flap, prying it open. Inside was a postcard.

On the front was a picture of the sun setting behind a dramatic, rocky island, jutting out of a clear cerulean sea. On the other side were words in block capitals, reading:

BEST WAY TO DIE: BORINGLY, IN HAMMERSMITH, OR IN IBIZA WITH STYLE?

And below the words was a phone number.

Ziggy

Ziggy was in the middle of his A-level exams, which were going OK. More than OK, maybe. Hopefully well enough to get him the grades he needed to take up his place at Bath university in September.

The only thing taking the edge off his excitement about his potential new life was his ongoing concern about leaving his mother behind, despite all her assurances that she'd be absolutely fine, and that it was her job to worry about him, not vice versa.

Alicia, who Ziggy fell more and more in love with every day, was going to Bristol, which was only fifteen minutes away from Bath by train. She was still adamant that she and Ziggy were no more than friends, despite him trying to persuade her otherwise. However, after Ziggy's last "relationship," which had gone from a quickie in a cupboard to dysfunctional parenting at warp speed, maybe it was good to take things at a glacial pace.

A letter dropped through the door of Ziggy's flat, landing with a whisper on the mat below. The only letters they ever got were bills or junk mail. But this looked different. He picked it up. It was addressed to him.

He opened it and pulled out the two sheets of paper inside. One was an official typed letter from a solicitor's office. The second was a handwritten note. He read the handwritten one first.

Dear Ziggy,

A while ago you did me the great honor of asking me to be Kylie's godmother. I do hope it's not too late to accept?

I have a gift for her, and for you and your mother. Before I left, I transferred the deeds to my apartment into your name. I hope it'll provide a safe and comfortable place for you all to live. Or you could sell it and move elsewhere. The keys are with my solicitor, an old friend who doesn't ask too many questions. He can also tell you where to find me, should you wish to visit, which I very much hope you will.

With all my love,
Daphne x

PS. If you still have that stone that Kylie swallowed, take it to Christopher Thomson at Hatton Garden. He'll give you a good price for it. It should buy you quite a few plane tickets, and pay for your first year's tuition fees.

PPS. Don't trust the yucca plant.

Lydia

ydia inhaled the smell of fresh paint. The final touches were being put to the renovated and re-vamped community center which now, much like Lydia herself, had a whole new lease on life.

The hall was filled with large, framed prints of the photographs, curated by William, of the community coming together to save the building: the nativity, *Me and My Dog*, and the sit-in.

They'd replaced the signage, so it was back to being named Mandela Community Center, ready to welcome a rainbow nation of occupants. They had a grand reopening planned on Monday. Lydia had been baking furiously for the occasion and Maggie and Art, their local celebrities, were going to be the guests of honor.

Lydia's phone pinged in her pocket. She squinted at it. Another message from Jeremy. He'd split up with Kitty and had been pleading with Lydia to take him back, just as Daphne had envisaged. Lydia should have been thrilled by this turn of events, but instead she just found his protestations of adoration a little . . . irritating.

For the first time since the early days of her marriage, Lydia had started to really like herself. She'd rediscovered her self-respect. A sense of pride. And she was never letting anyone take that away from her again.

Lydia had instructed a local agent to sell the house, and she would take her half of the capital and buy somewhere smaller and cozier for her and Maggie, with room for the girls to stay whenever they came to visit. It would be a new start.

All she needed now were some new members for her club, since William, Anna, and Ruby were the only ones left, now Art was so busy. She pulled a piece of paper out of her bag and pinned it onto the brand-new noticeboard outside the entrance hall.

ARE YOU OVER SEVENTY?
WOULD YOU LIKE TO MAKE SOME NEW FRIENDS?
WHY NOT JOIN THE SENIOR CITIZENS SOCIAL CLUB
AT THE MANDELA COMMUNITY CENTER?
CALL OR TEXT LYDIA ON 07980 344562.

EPILOGUE

Art and Daphne

The view across the Balearic Sea to the rocky island of Es Vedrà, as the sun was setting, was much the same as the postcard Daphne had sent Art, just a few months previously.

Daphne gestured to the waiter and ordered more cocktails.

"I didn't know you could speak Spanish," said Art.

"I've been doing Duolingo," said Daphne.

Art snorted. "Is that some kind of oral sex?"

"When will you ever grow up, Art?"

"Why on earth would I want to do that?"

Art felt something nudge his leg and looked down to see a mangy, skinny dog staring up at him with brown eyes that looked as if they'd seen too much. He reminded Art of the first time he'd met Lucky who, once he'd started talking, had gone from strength to strength. Art had gone with Lucky's foster carer to drop him off for his first day at primary school, and had wept alongside all the proud parents.

He surreptitiously slipped the dog a piece of chorizo.

"Do not feed the dog," said the waiter from behind him, making

him jump. "He is . . . how you say? *Callejero.* A stray. The more customers feed him, the more he begs."

"Sorry," said Art, then waited for the waiter to turn his back before dropping a large chunk of bread to the floor.

"Oops, silly me," he said. "Stupid arthritic fingers."

"I'm going to miss you, old man," said Daphne.

"I wish I could stay here forever, Daffy," said Art. "But I have
loads of work lined up, and Kerry's finally agreed to a brief meeting,
on neutral territory. And she's bringing my grandchildren! I can't
tell you how excited I am. But I'll be back soon, I promise."

"How many times do I have to remind you that my name's
Anna?" said Daphne, stubbing out her cigarette in the plant pot
next to her. "And that's OK. I'm thrilled for you. Really. Besides, I
never wanted a permanent lover. Part time is better. I'm less likely to
get bored of you."

"You're still not very nice," said Art.

"Well, you're still far too nice," said Daphne. "So between us,
we're perfect."

Art reached for Daphne's hand, lifted it to his mouth, and kissed
it. She felt a shiver run from her neck down to the base of her spine.
The sort of thrill she remembered from a long time ago, that she'd
never expected to feel again.

"I have a part-time family, too," said Daphne. "Ziggy said he and
Kylie will come out again as soon as his university term ends, early
December. Did I tell you she's my goddaughter?"

"Only five or six times," said Art. "And be careful, Daffy, because when I look at you now, I'd almost think you were capable of
love."

"Actually, you're the one who should be careful," said Daphne.

"Because when I look at you now, I'm starting to think I just might be."

Neither of them said anything for a while, not wanting to break the spell; they just watched as the sun disappeared over the horizon.

"All I need now is a dog. I miss Margaret," said Daphne.

"By the way, Anna's getting married again," said Art. "Sixth time lucky, perhaps."

"He's a brave man," said Daphne. "I hope he sleeps with his eyes open and is very careful what he eats."

"There's a boules tournament this evening in the village square. Do you think we should go?" said Art.

"Best way to die: While playing boules with the geriatric villagers, or while dancing on a podium at Pacha?" said Daphne. "We should remember what Dylan Thomas said."

"What did he say?" said Art.

"'Do not go gentle into that good night, Old age should burn and rave at close of day,'" said Daphne. "It's the closing party tonight. Let's go burn and rave."

"OK. Just promise me you're not getting on a podium," said Art.

"I'm promising nothing," said Daphne.

They walked off, back to Daphne's apartment, the stray dog tailing a few feet behind them.

Daphne stopped and stroked him behind his ears.

"There are younger, prettier dogs you could adopt, you know, Daffy," said Art.

"Pah. I prefer my friends to have experience, wisdom, and a few guilty secrets," said Daphne. And the dog followed her home.

Author's Note

At the time of writing this, I am fifty-four years old, about the same age as Lydia.

My eldest child has just left home for university and, like Lydia, I'm dealing with the menopause. The only time I'm ever described as "hot" these days is when I'm having a hormonal flush.

This time of life can be really *hard*. After decades of putting children first, an empty nest is a frightening thing, especially if you've been a stay-at-home mum. You feel like you've gained all these skills—multitasking, catering, diplomacy, tutoring, psychology, to name just a few—and yet you're viewed as redundant.

And we seem to be redundant in literature, too. So, I wrote Lydia, in the hope that if you're my age, you'll read this novel and know you're not alone in finding it all just a bit . . . overwhelming.

The strange thing about reaching your fifties is that, although your outsides might be gradually falling apart, on the inside you don't feel any different from the way you did in your twenties. I still don't feel like a "proper adult," and I don't expect that I will at seventy, either.

I look at my parents, in their eighties, and their friends, and they are all surfing the internet and traveling the world. They're nothing like the helpless, harmless older people who I encounter in novels. It often feels like the only role of a pensioner in fiction is that of a sad, lonely, hopeless technophobe, adrift in modern society, who is then saved by the kindness of a younger person.

Well, bollocks to that, as Daphne might say. That's not the kind of senior I intend to be, nor the one I want to read about. I wanted to create older characters who are *bossing it*. Pensioners who are showing the younger generation how to navigate life, rather than vice versa.

This doesn't mean they're perfect, or even aspirational. There's nothing more boring than a character without flaws. By the time you reach your eighth decade, you're bound to have collected many bad habits along the way, and to have a fair few secrets and regrets in your past. And my characters certainly do!

Then I started researching the Hatton Garden jewelry heist of 2015, carried out by a gang of eight men who were almost all in their sixties and seventies. It made me realize that the invisibility of aging is the best disguise. I also wondered whether, if one of the gang had been a woman, she might have been able to get away with it. Maybe she'd still be at large, in hiding, but with a collection of fabulous jewelry . . .

I loved the idea of older people who refuse to age gracefully, or to play by the rules. And I had a vision of a minibus, the kind that you see every day taking groups of kids or old people on day trips, being pulled over on the motorway. I imagined a policewoman looking for one particular escaped felon, but everyone on that bus off-loading their guilty consciences and confessing to some heinous misdemeanor.

That scene became the prologue to this novel. I then spent the next year having a great deal of fun working out who these passengers were, and what they'd all been up to!

I hope you had as much fun reading it, and I hope that you'll never look at a septuagenarian, or a yucca plant, in quite the same way again.

Acknowledgments

Whenever I talk to my children about my job, they roll their eyes and say "Mummy, making up stories is not a proper job." And they're right, it isn't. It's way better than a proper job. It's a joy and a privilege to be able to share the strange workings of my imagination with people all over the world.

Writing novels is a most peculiar pastime. For much of the time, it's incredibly lonely. There's just you, tapping away at a keyboard at 5 a.m., when most normal people are asleep, talking to your imaginary friends and trying to get them to behave or, in this case, misbehave. But then, once the initial feverish and shabby drafts are done, taking that story into the world becomes an exhilarating act of teamwork.

During the lonely times, my writer friends keep me grounded, in that they're the only people who can properly understand the crazy insanity of storytelling—the small triumphs and the huge insecurities. I have found many over the last few years, through that lovely corner of the social media platform formerly known as Book Twitter, in Facebook groups, and at events and festivals. I can't name them all, but a special shoutout to Ruth Jones, Beth Morrey, Natalie Lewis, and Annabel Abbs, as well as Write Club (who I met through Curtis Brown Creative), The Savvy Writers Snug, and the Debut20 Facebook Group.

A huge thank-you also to all the book bloggers and bookstagrammers who are tireless cheerleaders for authors, bringing our stories to new readers with fabulous creativity and perception.

Whenever I hit a writer's block or convince myself that nobody is ever going to want to read anything I write ever again, it's readers who keep me going. Thank you to everyone who's taken the time to leave a review, to come to an event, or to message me. Your words keep me going. A special mention here for The Good Housekeeping Book Room on Facebook, who have been such enthusiastic champions of my books and of reading in general. In a stressful world, you guys are a special oasis of loveliness.

And now onto the teamwork.

I am hugely privileged to have two of the best team leaders in the business: my editors, Sally Williamson at Transworld in the UK, and Pamela Dorman at Pamela Dorman Books in the US, aided by the fabulous Marie Michels. The books that you read are one hundred percent better than my first drafts, and that is entirely down to their skill, creativity, and diplomacy! I am so lucky to have had them by my side for the past five years.

Huge thanks also to Lara Stevenson and Cara Digby-Patel on Sally's team, and Jane Glaser on Pam and Marie's.

It is quite probable that you'd never see my books were it not for some incredibly talented marketing and PR people working their clever magic. In the UK, Becky Short and Melissa Kelly, and in the

US, Molly Fessenden, Chantal Canales, Mary Stone, and Julia Rickard.

There are so many more dedicated and talented people on the team—the cover designers, proofreaders, salespeople, and more, and you can find a list of them all at the very end of this book.

And now, I must talk about my agent, Hayley Steed at Janklow and Nesbit. It's difficult to describe the role of a literary agent. They are your creative partner, your business partner, your cheerleader, your psychiatrist, your parent, and your friend, all rolled into one. And Hayley is the best of all these things. I have loved sharing this journey with you, Hayley, and look forward to many more years of adventure.

Thank you also to Madeleine and Giles Milburn, Elinor Davies, and Hannah Ladds at the Madeleine Milburn Agency for being such wonderful champions of my work.

If you are reading a translated edition of this book, then that is thanks to the brilliant foreign rights teams at the MMA—Liane-Louise Smith, Valentina Paulmichl, and Georgina Simmonds, and at Janklow and Nesbit—Mairi Friesen-Escandell, Nathaniel Alcaraz-Stapleton, Ellis Hazelgrove, Maimy Suleiman, and Janet Covindassamy.

It is my dream to see at least one of my made-up worlds on the big screen, so a big thank-you to Emily Hayward-Whitlock for (hopefully) making this happen.

Thank you to Selina and Paul Burdell, whose gorgeous house in Ibiza inspired Daphne and Art's final chapter. I can't think of a more beautiful place from which to evade justice.

And finally, a massive thank-you to my family. To my children—Eliza, Charlie, and Matilda—for putting up with me spending so much time in imaginary worlds, for being my greatest supporters, and for making me laugh, every single day. Also, my mum and dad, who encouraged me to believe that I could do anything, and who are brilliant examples of how to rock your eighties.

I have the best husband in the world, who, thanks to my (possibly overly complimentary) descriptions of him in my memoir, *The Sober Diaries,* has his own fan group on Facebook. John says that everything I write is "brilliant." This is obviously not true, but since I threw a copy of an early manuscript of *The Authenticity Project* at his head and banished him to the sofa when he was a little more honest, he's now a bit reticent.

Thank you, John. For everything.

How to Age Disgracefully was brought to you by:

<u>Publishing</u>
Brian Tart
Andrea Schulz
Patrick Nolan
Kate Stark

<u>Managing Editorial, Production Editorial, and Production</u>
Tricia Conley
Diandra Alvarado
Tess Espinoza
Nicole Celli
Madeline Rohlin

ACKNOWLEDGMENTS

<u>Proofreaders</u>
Jennifer Tait
Hanna Richards

<u>Art</u>
Jason Ramirez
Lynn Buckley
Monique Aimee

<u>Interior Design</u>
Claire Vaccaro
Cassandra Mueller

Andy Dudley and the Penguin sales team